WHICH WAY TO HAPPINESS

LAURA DANKS

Print ISBN 978-1-913942-06-9

To Pete.

"You CAN have it all. You just can't have it all at once."
Oprah Winfrey

CHAPTER 1

L iz leaned against the door frame and watched her boss. He was blowing his nose with an unflattering sound, a kind of baby-elephant trumpet mixed with a kazoo jamming session. When he threw the tissue in the wastebasket overflowing with used Kleenex, she realized the rumor was true. The big honcho was sick with one of his severe hay fever allergies.

With his broad shoulders hunched and the tip of his dribbling nose matching his ginger hair, Connor O'Brien looked terrible. His eyes were dull and bloodshot, and his skin had an unhealthy gray tinge. He sneezed and sneezed, and Liz remembered that she had seen Connor suffering with hay fever every summer since she first started working for him fifteen years earlier, only this time he seemed much, much worse. He was vicious when he was sick and a compassionate "good luck" look from a passing colleague was a timely reminder of what was waiting for her behind the door.

With the brightest of smiles, Liz knocked on the glass door and crossed her fingers.

Connor looked up and gestured to come in.

"Are you all right?" she asked against her best judgment. Up close he looked a hell of a lot worse than he had from the corridor, and she couldn't stop herself.

"I'm fine, just the usual hay fever. I'll be A-okay tomorrow." He sounded winded as he pronounced every syllable with a bunch of nasal extra consonants. She knew then, his sinuses were completely blocked.

"Sure. Did you try some manuka honey?" Her suggestion was only half serious: she knew it'd be weeks before he recovered from the acute phase. She was annoyed that he was pretending otherwise. This macho routine of his hadn't suited him when he was in his forties, it seemed completely out of place fifteen years later.

"I don't need any pointless new-age remedy. I'll be fine tomorrow," he insisted. "I need some help for the meeting tomorrow."

A spark of joy bounced inside her chest, but with masterly professionalism Liz kept her face neutral and her voice even. "Of course, I'll be happy to assist. Is this the new project you've mentioned?" *The possible award-winning one*, she reminded herself. Connor was always over-protective of any project with some real prize-potential and usually kept his claws into those assignments to make sure his name was the one on the trophy.

Maybe it didn't make her the nicest person in the world, but this was a great opportunity and if Connor's recovery wasn't going to be as miraculously quick as he hoped, she could get a shot at leading a project, one that could finally launch her career. Hadn't she waited long enough already for her moment to come? She had spent the past fifteen years working her fingers to the bone only to see someone else, usually (read always) a male colleague, get promoted or rewarded instead. It was never her turn to shine and now that she was turning forty, she had to compete against younger and more computer-savvy men as well. Liz wasn't a careerist by nature, but she was tired of being brushed aside. For once, fate was shining its lucky spotlight on her. Who was she to refuse this benevolent intervention?

Connor took another tissue from the almost empty box and dabbed his watery eyes. "It's a new client, office refurb. All very hush-hush but Ted Malone's backing it, so it'll be a big deal."

He sneezed a gazillion times. Liz waited for him to compose himself.

"I have no other information. They wouldn't tell me anything before the NDAs are signed."

"Non-disclosure agreements? A bit dramatic for some office refurb."

"They are going through an acquisition. I bet that's Malone's doing," Connor said, drying his nose. "Apparently, there is a lot of red tape wrapped around the deal, something to do with their secret software." *Sneeze, sneeze.* "Anyway, I have very few details." *Sneeze.*

"Are they a start-up?" Liz asked, testing the water.

"Yes." He opened the desk drawer and dramatically looked for something. When he didn't find it, he slammed it shut and looked at her with a lost expression. "There's so much to do for tomorrow," he said, closing his eyes.

She had never seen him like this and despite her best judgment, empathy was taking over. He'd take advantage of her kindness—after fifteen years she knew his MO—but she couldn't really look the other way: he reminded her too much of her father. People always said they could have been brothers given their resemblance, she wondered if that was the main reason she was still working for him. It was likely and it was why she cared about him, even if he was a difficult man, another trait he had in common with her father. Still, she couldn't stop feeling protective of him. "Connor, why don't you go home? I can call you a car."

"No, I can't." He rubbed his hands over his face. "I need to get something prepared for tomorrow. A mood board, some sketches, something to show them we care."

Liz knew what he was asking: subtlety wasn't Connor's forte. He'd used this technique many times before, it was always the same routine. "I could get something together," she said. She prepared for the fake concern.

"It's very short notice... Are you sure you can handle it?"

She would now minimize the effort she would have to put in to meet the super-tight turnaround. She wanted to remind him she was collaborative, a safe pair of hands, someone he could count on in a moment of need. "I could come up with something half decent if I work on it all night."

He'd grab what she offered without a thank you. "Great," Connor said without any real appreciation of her commitment, and as always dismissing her effort as if it was a given she would pull another all-nighter without being paid for the overtime. She knew she should put her foot down. She should at least demand some recognition once the project was over but just as she was building up the courage to ask for it, Connor's phone rang and his attention immediately shifted. Without even excusing himself, he picked up his cell and took the call.

Her time with him had expired so she walked back to her desk, dreaming of the day she'd have her own studio. It was with an anger-clenched jaw that Liz went home, resigned to canceling her plans for the evening. Another blind date, one of the many she regretted accepting, or so she told herself.

As predicted, she stayed up all night to work on the presentation. By 3am she was tired and fed up. She cursed Connor and then reminded herself that there was a family tie that connected her to him, one that had kept her from leaving his firm all these years. Her father and Connor grew up in the same village in Ireland and when she decided to move to Boston after finishing uni, Connor was the one who helped her out, giving her an apprenticeship. She owed him for that, her father's words, and

Connor seemed to agree. But for how long would he take advantage of that? Wasn't fifteen years enough to pay her debt?

By 6am her eyelids were so heavy she decided to get some rest. She'd add a few more details in the morning.

When her alarm clock rang with the quivering of a thousand Tibetan bells, Liz buried her head under her pillow hoping to drown out the noise. The insistent jingle soon proved stronger than the makeshift barrier. Irritated by the drilling sound digging into her drowsy brain, she fumbled in the dark until her palm found the snooze button. The returning silence felt like a blessing and she rolled onto her back, gathering her sheets all the way up to her chin. Inhaling the scent of flowers and sunshine emanating from the linen, Liz snuggled back into torpor, only vaguely remembering the presentation and the meeting with the mysterious new client. Burrowed in the warmth of her cover, she chased the ephemeral slumber that still lingered around her.

Liz, get up! Her conscience was shouting at her and she had to listen.

She twisted and turned under the cover, fighting the part of her that didn't want to get up. But eventually, muttering to herself, she swung her legs to the side of the bed and sat up. She rubbed her face, then reluctantly stood up. Her eyes stung when she opened her curtains and the faint light of dawn filtered through her window. The city was stirring with a cacophony of engines roaring to life and the snarling of drivers joining the traffic.

She watched for a few seconds and her brain started to buzz with more ideas for her presentation and when a smile tugged at her lips, she knew her good mood was back. She rushed into the bathroom filled with renewed energy.

Liz was one of those people who sang in the shower, but today she was too busy to indulge in melodies. Today it was all about work. When the water ran lukewarm, she got out of the shower, used a towel to wrap herself into a cottony burrito and sitting in the middle of her bed, she started to sketch.

An hour flew by without her noticing. Her creative juices were flowing, a river of ideas flooding her mind. She drew, colored and printed out a photo she found online that inspired her. She collected fabrics and samples she wanted to take to the meeting, completely forgetting that she still needed to get dressed and that her allocated slot with the client was coming up. Brochures and swatches were piled to her side, but her creativity had taken over and she knew better than to try to tame it.

When her phone rang, she let it go to voicemail while she tinkered with the final details of her best work to date. When her phone rang again, she checked the caller and recognizing the office number, she decided to answer. "Elizabeth speaking."

"Liz! Where are you?" The voice of her colleague and flatmate Simone on the other side of the line sounded frantic.

"At home, why?"

"What are you still doing at home? Did you forget about the meeting?"

"No! Of course not." Liz's tone was defensive. "I'm working on my presentation."

"Well, if you don't get here in the next half an hour there will be no presentation."

"I'm not scheduled until eleven thirty—" Liz lifted her cell to her nose and almost suffered a heart attack at the sight of the time. It was already two minutes past eleven and she wasn't even dressed.

"Oh my God, Simone, I'm going to be late. Call me an Uber!" Liz said before throwing her cell on the bed and running to her closet.

CHAPTER 2

F rom the balcony, Hudson looked around the offices admiring the beauty of it. It was truly spectacular and as an architect himself, he knew that this space was proof of the quality of the people who carried out the project. He walked toward the terrace and stood in awe of the scenery. He'd seen many exciting and inspiring workplaces in his career, from London skyscrapers to the grandiose eccentricity of the buildings in Silicon Valley, but in his mind, nothing compared to the understated elegance of Connor O'Brien's office.

He loved the terrace the most. It stretched out from the cafeteria like a jetty into the sky, expanding over a sea of mismatched rooftops and interconnecting alleys. Hudson took a minute to think about the journey ahead. He wasn't one hundred percent happy with having Malone as a major stakeholder but he and Tom, his best friend and co-founder, had worked too hard to turn their backs on it now.

Hudson had pushed aside his personal life for years and, dedicated his mind and soul to building STYLE – he needed it to be successful. His software was radically ahead of any competitors and Hudson knew it would thrive, but with their new stakeholder on board they would fly. Ted Malone, media tycoon and unscrupulous entrepreneur, was as cruel as he was brilliant and in a few months, he'd own fifty-one percent of STYLE.

Malone was a man of great intellect who didn't mind paying an expensive price tag to hire the best player for his team. Which, combined with his lack of scruples, made him one of the most powerful men in business. That was part of the reason why they agreed to sell him STYLE. He was not a man one could say "no" to without devastating results. Also, it was true that with Malone's influence vouching for STYLE they would immediately join the big league. Still, every time Hudson heard Malone's unscrupulous approach he felt a shiver down his spine. "One needs to be Machiavellian about business and put ethics aside." That was Malone's favorite quote, one that Hudson could never come to terms with.

Doubts hit him hard, but he hoped that once Malone had control of the company he would play a fair game. He feared that wouldn't be the case and the worries about what Malone might be planning kept him up at night. He didn't trust the man and there was nothing he could do to settle in this partnership. To distract himself, Hudson stepped out the double doors and walked to the rail.

On the curb below, Liz had just arrived in front of the COBA's building.

It was a short walk from the Uber to the entrance, but today her high heels felt like stilts under the weight of the material she had amassed for her presentation. She pulled the glass door open and watched the people crisscrossing the atrium to get to the lifts, to the cafeteria, to the side entrance or the courtyard. There were men in suits and interns in shorts, women walking at different speeds in a variety of attires that stretched from jeans and T-shirts to sophisticated dresses. She watched them saunter, strut, swagger, while waiting for her breathing to slow and her pulse to return to normal. She wasn't late, she made it with a few minutes to spare, and would use those to pull herself together. Balancing three folders on the curve of her arm she stepped in, careful not to bump into anyone as she walked across the atrium. Rummaging through the oversized tote pressing against her thigh, she searched for her keycard.

"Come on," she grumbled, struggling to keep her folders from slipping down. "You've done this before with an umbrella and a takeaway coffee in your hand too," she reminded herself. When she touched the nylon lanyard with her fingertips a smile appeared on her face. She freed her ID with a tug and smoothly swiped it at the security gate. The barrier opened with a mechanical noise. She was tense, hot, and waved her free hand in front of her face. Her grandma's ring slipped down her sweaty finger and she stopped the flapping. It needed to be resized but she never seemed to find the time.

She called the lift, and while waiting for the doors to open she rehearsed her presentation. Parts of her plan were a little left-field but she felt this project was her one shot at winning an award.

The elevator arrived empty and Liz took advantage of that to put on some makeup. She did the best she could, hoping the client she was about to meet wasn't one of those misogynist types who liked *his* women smiley and tarted-up. She really needed to get along with this guy and she wished Connor had more information for her. When the lift stopped with a gentle bounce, she took a deep breath and walked out.

"Showtime," she whispered to herself as the rubbery floor absorbed her hasty steps. The double-height entrance was a hyper-modern open space from which the rest of the office pivoted off. Connor had designed it to impress and he had certainly succeeded. Above the imposing mahogany desk, which displayed several media awards, sharp letters spelled the words "Connor O'Brien Architects" known in the industry as COBA.

To the left, there was a floor-to-ceiling whiteboard where people wrote messages on cloud-shaped sticky notes. Sitting on a tall stool behind the desk was Simone, model-turned-receptionist extraordinaire.

"You made it! And with ten minutes to spare," Simone said, her sculpted eyebrows raised in a perfect arch. She was gorgeous in a purple sleeveless pantsuit and glorious afro.

Liz stepped closer. "Yes, I'm going to pretend it was a very calculated move."

"Well, you look great, as if you had hours to get ready." Simone was teasing.

"Talking about looks, when did you get the new hair-do?" she asked.

"I stopped at the salon this morning: that's why I left so early." She patted her hair. "What do you think?"

"Absolutely gorgeous. I can see you moved on from your eighties mood."

"Yes, baby, the eighties are out and the seventies are back in."

"I can't keep up." Liz smiled, the only trend she followed was the one found in *Elle Décor*. "Anyway, better go and set up. Is the client here already?"

"Yes, two of them. Be warned, they are handsome."

Liz waved her hand to dismiss the topic. "Don't start. Only a fool mixes work and pleasure," she preached.

"I know, I know." Simone pretended to yawn. "They are up in the cafeteria. You can get things ready in the boardroom. Do you want a coffee? I can bring you one?"

"No, I'm fine, I'm hyper enough without the extra caffeine," Liz answered with a wink, Simone had been her best friend since the first day they met five years earlier. As flatmates, Liz could be herself with Simone.

"See you for lunch, then. I want to hear all about it," Simone said, giving her a thumbs up.

"Sure." Liz waved, walking upstairs to the boardroom. It was deserted and Liz quickly started to empty her portfolio. She had a few minutes to spare but the clock was still ticking.

Hudson looked at his watch. It was almost time for his meeting, so after one last intake of the vibrant city below, he lifted his gaze to the horizon and drank in the view. The sun was pleasantly warm, the wind was fresh and fragrant with the scent of lavender potted all around the perimeter of the terrace. It was with some regret that he walked back into the cafeteria.

That was when he saw her.

He noticed the hair first: it was the color of maple trees in the fall shining with copper-colored rays under the light. The rest of her looked just as fiery. Energy emanated from even the smallest gesture. Hudson watched her spread fabrics and samples across the table. Unable to look away, he walked the perimeter of the glass room until he reached the door, then he leaned casually against the wall following her fluid movements with his gaze. Her mannerisms spoke of confidence and determination. She was beautiful in an unusual, powerful way and when she turned and focused her emerald eyes on him, unease spread around his limbs. He had seen and dated attractive women before but no one ever had such a strong effect on him. He smiled at her, looking for something to say, but his brain was nowhere to be found. She spoke first with no apparent difficulty. He was disappointed, she hadn't been affected by him in the same way.

Liz's heart stopped when she saw him. He was looking at her and for a second, she was lost.

"Please come in, take a seat." She welcomed him, pretending that his presence wasn't unsettling but then resumed her preparation to have an excuse to look away from his gaze.

"Sorry, I'm a bit early," he said, and Liz knew he was the client she had been wondering about.

"No problem, I'm almost done." She shifted a plan and took a deep quiet breath.

⁊

Hudson moved closer. "I can see the Corbusian approach. Is that your inspiration?" He looked at her other sketches. She was talented, that much was clear.

"Yes, amongst others." She looked up. "Are you an architect or just a nerd?" she asked, wrapping her chin in her fingers. He found the gesture irresistible.

"Guilty as charged on both counts actually." He hoped she would laugh and it pleased him when she did.

"Which one are you?" Hudson asked, pointing at one of her sketches.

"Neither, I'm an interior designer. Architecture is too *square* for me. And I'm too cool to be a nerd." She pursed her lips in a playful pout. "But I meant no offense."

Hudson laughed. "None taken, I found interior design a bit too *fluffy.*"

"Is that so?" She pretended to be upset, but there was fun in her narrowing eyes.

He threw her words back at her. "Sorry, I meant no offense."

"Touché."

She placed the last of her samples down and stepped away to look at the overall effect. She was clearly happy with it because she moved next to him. Surprisingly, his stomach tightened in reaction to her proximity. He ignored the feeling.

"We will have to agree to disagree," she said with a wink, but he shook his head.

"I think we should continue this discussion over dinner," he suggested, and she blinked twice.

"It is an appealing offer," she said.

"But?"

"But I don't date clients."

Before he could come up with an effective reply, Michael, the architect assigned to this project, entered the room. A few other people followed him, including Tom, Hudson's business partner.

"Hudson!" Michael said walking over to them. "You've met already," he added, and Hudson turned his gaze on Liz.

"Not officially. Sorry, I didn't introduce myself properly earlier. Hudson Moore."

"Elizabeth Walsh. Glad to be working together on this." She shook his hand.

"Me too," he answered, staring into her eyes.

"I'm Tom Brown, STYLE co-founder." Tom muscled his way into their bubble. "Nice to meet you." He extended his hand to her.

Hudson had to let go of her hand, so she could shake Tom's.

"Elizabeth, but please call me Liz."

"Liz it is."

"Are you an architect too?" she asked.

"Oh, no… I'm just the guy who looks after the money. So, as long as you stay within budget, I'm happy with whatever you creative types decide."

"That's a first," Hudson said, crossing his arm over his chest, and everyone laughed.

"Why don't we sit down and get started? Refreshments will be served in a little while," Michael said with a welcoming tone. Liz lifted her eyes to Hudson and their gazes met.

"I'm looking forward to seeing what you have for us."

"Game on." She walked to the board.

Hudson sat, and when everyone else was settled in one of the plush chairs around the large table, Liz started by asking Hudson and Tom hundreds of questions. When she was satisfied with the answers she started her presentation.

"These are just abstract ideas for an initial brainstorming. Once I've seen the offices and got to grips with STYLE's ethos and the company vibe, I'll be able to be more accurate." One by one, her sketches appeared on the large flat screen behind her. Then she moved to the side and turned the room's attention to the board she had prepared. "Does this fit with your vision?" she asked, looking Hudson straight in the eye.

She was spot on and he was pleased to tell her that.

"I'm glad I'm on the right track." Liz smiled and Hudson wondered what it was about her that made him nervous.

"Sounds perfect, Liz. Thank you for taking us through your thinking," Tom said just as the catering team knocked on the door.

CHAPTER 3

"Please help yourself," Michael said before rushing to Liz's side. "Great job," he whispered in her ear. He took two macaroons from a tray and passed one to her.

Liz bit into it with some satisfaction. "Yes, it went well. I'm really pleased." She turned her gaze on Hudson and studied him. He was definitely as handsome as Simone suggested, but then again, Simone is never wrong. In fact, he was so attractive she was having a hard time keeping her pulse steady every time their eyes met. She knew he was off limits, completely out of bounds but couldn't help herself, she was curious and intrigued.

His hair was long and a bit shaggy but the contrast of that casual look against his tailored dark suit only added to the appeal. He wasn't one of those alpha-males but he had charisma. She could see that from how the other people in the room inter-acted with him. His face was now slightly turned and she looked at his profile, he had a crooked nose and she wondered if a fist landed into it to make it so. He was taller than her, his body was athletic and muscular, the physique of someone who had an active life but didn't spend hours at the gym to sculpt his six-pack. *Okay, Liz, stop picturing him without a shirt on.*

She noticed the stubble, unsurprised he was following the trend like any other forty-something she knew. She stared at the grin that seemed to always be on his lips and then lifted her gaze again to the tempestuous inquietude in his eyes. He was attractive, undeniably so, but it was when they shared a joke that she felt the connection. That was when her heart started to jump around in her chest. It hadn't stopped yet. Hudson made her tick. She remembered the feeling, one she had not felt in a long time. She sighed, then reminded herself he was her client and that made any other possibility out of bounds.

She heard a voice calling her name and turned. "Hello?" Sofia, COBA's in-house lawyer waved a folder in front of Liz's face. She frowned. "I have the NDA that you have to sign."

Liz snapped back into her professional self. "Of course, sorry." She took the folder but her gaze fell on Hudson. He was talking to Michael and she wondered if they were talking about her. The possibility made her pulse accelerate and she strained her neck, hoping to hear their conversation.

Sofia nudged her. "Liz! Come on, I need this signed."

"Oh, sorry, Sofia." Embarrassed, Liz opened the folder, skimmed through the text and signed her name. Then returned it to Sofia with an apologetic smile.

"Are you all right? You look flustered. You're normally one of the few that has her shit together around here."

Liz hid the emotions that were gurgling inside her chest with a small laugh. "Yes, all good. I've just finished a long presentation. It's probably that."

Sofia didn't look convinced, but without a word she collected the paperwork and returned to her office.

Michael flanked Liz again. "So, what do you think of the client?"

Liz purposely focused her answer on the company and not its CEO. "Well, hard to tell without a demo, but from what Hudson told us, STYLE has an exciting product offering."

He nodded. "And what about the guys?"

"They seem okay," Liz said, uncommitted.

"I spent the morning with Tom and Hudson and I've developed quite an admiration for them. Tom is clever with numbers, if you make a case he'll give you some leeway for your budget. Hudson is very smart and I respect him for following his dream and trusting his guts." Michael lowered his voice. "Although if his software is successful it may make it harder for interior designers to make a living."

"I don't understand."

"I'm not sure if I'm right about the capability, but if I were you, I'd try to get more info about it. Anyway, you can ask them about it on the flight."

Michael's sentence left her perplexed. "On the flight?" Liz's usually smooth brow folded with questions.

"Yes. To London. You need to inspect STYLE's European offices."

"What?" Liz looked at him in shocked surprised. "Connor didn't mention any travel."

Michael raised his shoulders as if to say, *Why are you even surprised?*

"I'm afraid it's necessary. Their Milan office is a listed building protected by the Beni Culturali and you will need to get them to sign off your plan before starting any work."

Liz turned her eyes on Hudson for a split second, then returned to face Michael. "I can't go to Europe; my calendar is packed." She used the first excuse she could think of. The trip made sense, and given the project's tight deadline: the sooner she spoke with the Italian conservation officer, the sooner she could draft her plans, but the idea of traveling with Hudson made her uncomfortable. It was stupid but she was determined to keep him at a safe distance.

"Just shift some of your workload onto my team. They will be happy to help."

She tried to appear calm and collected, despite the storm raging inside her. "I'm not sure my clients are going to be okay with that." Liz's tone was sharp.

Michael went straight to the core of the problem. "Connor dumped this on you and I'm afraid you have to take it and run with it."

She opened her mouth to respond but closed it again, knowing he was right. "Fine, I'll shift stuff around. I want the project: it's a good one for my portfolio."

"It's just the project you are interested in, or the client too?" he asked.

Liz looked at him. They had gone out a few times; she liked him, she knew he liked her but she had told him that since they were colleagues nothing could ever happen between them, she never mixed business and pleasure. She was going to stick to that resolution. Career before love, she swore by it and wasn't going to change her mind now that success seemed in reach. "Just the project," she said.

She wasn't sure he believed her.

"Okay then. Let's wrap up this meeting." They went to Hudson and Tom to shake their hands again. Hudson turned his attention to her and she wished her dress had pockets so she could shove her trembling hands into them.

His eyes were curious, inquisitive as they studied her. Was he trying to read her thoughts? The idea made her feel uncomfortable so she decided it was time to say her goodbye and put some distance between them. At least for now. "It was a pleasure to meet you." She extended her hand to him and when he took it, an unexpected current ran up her arm and down her spine.

"The feeling is mutual," he said, and they both dropped their hands at the same time. *He is my client.* Liz repeated those words to herself as if they were a mantra.

"Well, see you tomorrow morning then."

"Tomorrow morning?" She frowned, realizing she had very few hours to get everything ready.

"Yes. Sorry about the early flight. We'll spend the night in London: Tom and I have a meeting there in the morning; then we'll travel to Paris, and then fly to Milan the day after. We are due back in Boston on Saturday."

"That's quite a schedule." She took a deep breath.

"Are you okay with that? We sent the schedule to Connor's PA a week ago at least, I hope you were informed." The caring tone of his question floated between them.

"Yes, of course," she lied, "it's no problem." She didn't want to admit she had been roped in at the last minute and she was feeling overwhelmed. She pretended otherwise. "I'll see you at the airport," she said, then turning to Tom she smiled.

"Thank you, Liz, for accommodating us." Tom took her hand and gave it a friendly shake.

"I'm looking forward to seeing the offices." She forced the smile, hoping to disguise the tension she felt, and with a nod in salute, she walked out of the meeting room.

She wanted to stop and take a deep breath but the walls were made of glass and she didn't want anyone seeing her distress, so went straight down to Simone. "Can you take your lunch now? I need help," Liz asked and her voice shook.

"Absolutely, babe. That's what BFFs are for," Simone said, covering Liz's hand with hers. "Now, tell me what's going on."

CHAPTER 4

"Sorry, tell me again why are we having this frantic shopping trip?" Simone asked as she tried to keep up with Liz who was powerwalking through the mall like a possessed woman.

"Because I'm going to London tomorrow," Liz said breathlessly, "then Paris, then Milan and I'm panicking. Should I buy shoes too?" she asked, more to herself than Simone.

"Okay, I get that you have some unexpected travelling coming up, but why are you stress-shopping? Isn't this just a business trip?"

"Yes, but—" Liz kept marching, unwilling to speak her reasons out to loud and validate them.

Simone reached out to catch her arm, forcing her to stop. "I never saw you this nervous about a project. Actually, I never saw you this nervous full stop. What's going on?"

Liz shook her head. "It's so last minute and I'm freaking out. I want to make a good impression." And that was part of the truth, she wanted to be her best self.

Simone lifted an eyebrow, her signature move. "I know you like to plan, so why are you not planning?"

Liz was confused.

"What I mean is, why aren't you approaching this logically? You are just running around, mentioning clothes and shoes when your wardrobe is full of perfectly good items."

"But—"

"Wait. Take a deep breath."

Liz did as she was told.

"Have you worked with important clients on high-profile projects before?" asked Simone.

"Yes, and yes."

"So, why are you falling apart?"

Liz shook her head, unwilling to admit that Hudson put a strange sense of inquietude in her heart and she was equally scared and excited about working with him.

"Something is clearly bothering you. Let me help."

"I'm just overwhelmed. Too much to do in so little time."

"I've seen you working on tighter schedules, so it's not that."

Liz sighed and stopped rushing around. She wanted to confide in her best friend but she wasn't ready to talk about Hudson. To admit he made her nervous and that she was dreading the upcoming trip. She felt vulnerable under his gaze and she worried he'd see her heart quivering.

"I don't like to be unprepared," Liz said, chewing on her thumbnail.

"Yep, you are a planner, no doubts about that."

"You make it sound like a bad thing." Liz started to fret again.

"Sorry, I didn't mean to." Simone touched Liz's arm. "You are going to kill it, because that's what you always do. It doesn't matter what you wear."

"Thanks for the vote of confidence." Liz wasn't sure she could pull it off if Hudson watched her with the same intensity as he had watched her in the boardroom earlier. She needed to find the perfect clothes to be her armor.

"I mean it, Liz." Simone laid her hand on her friend's shoulder. "But if it makes you feel better, I'm sure we can find you the right dress for Milan and for Paris. Then I'm going to help you pack tonight."

In the mall people were passing by, minding their own business, eating, chatting or looking at their phones. There was music playing and lights were shining from the shops on either side. She felt slightly dizzy, out of control for the first time since she could remember and realized that she didn't like the feeling. It was pure panic.

"Liz? Are you listening?" Simone's voice brought her back from her introspection.

"Sorry, what did you say?"

"What's up with you?"

"Nothing. I worked all night to finish the presentation and I think I'm about to crash."

Simone didn't look convinced. "Let's have lunch."

"But—"

"No buts! I need to eat and you need to relax. Let's go to Gino's and talk this through." Simone held Liz's hand. "I have a plan, girl. Everything will be okay, trust me." They walked to the best Italian in Boston. Simone squeezed her fingers.

Liz nodded, then took a deep breath and followed the scent of Italy. The familiar mix of roasted garlic and fresh herbs was reassuring and comforting. They sat at the table in a quiet corner sipping their cold drinks while Simone told Liz exactly what they were going to do next. With every line they ticked off the to-do list, Liz's stress level decreased.

"That works," Liz said, smiling for the first time since they left the office. "You are a genius, Simone. My navy shirt-dress with my suede ankle boots for Paris is the perfect combo. The red pencil dress with high heels will go down well in Milan. It works and I don't have to go shopping after all."

"There you go, all sorted," Simone said, popping one of the olives from the ceramic pot into her mouth.

"Yes. I can get a blow dry right next door, then go straight home to pack my bags, get my passport, check in and make sure the visa came through okay." She rolled her eyes at the pain of it all.

"I can book you a car to the airport, so you have one less thing to worry about," Simone suggested, raising her glass. Liz did the same.

"Thank you for everything, you are my savior." Liz reached out for her friend's hand. With a well laid-out plan in front of her, and Hudson pushed as far away as possible from her thoughts, she felt in control again.

"This is what friends are for," Simone said supportively. Then she turned serious. "As a payment, I want to know what put you into this state, and don't give me any BS because I know you too well to believe that it was a change of schedule that got you this flustered."

"This project got me worked up." Liz laughed but her giggle was shaking with nerves.

"The project or the client?" Simone was the second person to ask her that. Were her emotions so easy to read?

Maybe my poker face isn't as good as I thought. Simone was looking at her so Liz lowered her eyes and took a deep breath. She recalled the moment when Hudson shook her hand, at the strange current that stung her palm, the electricity that buzzed in the air and kicked her system out of whack. She could still feel his gaze on her, his unreadable expression. His eyes were deep with a dark rim around the blue irises. She had felt something that she'd never felt before and that scared her. "I don't know." Liz returned her gaze to her best friend. "Maybe? Hard to tell."

"Look, you are a grown-up and you're smart, but since I've known you all you've done is work. You are turning forty in two months. Aren't you ready to have something else in your life, other than a career built on the crumbs Connor throws at you?"

"Oi." Liz wasn't impressed with the lecture.

"I'm sorry, hon, but I'm just calling like I see it. You are so much better than this freelance role he gave you when you finished your apprenticeship. He treats you like his personal assistant and you work full-time but get paid by project. How's that fair?"

"Connor gave me a chance when no one else would."

"Bullshit. And even if it was true, you've paid him back in full three times over. You are great at your job and he's taken advantage of you."

Liz shook her head. "I don't know about that."

"I do. Carlton Studio headhunted you last year, offering you a great package and a corner office, they don't do that with every yahoo they meet. You clearly impressed them."

"I guess I did, it was pretty flattering actually."

The waitress placed the extra-large pizza in front of them, Simone thanked her then continued with her prodding. "So why didn't you take it?"

The question was legitimate, one that Liz had asked herself many times before. "I guess I'm not ready to move on."

"But why, Liz? What are you waiting for?"

Liz looked down at her hand, her grandmother's ring shining on her finger. Family ties. "I don't know. I can't explain it properly but when I moved here from Dublin it was only temporary, maybe a year or so, just until I got some experience." She twisted the ring round and round.

"But you stayed. It has been fifteen years now; this is your home. Isn't it time you started your life, here and now, instead of pretending that one day you are going back to Dublin?"

Everything that Simone said made total sense, and yet there was something stopping Liz from taking that one final step. Connor's connection to her father was the only thread keeping her connected to Ireland, if that went too, she feared she would be completely alone.

"Listen, I'm not trying to tell you how to live your life but there are too many things holding you back and it's time you let them go. And that includes your grandmother's ring."

Liz's expression was colored by the dread she felt in her chest. "This ring is a symbol," Liz explained.

"I get that, I really do," said Simone. "She wanted you to be self-reliant, to know that you didn't need a man to put a ring on your finger, that your professional success comes before becoming someone's wife but I'm worried you've taken her advice a bit too literally. She gave it to you to help you get back on your feet after your break up, but that was ages ago, isn't it time you start looking for someone?"

"Maybe. I just haven't met anyone worthy enough to replace this ring with a new one."

"Did you give anyone a chance?"

Once again Simone had been on the mark. Maybe a change was necessary, maybe it was time to stop waiting for the future to happen and start living. Now. "I promise I will. As soon as the right person comes along."

"How about the hot CEO from this morning? Too clichéd? An affair with the client is a classic trope."

"Oh, stop it, I'm *not* going to date a client. It's not me, also Connor would skin me alive."

"Screw Connor. He had more *affairs with clients* than I care to remember."

They both laughed.

Simone took a slice of pizza and folded it in half. "Do you remember the McKennas and their home in The Hamptons?" Simone took a bite and chewed, making a funny face. When she crossed her eyes, Liz almost choked on her drink.

"OMG, the McKennas were awful, an absolute nightmare. I don't like to talk about my clients like that but that couple drove me up the wall." Liz giggled and realized that what Simone had wanted was to lighten up the discussion.

"Connor's fault. He slept with her and after she agreed on a much bigger budget than originally discussed, he dumped her on you."

"He did, the bastard. And even with the project all sketched out the McKennas kept arguing. She wanted everything to be gold and glam, very nouveau riche; while he wanted to cut corners everywhere to save money. I think he knew about his wife's affair with Connor too. I swear, it was so awkward."

"I could forgive her for her taste and even for the affair; but she wore real fur and that's where I draw the line," Simone said, and they scowled at the idea of those poor animals.

"The husband smoked cigars," Liz added in mild disgust.

Simone nodded in disapproving agreement. "Poor you, honestly you had the patience of a saint with them. How many times did they make you change the drawings and the color schemes?"

"Please, don't remind me. At least a dozen. They insisted until I ran out of possible combinations." Liz pinched a slice of pizza too, placed it neatly on her plate and cut off a bite-size chunk. "She spent half of their budget on ugly designer pieces only to show off. He was fuming as he wanted money to buy a boat and shouted at everyone working on the account."

"Yes! I remember that. So embarrassing, and you were stuck in the middle."

Liz chewed on her pizza and her thoughts returned to Hudson. Connor dropped her in the middle of this, too, and this time there was so much more at stake.

"Anyway, I'm not going to pressure you anymore but I think it's time you break free."

"Thank you." Liz squeezed her friend's hand and felt positive again.

When all the pizza was gone and the details were ironed out, Simone returned to the office and Liz went to the salon.

By five o'clock, Liz was home, her travel documents were ready for tomorrow and the taxi booked. With relief she entered her room and plonked her baggage onto her bed, then careful not to ruin her newly polished nails, she zipped it open and started to fill it with the chosen ensembles.

She placed the shoes at the bottom, then folded the dresses Simone suggested as precisely as she could, then added some casual clothes too and wedged her toiletries bag in the neat little gap she had purposely created. She worked quickly which meant she was done sooner than expected.

She decided to cook some dinner before Simone suggested getting yet another takeaway, that girl was a bad influence when it came to junk food. *One minute on your lips, a lifetime on your hips.* She chanted in her head as she walked to the kitchen. In the hallway, she spotted the picture of her family hanging on the wall. The house where she grew up, her parents, her two younger brothers and her grandma grinning at the camera. She felt the longing but also the distance. Simone was right, her life was in Boston now, if she liked that or not.

CHAPTER 5

Hudson was sitting in one of the armchairs toward the back of the first-class lounge when Liz entered. She looked beautiful and the sight of her sucker-punched him in the guts. He had not forgotten the effect she had on him—but the space of almost twenty-four hours amplified its force. He watched her as she walked toward him. Her eyes looked tired as if she had not slept well. His instinct was to soothe but he didn't know her well enough to start with that. He'd have to work his way up to that level of intimacy.

"Morning," Hudson said as she sat on the chair opposite him.

"Morning," Liz replied, and he knew he should return his attention to the email he was working on. She didn't look like the same person he met the day before. Something was off. He didn't want to be too forward but when she started fidgeting on the chair, he turned his gaze on her again. Yep, she looked miserable. "There's coffee and a breakfast buffet to the left. If you fancy something, I'll happily get it for you."

She seemed surprised and slightly embarrassed by his offer. "I'm not hungry, but thank you." She was obviously in a bad mood and it seemed safer to return his attention to work. He just couldn't concentrate. "What's wrong?" he asked her, unable to stay out of it even if he had promised himself he would.

"Excuse me?" She was raising her defenses.

"You look... troubled." He hesitated on the last word but it seemed appropriate for the way she looked. He noticed a small crack in her defenses: her hands were shaking. He wanted to reach out, to touch her but she didn't look ready for such a gesture. "I don't mean to pry but did something happen last night?"

Her eyes hardened in a way he had not expected.

"Can't a woman be unwilling to smile without a man jumping to the conclusion that she is upset and something happened?"

Taken aback by her remark, Hudson didn't have the time to formulate an explanation. She took advantage of that. "Nothing happened." Her shoulders squared, her chin snapped up and he could tell she was spoiling for a fight. He was tempted to take her on but not when she looked so miserable already. She wasn't fine, they both knew that, but he decided she was entitled to her privacy.

"Sure, my bad," he said, then unable to let this go he added, "I'm here if you need someone to talk to. I'm a good listener."

She blinked, and he could see she was surprised by his offer. "I mean it," he said and reached out to touch her hand, he wanted to reconnect with her. But he felt her quiver, then she pulled away.

"Thank you." She smiled, her combative expression softening. "But everything *is* fine. I'm just tired. I've not been sleeping well."

"Sure." Hudson agreed she might have had too few hours of sleep but the fatigue was only a part of it. He could see there was something else, something she wasn't telling him. And to be honest, fairly so. After all, he was just a stranger, just another client. The fact that she had filled his dreams all night, didn't mean she had felt anything towards him. Disappointed, he returned to his emails and silence descended between them until Tom arrived.

"Sorry I'm late. My little boy gets clingy every time I go away for work." Tom sat in one of the armchairs placing his plate and his mug on the coffee table in between them.

"That's cute. How old is he?" Liz asked, suddenly finding her charming smile again. Hudson pretended not to be hurt by her double standards.

"He's turning four in a couple of months." Tom took a sip from his mug.

"That's such a great age. They are still all chubby and sweet but they are also articulate and quite independent."

"Yes!" he said as his face lit up. "That's exactly what Ava, my wife, said."

Liz smiled.

"How do you know so much about children?"

She laughed. "I have two younger brothers and I used to babysit a lot when I was at uni. It was better than being a waitress, I guess."

"How could you choose kids over a pub?" Tom asked with a surprised expression, and they all laughed. "Are you from Ireland originally?" Tom's question drew shadows over her eyes.

"Yes, just outside Dublin. I guess I haven't lost the accent."

"Still there, but why lose it? It's so charming."

She smiled at Tom's words.

"Do you go back often?" he asked.

"Not often enough."

Hudson heard the pain in her words and decided to change the topic. "I can see our flight is boarding," he said, pointing at the screen in front of them.

"Ah, yes." She seemed relieved.

Tom chomped into his pastry. "Right, I'll be two minutes."

They waited until Tom was done, then headed for the gate. Discreetly, Hudson kept his eyes on Liz while Tom chatted about inconsequential stuff.

Liz was exhausted from the lack of sleep and saddened by nostalgia, but it was the emotions she felt when she saw Hudson that turned her mood sour. She wanted to feel nothing, instead she felt too much and that made her angry. She was sorry she took her frustration out on him but it couldn't be helped; she couldn't allow herself to fall for him, so indifference would have to do.

Luckily for her she really liked Tom, he was funny and easygoing and his excitement about the arrival of his second child was contagious. She welcomed his company and in the spur of the moment, she offered to design the nursery for the new baby as well as give him some pointers to update his four-year-old's bedroom into a suitable big brother's room. Tom was thrilled but Liz had to confirm many times that she was genuinely happy to do it and was looking forward to meeting his wife Ava before he finally relaxed.

When they boarded the plane, Tom taking the seat near the window, Liz felt the tiredness hitting her and the idea of being forced to sit for several hours seemed very appealing.

Liz looked at her ticket to confirm her seat. She was in the middle and her pod was connected to Hudson's one. They sat simultaneously and with the barrier between them lowered, they found themselves in an alcove. Liz held her breath, hoping he'd not hear her fast beating heart. The set-up was intimate and she worried that a flight of almost seven hours would offer too many chances for them to deepen their connection while all she wanted was to stay away from him.

"Looks like you are stuck with me." Hudson's laughter was self-deprecating, and she offered him the smile she had withheld so far. In a world where mediocre men were becoming successful by being boastful and loud, she appreciated his quiet charisma and his humble approach.

"I'm okay with that as long as you promise not to turn into that character from *Airplane!* ...can't remember his name..." She tapped her forehead with her finger.

"Ted Striker?" Hudson offered.

She laughed. "Yes, that's it!"

"Aren't you too young to remember something that came out in the eighties?"

She was flattered. "I'm turning forty next month. So not that young."

The flight attendant came over to check the overhead lockers and the seat belts, they waited in silence for her to leave, Hudson spoke first.

"Surely in a world where people live to be 100, forty is the new twenty..."

"Very true, there's still life in these old bones," she said and they both laughed, then she turned serious. "And how old are you, if I may?"

"Forty-two but only just." He lifted his hand in a charming gesture. No, this wasn't the *distance from him* she had planned. "Are you put off by older men?"

"Not if they are wise." She smiled, wondering if Simone had been right, maybe it was time she gave someone a chance. Would it be that bad to be swept off her feet? Forty maybe was the new twenty, but the truth was that while she was still young, she wasn't getting any younger.

"I am wise," he answered and she blushed. *Is he flirting with me?* She had been out of the game for so long she wasn't sure. She had been with Sean since they were fourteen and after they split up, she dated a few people but with not much enthusiasm. She was over Sean but he broke her heart and she had lost faith in relationships. But Hudson awakened something in her that had been dormant for a long time. She felt the connection with him immediately, in fact even if she was exhausted from two consecutive sleepless nights, his vicinity had given her an inexplicable charge.

"So, your brothers, are they in Ireland?" he asked.

"Yes, they live in Dublin, near my parents. They have kids, which is good to keep my ma busy and off my back about not having started a family yet." Liz didn't like to admit that her mother had given up on her and accepted she might never get to see her daughter walking down the aisle. She wasn't one to open up with a stranger but she felt she could tell him everything. He was a good listener, after all.

"I know women get a lot more pressure than men do, but I can sympathize. There's so much expectation about getting married and starting a family, especially after forty. I get some from my father and from Tom too sometimes." He lifted his shoulders.

"I know, right? If we don't want to have babies, it's not people's business…"

Hudson looked at her. "I do want a family." His eyes seemed to say what his words had not, she felt warmth radiating inside her chest. *Why is she looking at me like that?*

"But you are not married?" The question was out before Liz realized that just turned her into one of those people she had criticized for being nosey.

He answered anyway. "No."

"Have you not met the right person?"

"Not until recently but I think she's taken." He looked down at her grandmother's ring on her finger and Liz realized he probably assumed she was engaged. She was about to explain the misunderstanding but the flight attendant appeared at her side, carrying a tray with half-filled flutes.

"Champagne?" she asked, aiming her best smile to Hudson. Liz was annoyed but not surprised, Hudson was a man in his prime, one that available women would consider a catch.

"No, thank you," Liz said.

Hudson shook his head to decline as well but when he smiled the flight assistant blushed slightly. "Can I offer you something else instead?" she asked.

"No thanks. I'd better get some work done," he said, reaching for his laptop. Disappointment washed over the woman's face as she moved on to the next row of passengers. Liz wanted to keep talking to him but she wasn't going to be one of those nuisance companions who doesn't know when to back off.

"I'll let you get on." Liz tuned into a movie, staring at the screen with little interest. Her focus was still on Hudson. She wanted to know more about his life to figure out who he was. The flight attendant returned with food and drinks. It looked delicious but Liz picked at it in between yawns. Tiredness was winning this battle of wills. She needed to sleep, that much was obvious, just as it was obvious that she was stubbornly fighting it, too self-conscious about snoring or dribbling in front of him.

"Why don't you get some rest?" Hudson suggested. "Nothing amazing is going to happen but if it does, I'll wake you." His gaze fell to her lips and she wondered how it would feel to be woken up with a kiss. The images from childhood fairy tales popped in her head and squeezed her heart. She blinked the thought away as completely inappropriate and banned any romantic idea from her head. *No fraternizing with the client!*

"I could do with some sleep," she said and rested her head back. "Promise you'll wake me up if something extraordinary strikes?"

"Such as?"

"I don't know, a unicorn on a rainbow? I'm sure if something special happens you will know it's special," she said.

He laughed at her remark. "I promise."

She frowned. "How do I know I can trust you?" She asked the question looking straight into his eyes, wondering if she was ready to trust again. She had trust issues, she had been working on them, still, she found it hard to put her faith in someone else.

"You'll have to take a chance on me," he said, setting a challenge she knew she wasn't ready for.

"I'll think about it," she said, putting on her noise-canceling headphones. That small possibility made her smile, she didn't fully understand why but she wanted him to win her trust.

He opened his laptop and started to work.

Liz kept playing with the ring on her finger. The idea of being engaged spurred in her both excitement and disappointment. Unwilling to elaborate on the reason why she felt such a strong emotion, she turned her gaze on Hudson.

She followed his long fingers as he typed, pressing the letter keys with quick strokes. She was fascinated by the motions of his hands but the more she watched him type, the heavier her eyelids became until all she could do was succumb to the fatigue and sleep.

She was dreaming of her hometown, of the beach she used to go to when she was young. The sea was high and she felt fear as the wind chased the cresting waves. She lay down in the sand and felt the gentle stroke of the water caressing her arm. She sighed when she saw Hudson next to her, holding her hand, calling her name. She heard his voice again and dream blended with reality.

"Liz," he called her name again and her heart started to beat faster at the sound of his voice. When she opened her eyes, he was there, looking at her, unavoidably wrapped into her dreamy bubble and she worried she had already let him in too much.

"Hi," he said and his voice shocked her brain awake. The tickle of his fingertips over her ear as he lifted her headphone made her shiver.

"Something extraordinary actually happened?" She used the joke to loosen the knot in her throat.

Hudson laughed and eased back to his seat. "No, I'm afraid it's just routine. We are landing."

"Right now?" She looked around. The other passengers were adjusting their seats and getting ready for the next part of their journey. "I slept so well." She looked down at her body tucked into a blanket. She was stretched out on her reclined seat and her feet were propped up on the footrest. Her head was supported by a pillow. "Did you do all this?" she asked and saw the answer in his eyes.

"I hope you don't mind, you looked so uncomfortable, I was trying to avoid you straining your neck.

"Oh... thank you," she said, fretting before checking her watch, she slept for over five hours. She straightened up and smoothed her hair, feeling immediately self-conscious.

"Excuse me," she said. "I better go brush my teeth before they switch on the seat belt sign and ground me to my seat."

"Of course." He smiled, then returned his attention to the emails in front of him.

In the safety of the bathroom, Liz looked at herself in the mirror. Her cheeks were flushed and her eyes shining with nervous excitement. She brushed her teeth and tied her hair in a ponytail, then, unable to lie to herself anymore, she admitted to her reflection that she was smitten by Hudson and she felt like a teenager dealing with her first love. She hurt with emotions she had not felt in a very long time.

She returned to her seat with an uneven pulse and strapped herself in.

Hudson, who had packed his laptop away, glanced over at her. "You look good."

She opened her mouth to say something but he was faster.

"I meant... better, as in you look rested."

She saw the embarrassment in his tense shoulders and came to his rescue. "Thanks, I know what you meant."

"Oh, thank God! I would hate you to think that I was hitting on you."

She smiled, remembering she was the one who made it clear she didn't date clients the first time they met, when he invited her to dinner, but his words stung. She had momentarily hoped that he would, she had momentarily planned to play along. She was glad the moment had passed.

After a brief announcement from the cabin crew, the plane landed smoothly into the dark of the evening, a chilly drizzle welcomed them to London. Customs and passport control were quick and they were soon in a cab to their hotel.

Liz realized she was ravenous when her stomach rumbled.

"Hungry?" Tom asked her.

"Gosh, so embarrassing, but yes, I'm starving. I've skipped both breakfast and lunch and now I think I could eat a horse." She refrained from rubbing her tummy when it rumbled again but her cheeks flushed in embarrassment. "As soon as we check-in I'm going to order a massive dinner from the room service."

"Nonsense!" Tom shook his head. "We are in a city with more restaurants than people. We won't let you eat room service. We'll go to dinner somewhere nice. Right, Hudson?"

He nodded in agreement.

"Sure, we can do dinner," Hudson said.

"I thought you had something booked in London?" Liz asked. She didn't really want them to change their plans for her, even if the prospect of not having to say goodnight to Hudson just yet made her heartbeat quicken.

"We have a meeting with our PR agency but not until the morning. We are all yours tonight." Hudson flashed a smile at her and Liz hoped he didn't see her quiver.

While Tom searched the internet for a good restaurant, Liz chatted with Hudson about London architecture. He was an interesting companion. Extremely clever, like Michael had said, he thought fast and spoke softly, without wasting any words. Perfectly balanced between aloof and caring, he was an intriguing package. He was friendly but never crossed the line and Liz was struggling to figure out if he liked her or if he was only being polite. His touch had been gentle, his laughter sincere and his eyes unreadable. It drove her crazy not knowing what he was really thinking of her. *Do you like me?* she wanted to ask while the fluttering of emotions that Hudson brought into her life made her feel alive.

She remembered her feelings for Sean, he had been her best friend and companion of many adventures. Their relationship had been an easy ride and while they were together, they never argued but she never felt for him the spark she felt for Hudson. Why was Hudson so special?

"I've got the perfect place," Tom announced with a grin and Liz put her questions aside for now.

CHAPTER 6

Hudson looked up from his laptop and rubbed his stiff neck. He had felt the tension building as he typed but he had been too immersed in the work to take a break. Now he'd pay for that with a headache. As he stretched his arms out to loosen his shoulders, the idea of going for a run tickled his restless muscles. He longed for the slow burn of a good workout that would deliver a storm of endorphins to his brain to help him with jet lag.

Exercise was exactly what he needed, but somehow, even if he was full of good intentions, he couldn't quite work up an appetite for any sort of physical activity. He wondered what was wrong with him as he was usually at the gym before half of Boston was even up and he was running on the beach when most people were having cocktails and pints of beer.

Frustrated with himself, he slid the laptop onto the coffee table in front of him and stood up from the armchair he had occupied for way too long.

He blamed stress for his disjointed, anxious mood even if deep down he knew the cause of his unsettled mind was a woman with hair of fire and eyes that sparkled.

He grunted at the corny taste of his thoughts and willed himself not to turn into a walking cliché. Yet he couldn't help himself, he was all about the candlelight and the flowers, the dancing and the romancing. It was just the way he was. Still, Liz was working for STYLE; and this trip wasn't a couple's getaway. *Also, she is engaged*, he reminded himself.

Pinching the bridge of his nose, he took a deep breath and forced Liz out of his mind. He had so much on his plate already with the new offices, the acquisition, and the launch of STYLE's technology, he didn't have the time to be distracted by frivolous dreams. And yet, Liz was all he could think about.

Why right now? And why her? He turned his gaze back to the city outside his window; with the sun shining above it. It looked beautiful in an unexpectedly joyful way, as if the reins that kept London going at neck-breaking-speed were now lax, giving its dwellers the permission to slow down. He scanned the road below, watching the stream of people that walked unhurried enjoying the sun. A café with the red canopy stretched out over its outdoor tables looked inviting, and he realized that only an aorta-clogging, fat-filling, mouth-watering full English breakfast would kick his system back in gear and the woman out of his mind.

His phone vibrated in his pocket. Tom's name flashed on the screen.

"Hey," he answered, relieved and disappointed that it was his business partner calling.

"I was checking you were up," he said with a groggy voice. "I'm struggling to get out of bed."

"I've been awake a while. I needed to catch up with few emails," Hudson said, carefully omitting the fact that he had spent half of the night wondering about Liz and the other half telling himself that he shouldn't.

"Aren't you full of virtues!" Tom's ironic tone wasn't lost on him.

"More than you, that was established a long time ago," Hudson answered.

"I can neither confirm nor deny those rumors," Tom said with a chuckle.

"The meeting with Rachel and the team is not until ten. Why don't we go for breakfast at Borough Market first?" Hudson suggested.

"Oh yes, to that little café we went to last time we were here?"

"That's the one," Hudson confirmed, remembering that the food had been mouthwateringly delicious.

"Okay, give me half an hour. We'll get an Uber," Tom said, but Hudson was restless.

"I need to get out of here. I'll walk. See you there when you're ready."

"Yes, see you there."

Hudson slid his mobile back into his back pocket and stood for another minute in front of the window, wondering what Liz was up to.

Liz opened her eyes and stretched out like a kitten. She was still exhausted from her patchy sleep but she felt better than the previous day, so at least it was a step in the right direction. All she wanted was a massive breakfast in bed and maybe an indulgent long bath; but the sun was shining and action was required. She had spent too much time already thinking about Hudson and fantasizing about Paris, their next destination. She imagined the two of them taking a romantic walk down the Seine and she sighed. *We are going to France for work*, she reminded herself, and wanting to shake off her dreamy mood she decided she needed a good workout. She knew better than to believe a man's promises, even more so when the man in question had not made any.

She mentally waved goodbye to the opulent bathtub and put

on her gym kit. With her hair in a high ponytail she left the room, ready to kick her infatuation for Hudson into a strictly-platonic client relationship. Failing that, at least she would have burned enough calories to indulge in the tray of Danish pastries she was planning to drown her sorrows in.

§

On the other side of town, Hudson sat at the table in a restless mood drinking his second coffee already. He, too, was trying to stop thinking of Liz in a romantic way, he wanted to squeeze the need for her into a neat box and lock it away. He had not succeeded so far.

"Smells great in here," Tom said, sitting at the table and pulling Hudson out of his reflections.

"Finally, man, I'm starving," he said, passing him the menu and hoping his friend would not spot what was brewing under the surface.

"I'm hungry too but my body wants dinner… not breakfast."

"Oh well, given what they serve here your stomach will not notice the difference."

"That's true." Tom read from the menu. "Venison sausages, wild boar bacon, quail eggs and even bone marrow! No animal's safe around here."

They laughed and Hudson looked at his oldest friend, his business partner and the brother he never had and wondered if he should confide in him. Their friendship was based on all the many things they had in common and the affection they held for each other. Over the years, they helped each other out of dips and celebrated their successes, and Hudson considered Tom family even if they were not related. Hudson never kept anything from him before but somehow this seemed a secret too important to be said out loud just yet. So, he returned the topic to food. "It's gonna be 2,000 calories at least," he said.

"Once in a while won't kill us. Also, all the meat is organic," Tom said, trying to ease his conscience.

"Okay. Let's get a salad for lunch, to balance this out."

"We'll need to eat salad for a week!"

Hudson was finally relaxing as the waiter arrived. He was a tall guy with a hipster beard and a blue apron around his waist, a scruffy notepad in one hand, and a chewed pencil in the other. "What can I get you, lads?" he asked, scribbling something on the top right corner of his pad.

"Two ultimate full English, thanks," Tom said, ordering for both of them.

"And to drink?"

"Black coffees?" Tom said, and Hudson confirmed the choice with a nod.

"Sure. Won't be long." The waiter tucked the pencil in his breast pocket and walked to the kitchen with calm purpose.

"We are about to have the mother of all fry-ups," Tom said, returning the menu into its holder.

"Artery blockage comes included in the price." Hudson enjoyed Tom's horrified face.

"Please don't you start again. For once my wife is not here to tell me off, so let me enjoy the moment. I want to eat guilt free.'

"You know she is right. She is always right actually and without her you'd have probably put yourself in an early grave by now," Hudson said.

"Don't I know it." Tom shrugged. "Still, I'm out of her sight. Let me have this moment of gluttony."

"Sure, I won't ruin it for you." Hudson's tone was lighthearted but his smile didn't reach his eyes, he saw a redhead walking into the restaurant and his thoughts went straight to Liz again.

"Are you okay?" Tom asked.

"Yes, fine," Hudson answered, too quickly for it to be the truth. Tom knew it.

"Look, Hudson, we've been friends for twenty years. We've

worked together every day for the past decade and I'm not buying it. Maybe you can fool everyone else but you can't trick me with your controlled façade. What's wrong?" Tom had a determined look that demanded an answer.

"It's probably just jet lag." He heard the lie in his own voice.

"Hudson." Tom shook his head. "I'm not an idiot. This distant melancholic look started after the meeting at COBA. I want to know why."

"It's nothing. Lots to juggle that's all."

"Okay, so your weird mood has nothing to do with Liz?" Tom asked.

"Liz?" Hudson tried to pull off an innocent tone.

"Yes, her."

"Why?"

"You seem quite taken by her."

"I think she is talented. That's all."

"And beautiful."

Hudson nodded, that much he could admit. "But she's also engaged."

Tom sighed. "Yes, I've noticed the ring. She doesn't talk about the fiancé much, does she?"

"Not everyone is like you, Tom. Showing the family photos to the first person they meet."

Tom shrugged. "I like to show off my family. You are a bachelor: I'm not expecting you to understand."

"Great. The bachelor card." Hudson hoped his tone was not too bitter.

"So are you going to tell me why the frustrated look?"

"Work of course." Hudson shook his head. "Maybe given that you have time to spare to show off your family I should put a few more tasks on your to-do list, and lighten mine."

"Nope. Thank you, I'm fine. Message received." He lifted his palms up. "I will keep my nose out of your affairs."

"Good choice." Hudson's tone was friendly but firm.

"But I have something I want to get off my chest."

"What is it?"

Tom took a deep breath. "I think Liz would be a good match for you."

Hudson was surprised to hear that, but he was also pleased, he felt exactly the same way.

"I shouldn't ask because Liz is engaged but how can you tell that we are a good match?"

Hudson thought this was pure torture, but so was not talking about her.

"The way you interact, you know, the banter and the laughs. There's definitely a connection between you. Also, the way you look at each other, when the other one is distracted. It's cute."

"Well, she is engaged, I'm content to be a bachelor, so moot point."

"I'm not saying that you aren't, there's just something about seeing you with Liz that makes me think of wedding bells and a house full of kids."

"It's probably because you are getting sentimental in your old age," Hudson said in dismissal, then turning away from his friend, he looked at the people walking by.

Another beardy waiter came to the table, bringing over their coffees. Hudson thanked him and stirred the sugar in with a smooth round movement of the spoon. The noise of the metal hitting the side of the ceramic cup was now the only sound between them. They sipped the freshly-ground ethically-sourced Colombian coffee in silence.

Tom spoke first. "Are you ready for Paris?"

"Yes, those guys are going to be up for the change. They've wanted a revamp of their office for ages. They are going to love Liz's ideas." Hudson focused on the black liquid rippling after he took a sip.

"Agreed. They will rally behind the refurb. I'm a bit more

worried about Milan. It's going to be harder to get their approval," Tom said.

Hudson nodded. "We'll need to prep Liz, so she takes a co-operative approach but she also stands her ground on what goes on the plan and what doesn't. The Italians think art and design run through their veins and they will want to have a say. The only way is to convince them it was their idea."

Tom laughed. "Yes, if she manages that, they will swallow the changes—otherwise I think they will fight her all the way," he said with sheer conviction.

The waiter returned with two black skillets piled with food. He placed them in front of the two men with a smooth arch of his elbow. "Careful, guys, they are hot," he warned them before retreating to the kitchen again.

Hudson looked at his plate in silence. "Joy for the eyes, massive blow to the cholesterol. Exactly what I need."

"Better dig in before our conscience bends our will." Tom picked up his fork. Hudson did the same.

CHAPTER 7

Liz was waiting for Tom and Hudson outside the ticket office at St. Pancras International. She had had a great morning: a powerful workout and half hour in the sauna and yet she was anxious again, almost palpitating every time she thought she had spotted them—him—in the crowd. She didn't want to admit that Hudson was at the core of that malaise. She didn't want to admit she missed him and was looking forward to seeing him.

She looked around and saw a couple wrapped in an embrace. She had a suitcase at her side and the intensity of their kiss talked of goodbyes. Liz was transported back fifteen years earlier. She was so young and so in love, she remembered the feeling so well. It was euphoria and despair; it was promises and a broken heart. *"It's only for a year."* Sean kept repeating those words to her as if that was going to make the separation less painful. *"We'll get married the minute you are back, okay?"* Sean had insisted on that even if she said that as long as they were together nothing else really mattered.

She cried herself to sleep each night for her first month in

Boston. She was homesick and lovesick and all she wanted was to go back to Sean. But Connor had given her an opportunity she couldn't waste—her father told her she couldn't be rude to him and quit, she had to stay and finish off the internship she had started. The memories of what happened after brought tears to her eyes, and she blinked the past away. Then she wondered how Connor was feeling: she hoped he was recovering from his bad hay fever allergy attack and reminded herself to send him an email later on.

She checked her makeup again, patted her hair down only to run her fingers through it a minute later. Hudson had stirred in her feelings she had not felt in a very long time, emotions so strong she wasn't sure she could actually handle them. Her mouth was dry and her stomach knotted. Her palms were wet with emotive exertion and when she felt the heat rising to her face, she knew she needed to calm down. *You are not thirteen*, she reminded herself.

Taking deep breaths, she discreetly flapped her hands, hoping to dry out her palms, wiggling her fingers until a too-vigorous-flick sent her grandmother's ring flying in a parabolic arc. She swore under her breath, grumpy at herself for not having had that ring resized and watched it rolling on the floor before it eventually settled a few meters away. She ran to it but a man was already picking it up.

"Thank you!" she cried out, then flashing her most friendly smile she placed herself right in front of the stranger. But when he tilted his face to her and she realized she was staring into Hudson's eyes, her words died on her lips.

Down on one knee, holding an engagement ring in between his fingers, Hudson's gaze was intense. The air between them was charged and her heart jumped into her throat, cutting off her air supply. In a moment of that suspended time, Liz's chest exploded with emotions that took her apart. The majestic architecture around her, the ring–knee combo and Hudson's handsome face belonged in a reality Liz had been refusing to think about. Until now.

Yes, I will, she thought before her rational side slowly kicked back in, forcing her to put herself back together. The pieces didn't seem to fit as well as they had before. Eyes opened wide, mouth gaping, she was too dazed to find something clever to say. She forced herself to return to her practical, career-focused self but she knew that this exact moment was going to be an ever-lasting memory burned forever into her brain.

Hudson stood, his eyes unreadable. "Better put this back on your finger before your fiancé finds out it is missing.' His voice was filled with disappointment. She frowned.

"My fiancé? I'm not engaged," she managed. "This is my grandmother's ring, a family heirloom." She told him the truth because she had wanted him to know she had no strings. Not that it matters, he was a client, nothing was going to happen between them. But she felt it was important he knew she was single.

"There's no fiancé? No other half?" Hudson asked with surprise.

She shrugged before taking the ring from him. "Not for a long time." She felt she needed to be honest.

He stared into her eyes as if he were trying to read her thoughts, then took a step closer. Given that Hudson was a good few inches taller than her, Liz had to tilt her head back to keep eye contact. He did the opposite, and for a moment they were dangerously close. If she lifted her arms over his shoulders, she knew they would be kissing, she knew they both wanted to.

"Hudson..." she whispered, and he finished her sentence.

"We work together, it makes things complicated."

She followed his lead. "Yes." She swallowed. "You are a client and we are both professionals."

"We are." He lifted his fingers to her jaw and caressed her skin gently. When a sigh left her lips, he took a step back and dropped his hand. She was glad he had the restraint she was lacking.

With impeccable timing, Tom appeared around the corner. "Liz, good morning. How's the jet lag?" Tom leaned in to kiss her cheek.

"Bad. Sleepless night. And you?" she asked, happy that Tom had wedged himself between them and cut the tension.

"Struggled to fall asleep and struggled to get up, but I managed a few solid hours in between."

"That's good," she said, twisting the ring she had replaced on her finger.

"We better go. Passport control may take a while and we can't afford to miss this train," Hudson said, his tone neutral again. All trace of the emotions she had heard in his voice a few minutes earlier now gone.

Tom looked at Liz with a smile. "Shall we?"

She nodded and they followed Hudson who had started walking toward the entrance.

"So, tell me," Liz asked Tom as they stepped through the glass door, "how's the acquisition going? I hear you guys have hooked Ted Malone. That's a pretty big fish."

"Yes, it's a bit crazy at the moment." Tom's voice was even but he seemed to have lost the usual spark.

Liz pulled her case on the smooth marble floor. "Are you worried it's going to fall through?"

"That would be catastrophic, so we are worried, yes. Until it's all signed anything can happen." Tom pinched his nose. "You can't imagine the strain on both body and mind."

Liz nodded at his words. It was a castle made of cards: the smallest breeze could take it all down. Her eyes moved to Hudson, he was hiding the stress well.

"Are you looking forward to this trip?" Tom asked, changing the subject.

"Yes, actually. I've seen the picture and the floor plans of the offices online, but walking around the building and meeting the people who work there will give me a better sense for the space," she answered while Tom helped her lift her luggage onto the scanning machine conveyor belt behind his own.

"I agree, it's a good thing you are coming with us. I'm also glad we have these few days together so you get to know us a little better too. Especially Hudson."

At his words Liz turned her gaze over to Tom. "Why?"

Tom looked slightly embarrassed, but his answer was convincing when he said, "Because you will need to work on this closely with him to get all three offices done in such a short time and it's easier and faster the better you know him. Don't you agree?"

"Yes, yes of course. Establishing trust will certainly help."

She watched Hudson queuing at passport control a few meters away, their eyes met for a moment and in that very instant she realized it'd take a lot of effort to resist his charm.

Tom picked up both their luggage from the other side of the gate while they kept chatting about STYLE history. They passed passport control to find Hudson waiting for them on their platform. They boarded the train together and walked to their seats. Liz was facing Hudson and the tension seemed to immediately rise as they bumped their knees under the table. Tom sat next to him and kept the conversation going as they settled.

"So, all your family still in Dublin, then?" Tom's question took her by surprise.

"Yes, just me in Boston." She felt Hudson's piercing eyes on her so she kept her gaze on Tom as he asked her another question.

"I don't mean to pry, but don't you miss them? I go for lunch at my parents' every weekend, can't imagine not seeing them that often."

"It was hard at the beginning but then you get used to it…" Liz tried to minimize the longing she felt at times. Hudson's legs brushed against hers under the table again but this time felt intentional and she knew he was offering her his sympathy.

"I guess one does, human hearts are designed to be resilient, to mend after a break." Tom's words struck a note in her.

"With time wounds scab over and heal."

There was silence between them for a minute, then Tom spoke again. "We have a few hours to kill: why don't you show us the sketches again?"

"That's a good idea. In the last meeting I didn't quite get the chance to show you the details. I think it'd help to be all on the same page," Liz said, picking up her bag to retrieve her laptop. "I'd like your honest opinion," she said, looking straight into Hudson's eyes. "I want to deliver your vision, not mine." She moved her eyes briefly to Tom then back on Hudson. "These are your offices." He held her gaze until Tom cleared his throat.

"Sounds great," Tom said, shifting out of his seat, "and I'm sure you guys will come up with something amazing. After all, Hudson is qualified when it comes to understanding design and stuff."

"Where are you going?" Hudson asked him.

"I'm the CFO. My job is to handle money and budgets. I work with spreadsheets, not CAD, so I'm going to play with numbers and let you guys decide on Pantones and fabrics. You are the architect, right? You make the decisions. Plus, I trust Liz."

Liz looked at Tom, unsure of what to say.

Tom smiled. "I do. You guys are going to be fine."

"Sure?"

"Absolutely, all I want is a corner office, the biggest you have." He laughed, then moving aside he pointed at his empty seat. "Come next to Hudson, easier to see the screen."

Liz gracefully shuffled out of her seat and moved to the opposite side.

"You guys are going to do a great job together, I can already tell," Tom said, leaving Liz and Hudson to deal with their buzzing connection.

Liz opened her laptop and placed it between them. "Before we start, I have a question."

"Sure."

"You are an architect, right?"

"That's correct."

"And you created an interior design software?"

"Yes." He frowned.

"So, why did you hire COBA to refurbish your offices? Surely you could have done the planning yourself and just hired contractors to carry out the work? Cutting out the middleman would have saved you a fortune in fees but isn't that the point of your software? I mean, I speak against my own interest here as you are trying to put people like me out of business."

"Ouch." But he was grinning. "I have to agree, they are all valid points, which I've raised with Malone several times. He was the one who insisted we hire COBA for this project, he was unmovable on it."

"Makes little sense," she said.

"Malone is not a man who does anything without a good reason, but I'm with you on this one, I can't understand why going with COBA was so important. It felt personal."

Liz thought of what she knew about Malone—nothing flattering came to mind—in fact, all the stories she heard painted him as a cut-throat businessman who would happily use any tool or avenue available to get what he wanted. *So, why does he want COBA on this assignment?* she wondered.

"Now that you know you were not my first choice, does it make any difference?"

She blinked because Hudson's eyes were intense and she could only take so much of their depth before her cheeks turned hot.

"Not really. I was just curious. I'll just do my best work, as always." She moved her gaze on to the screen. "Shall we start with the mood boards?" Liz clicked on a folder named STYLE. "I've created several visualizations; they all have *Innovation* as a central theme, but I went from a fun and entrepreneurial fluid space to a sleek corporate look with several variables in between."

She opened several files and moved them across the screen so that they were all visible. "I also have 3D screenshots of different areas—but let's discuss the theme first."

Hudson and Liz looked at the colors and the details, and as they brainstormed, they started to agree on most things.

"These are impressive, Liz. Award-winning, even. You are very talented." Hudson's genuine compliment left her slightly shaken.

"Thank you," she said as his phone rang.

Hudson checked the caller ID and pursed his lips in annoyance. "Sorry, I need to take this. It's important. Do you mind?" he asked.

"Of course not," Liz said, shuffling out of her seat so that he could have some privacy.

"One moment," Hudson warned the caller, then covered the microphone of his mobile. "You stay; I'll go in the corridor," he whispered when he brushed passed her side.

"Sure," she said. He was about to turn when the train swayed and threw her backwards. Liz tried to keep her footing but her high-heeled boots were not the best gravity fighting tool. She braced herself for the inevitable fall but Hudson's arms reached around her and with alacrity he pulled her against his chest. "I've got you," he said, and she nodded, too breathless to speak.

Neither of them could move, the other passengers were staring, the caller was waiting and the train had returned to its smooth ride. But in his arms, her pulse was popping up and down like corn kernels in the microwave.

Hudson kept one hand firmly on her back and his gaze on

hers. Lifting his cell to his ear he said, "Call you back," and without waiting for an answer, he slid it into his pocket.

"You okay?" he asked Liz, who had found her balance, although her legs were not that steady.

"Yes, thank you." She forced a smile. "Sorry about your phone call." She squared her shoulders and straightened her back when he let her go. "I know you said it was important."

"You are more important." His tone was sincere and she so desperately wanted to believe him.

"Who was it?" she asked, trying to sound casual.

"Ted Malone," he said, and Liz felt her blood pressure dropping.

No one hangs up on Ted Malone. He was not a man you said "wait" or "I'll call you back" to. "That was ballsy, or maybe reckless." Her forehead crinkled and her brow furrowed. Everyone knew Malone was a powerful player who could make or break someone's fortune. Everyone knew he was not a man you put on hold. She remembered when Connor rebuilt Malone's house in the Hamptons a few years back and told her how much pressure he felt in delivering above and beyond what was expected. Connor argued with Malone about the type of stones to use on the patio. Eventually Malone's wife took Connor's side and the works were completed without further problems but Connor had encountered a few obstacles along the way, he had no proof they were Malone's doing but the suspicions were strong. At least COBA was still in business but many other who crossed Malone were not that lucky. Now Malone was acquiring STYLE, she just hoped that Hudson's grand gesture wasn't going to cost him.

"I know about Malone's reputation," Hudson said, taking a step away from her.

"Why didn't you take his call then?" Liz looked at him. *Did you really take such a risk for me?* she wanted to ask him.

Hudson shoved his hand in his pocket to retrieve his mobile, then pressing the redial button, he said, "I told you, you are more important," and with those words he headed out of the carriage, letting her wonder if she should believe that he really cared that much about her.

CHAPTER 8

A s if the two hours twenty-three minutes train journey Hudson spent next to Liz hadn't been painful enough to endure, she was now sitting, almost literally, on his lap as the two of them plus Tom had crammed into the back seat of the only cab left at the station. *What's a man to do?* Hudson clenched his teeth, annoyed that the harder he tried to keep his distance from Liz, the more she was pushed his way.

It was the driver's last ride before the end of his shift, and the front seat was occupied by the man's grandmother who'd arrived from London on the same train.

"We should have waited for another taxi," Hudson complained, struggling to ignore a strand of Liz's hair that, curling over her shoulders, tickled his jaw.

"It was the only taxi left," Tom answered as the driver followed the main road out of the station.

Meanwhile, Liz was sitting straight and rigid, trying to put as much distance between her and Hudson as possible, and he guessed she was probably feeling as uncomfortable as she looked. Staring at the road ahead, she was holding her entwined hands in her lap while focusing all her attention on the line of cars in front.

"We are going to be late." Tom tapped his fingertips on the briefcase he was balancing on his knee. Hudson could see Tom's stress level growing exponentially with every inch they crawled. He hated to be late and that very quality that made him an excellent chief financial officer, made him an awful travel companion.

"Est-ce qu'il y a une autre route?" Liz asked the driver if there was another route they could take. The taxi driver grunted something under his breath and then, without any warnings, he whirled the car into a U-turn with a frightening screech of tires.

Liz was thrown against Hudson's shoulder and instinctively put her hands on his leg trying not to fall off her seat. In response he wrapped his arm around her in support. The centrifuge force pushed them together, locked into another intimate embrace. He looked at her and the tension in his arm grew with her body against it.

"Sorry, transport seems to be against me," she mouthed, drawing his attention to her lips and in that instant, Hudson felt something he never had before. He knew she was the one he had been waiting for. The moment seemed to be everlasting, even if it was probably only a few seconds, but the squeeze to his heart scared Hudson more than the reckless driver.

"This guy drives like a lunatic!" Tom said, gripping his briefcase, but then he grinned when the road ahead was clear of traffic and the car could resume its speed.

Hudson released Liz from the embrace and she returned her hands to her lap but the moment they'd had left them both shaken. How long would they manage to keep away from each other?

Despite their ever-growing tension, Liz and Hudson put up a good show at the office and by the time they were done, everyone from the French team was eating out of their hands. Change was coming but Liz made it sound like an exciting opportunity and not a burden, and after insisting on a round of suggestions, all parties felt good about working together.

Hudson grinned at Liz. "You did great: thank you. Everyone is now looking forward to the disruption you'll cause. I call that success!" Hudson's joking tone made her smile.

"Well, thank you," she said.

"I mean it: you did great building trust with them. It will help once we are back in the States and they realize half of the facilities will be out of bounds for a month at least." She knew he was teasing her.

"You are a caring CEO, I bet you have thought of a way to soften the blow."

"I might have." He winked and she felt the need to touch him, to keep the connection. It wasn't only the physical attraction, which had been undeniable from the first minute she looked at him, it was something deeper. She liked everything about him even if she knew so little.

"Liz, there is something I want to ask you," Hudson said.

She raised an eyebrow. "What is it?" Her playful tone turned serious, her throat went suddenly dry.

"Do you like wine?"

Liz laughed, relaxing. "Yes, I like wine."

"Great, because we are about to go and drink some." Hudson turned to the audience and with his usual charm, he said, "Drinks anyone?" The room turned silent. "My treat," he added and the hoots from the crowd were a clear enough answer.

"I know a great place," Nadia said after a few people made suggestions that were turned down. "There is a bar in the Latin Quarter that does salsa nights: you guys would love it."

There were cheers and clapping at the idea, and Nadia

seemed pretty pleased that the team was behind her, Hudson shrugged his shoulders. "The people have spoken. Salsa it is."

"So here's another question: ballroom skill level?" Hudson asked, turning his gaze back on Liz.

"Oh!" She bit her tongue. "You'll need to find out."

"Okay, I'm game." Hudson stepped closer. She held her position but her shoulders tensed.

"We agreed on keeping this professional," she reminded him, even if her voice wasn't steady anymore.

Hudson looked at her. "I'll play by the rules."

"Oh, good," she said.

"And when we dance it will be just some friendly competition. Unless you're scared of losing?"

"Scared of losing? I don't think so. I can hold my own on the dance floor." She laughed, dismissing his words, it wasn't the possibility of losing that terrified her.

"Okay, I believe you," he said with a sincere tone, his gaze was still ironic.

"Fine, I'll have to show you then, but don't come crying when I humiliate you with my skills."

He laughed out loud. "Most likely the other way around," he said nudging her, and she shook her head.

"You really get on my nerves sometimes." And with that she walked to her chair to retrieve her stuff, stomping slightly with irritation.

❧

Liz left ahead of him and when they took the Metro, Hudson pretended not to care that she intentionally joined a different group, purposely ignoring him. He used that short separation to explore why he was so disappointed and how it could be possible that he missed her already.

The bar was at the edge of the Latin Quarter, and Hudson

recognized the location from the black-and-white photos he had seen in history books, capturing the waves of students who had marched these same streets in 1968. When he walked in, the place was a mix of rustic and ethnic with a cozy atmosphere. Wooden tables and mismatched chairs covered one side of the large space while the rest was dedicated to dancing.

Shots, red wine glasses and beer jugs arrived as ordered and everyone was in a positive mood. Hudson kept an eye on Liz, who had been pacing herself, sipping only a small amount and keeping her behavior extremely professional. He wondered if she ever let her hair down. She had been chatting with everyone, other than him, and he had been trying to convince himself that staying away from her was for the best. He noticed that Tom had been on the verge of saying something but after his warning about minding his own business, Hudson knew his friend had decided not to interfere. They stood shoulder to shoulder watching their team drinking and dancing.

"They are having fun," Liz said, coming to stand next to Tom. Hudson felt the buzz of her presence and felt compelled to ask her something, even inconsequential, just to have the excuse to talk to her, but a hoot from the dance floor caught their attention.

"Someone's showing off," Liz commented at the sight of Nadia's solo dance.

"Brilliant moves, Nadia!" Tom complimented her and taking that as an invite, she swayed her hips all the way to him.

"But, Tom, you are not dancing, eh? You guys have been standing here watching for long enough. Now it's salsa time!" she said with a cheeky smile.

Tom shook his head. "No, no, no. I'm not dancing, I don't even know where to start." Tom looked like he had tons of excuses ready to dish out, but she was not having any of it.

"Show me your moves, come on. You can't be that bad!" She

challenged him with another enthusiastic shake of her hips and pulling a face no one could say no too. Tom still tried.

"Nadia, I'm sorry but I can't dance. My wife says I have two left feet," Tom admitted with a nervous laugh while flapping his hand in front of him. But if he thought that would get him excused from embarrassing himself in front of his employees, he was wrong.

Nadia threw her head back and chuckled with a full, raucous laugh, holding Tom's hand while he reluctantly attempted to get into the rhythm, the glint in her eyes said she was not going to relent until Tom got it right.

"No, no, no." Nadia shook her index finger, then showed him how to move properly. Her cheeks were flushed, and her French accent was thickened by the wine she had drunk. She was having a great time and Hudson admired her for being so bold with her boss's boss.

"Just go with it, Tom. Resistance is futile," Hudson yelled at Tom when he looked back at him, hoping that his best friend and business partner was going to rescue him.

"You son of a—" Tom shouted with narrowed eyes. Hudson laughed, and Liz joined in.

"He really has no rhythm," Liz decided, watching Tom taking a few steps while holding Nadia's hips.

"He really is terrible," Hudson agreed, turning to her.

"I think it's time for you to show me all those skills you've mentioned," Hudson said, offering Liz a hand.

"Not that I have anything to prove but yes, I have skills and you are going to feel embarrassed about doubting me," Liz challenged him.

"Let's do this, then," he said, but when he placed his hands on her waist her body stiffened under his touch and he eased away.

"You okay?" he asked as he watched her strap her emotions tightly inside her.

"I am and I'm going to let you lead," she said, adjusting her hands over his shoulders. "But you have one song to prove you're good at this. Otherwise, I'll lead."

"Sure." Hudson looked at her, thinking that he liked her backbone, then lowering his voice, he said, "But what if it's you who's not good enough to be my partner?"

"You chose the wager," she answered without thinking too long about it.

"I admire the confidence," he said, tightening his grip on her waist again and feeling her quiver.

A burst of laughter from the back of the room broke their moment. They turned to watch Marcel stripping off his shirt while standing on one of the tables.

"What is he doing?" Liz frowned but Hudson laughed.

"There's my wager, you'll have to do the same." He pointed in Marcel's direction.

"What?" She looked horrified. "I'm not stripping."

He laughed again but imagining Liz dancing on a table in her lingerie was an image too powerful to handle. When he spoke, his voice was huskier. *God what is she doing to me?* "Not the stripping part." He shook his head but kept a firm grip on her. "I meant doing something spontaneous. Something fun. Like dancing on a table."

"Something spontaneous?"

"Yes, and fun."

"But why?"

"Because from where I stand, I can see you have your shit together but I think you are holding back, as if you are waiting to live instead of living."

"Well, aren't you a talented psychologist? We met two minutes ago and you have me all figured out already," she answered, tightening her hands around his shoulders. He didn't think she meant in affection.

"I'm sorry, I wasn't criticizing you, and no I don't have you all figured out but I'd like to get to know you better. The real you, the one you are keeping hidden."

They stood there as the next song started. People danced around them.

"Not sure there's more to me than what you see," she said.

But Hudson shook his head again. "I don't believe you. I've seen glimpses of it but only few and far between. You have a tight grip on things."

"This is a work trip, Hudson. You are my client and, as we already mentioned, professionalism is the only way."

"What if that's not enough for me?"

"It'll have to be." The words floated as they began dancing. They found their rhythm almost immediately and it felt as if their bodies knew each other already at a deeper level. When the song ended, Hudson dropped his hands and asked, "Do you want to lead?"

He was genuine and he could tell she knew. "No, you're actually very good." At those words he spun her around making her laugh. He decided that she could be spontaneous, she could have fun, all he needed was to get her used to the idea.

They did a few elaborate backs and forwards before they faced each other again.

"Where did you learn?" she asked.

"When my nan died, my grandfather married again. He married a professional dancer. I learned from the best. She's in a wheelchair now but still boogies like a devil," Hudson said. "And you?" he asked, placing his hands back on her hips.

"I did ballet when I was young, but then I decided that variety is the spice of life and moved to contemporary and ballroom dancing too." The music turned mellow and romantic and Liz lip-synched the words of the popular song playing.

He smiled and snuggled her into his arms following the rhythm. As he held her, his fingers molded around her curves, he loved the way she fitted against him. She was perfect. When Liz angled her head to the side, Hudson started to have a hard time remembering they were just two strangers on a business trip. She had warned him twice already about professionalism and knowing it was important to her, he decided to break the moment despite every cell in his body screaming for more. He spun her around again, then looped her back against him as she laughed.

"It hurts to admit it, and I'm *very concerned* that what I'm about to say will inflate your ego, but you are the best dance partner I've ever had. Thank you for reminding me how much I love dancing," she said, lifting her hand to his cheek in an unexpected gesture. He wanted more, so much more.

"Why did you stop?" He covered her hand with his.

"My ex didn't dance, and then when I moved to Boston work took all my free time." Her answer was simple and sad, he wanted to be the one who took her dancing and made her happy.

"Guys..." Tom stepped in between them.

"Tom, what's wrong with you?" Hudson noticed his friend's furtive behavior.

"We need to go." He was breathless. "I've ordered another round of shots and as soon as they are distracted, we leg it. Please?" He looked at them for a second and added, "Of course, you guys can stay if you are enjoying this torture, but I need to get out of here before Nadia catches me again and forces more dancing on me." Tom looked cautiously over his shoulder. He looked genuinely spooked.

"I'm happy to go back to the hotel," Liz said.

Hudson nodded too, hiding his disappointment behind his sympathy. "Sure, bud. I'm good to go as well, can't bear to see you being tortured." Hudson used his patented detached tone. Inside his chest emotions were swirling.

"I'll go flag down a cab before they notice we have deserted the dance floor," Tom whispered. He was already wearing his blazer and clearly determined to escape.

"You do that. I'll settle the tab and catch you up," Hudson said, then stood a second watching Liz. She giggled as she grabbed her things and then stepped through the door that Tom was keeping open for her. When she was out of sight, Hudson turned to the barman.

"Can I settle my tab, please," he asked, and the barman started tapping into the till.

"You guys make a great couple. When is the wedding?" he asked, leaving Hudson confused. "The redhead's your woman, right?" The barman smiled. "The ring is great, I've just bought one for my partner too, I'm going to ask him on our third anniversary next week." Hudson saw both excitement and trepidation in the barman's face and smiled.

"Congratulations," he said. "I wish I could give you a different answer but we are not engaged."

The barman looked at him with a scowl. "Don't let her get away, eh? Paris is the perfect city to propose, so don't wait, *mon ami*, you'll regret it."

"Right. I'll keep that in mind, thanks." Hudson paid with his card, then pushed fifty euros to the barman. "Make sure those guys there go home safely, all right?"

"Sure, sure," he answered, taking the money. "You remember my words, okay?" The barman grinned. "Paris is the city of love."

"Night," Hudson said before heading for the door.

CHAPTER 9

L iz entered her hotel room with a grin on her face. To her surprise she'd had more fun than she'd had in ages, and even if she attributed her good time to the beat of the music and the warmth of the wine, she knew that Hudson was the real reason for her mood. Liz forced him out of her mind and sitting with her legs crossed in the middle of her bed, she took a deep breath. It was almost midnight in Paris which meant it was about 6pm in Boston. She knew Simone would be home.

She picked up her cell and made the call. She waited, listening to the rings going unanswered and worried she had made a mistake working out the time—but then at the fourth ring Simone's voice greeted her from the other side of the Atlantic. "Liz! how are you?"

"I'm good, I'm good," she said, and the alcohol still in her bloodstream made her sound cheerful. "I'm in Paris."

"Are you drunk?"

"No!" Liz answered immediately. "Well maybe a bit tipsy…" She giggled. "Every meal comes with a glass of wine: it's hard to keep up."

"How's it going so far?"

"Really well, actually. I had a good day, the team here is excited about the office refurb and they like my ideas."

"Sounds great, and how's Paris?"

"Gorgeous, as always. We went to a salsa place in the Latin Quarter and wow, I have never been in that part of town before. It's so lively, reminded me of New Orleans. You'd love it."

"Sounds like you had a brilliant time. Any dancing?"

"Yes is the simple answer."

"Since when have I cared for the simple answer?"

"Okay, fine. I danced with a very handsome man." Liz laughed, feeling self-conscious about telling Simone she had tangoed with the client, so she kept that detail hidden.

But Simone was like a mastiff. "Who? A hot French man?"

Liz's hesitation gave her answer away.

"Oh my God, don't say Hudson Moore?" Simone whispered the name from the other side of the Atlantic but it echoed loud into Liz's chest.

"Yes, but it was by chance—he didn't ask me to dance or anything. We were forced onto the dance floor."

"But still. Hudson Moore, girl!" Simone sounded excited. "Is he a good dancer? I bet he is, he looks like someone who has moves," she said.

"Yes, I cannot lie, he's pretty accomplished," Liz confessed to her friend.

"I knew it!" Simone squealed like a teenager. "He's perfect for you."

"What! Wait, back off..." Liz took a deep breath. "Nothing is going to happen between us. We were pushed on the dance floor and it was less fuss to go with it than argue so we went for a couple of songs, nothing more. He may be perfect but he's also my client and I'm staying at arm's length. We talked about his double standards but Connor is really funny about fraternizing with clients. Do you remember he fired Christina for dating Harry Caviler? I don't want to end up like that."

"Yes, but I also remember she married him and now she lives in the $12-million mansion she designed for him." Simone made a good point but one Liz wasn't interested in. Marriage wasn't in the plans; her career was.

"Maybe it worked out for her, but I wouldn't want to lose my job to gain a husband. Sorry but my professional reputation is too important to me to risk it with a fling."

"Oh, Liz, a fling? Christina married the dude, it wasn't a fling. You can find another job easily, a better paid one too, but can you find another Hudson?"

Liz's breath was stuck in her throat and for a second, she couldn't exhale.

"You are making this a bigger deal than it is," she said eventually. "Hudson is an attractive man but I don't care for it," Liz said, finishing the discussion. They chatted for a little while longer about the food and the office but Simone's words buzzed in her head for a long time after they had ended their conversation. Despite reassuring herself she didn't—truly didn't—care for a relationship with Hudson, Liz spent most of the night thinking of what she actually wanted from her life. Was working for Connor genuinely enough to make her happy? Was Hudson really just a fling?

Liz woke up early and when she looked in the mirror, she saw the signs of a bad night's sleep coloring the bags under her eyes in deep purple. She took a shower and while the hot water relaxed her muscles, the Adele song she bellowed gave her a burst of energy. She dressed and hiding her tired eyes with expertly applied makeup, she went down for breakfast.

Artfully, she sat away from Hudson, pretending she had work to do and hiding behind her laptop she played with her plate of food until the waiter eventually took it away untouched. When Hudson left the dining area with a quick wave in her direction, she sighed with relief.

She went back to her room, repacked her bag and checked

out. Tense, she sat in the lobby waiting for the airport transfer. With nothing better to do she stared at the book in her lap. Hudson and Tom arrived shortly afterward; sitting in the two armchairs opposite hers, they chatted inconsequential matters. She tried her best to keep up with the banter but her heart wasn't in it.

"Are you okay?" Hudson asked her.

"Not really."

"What's wrong?" Tom leaned forward in an emphatic way.

"Just a tension headache, nothing serious." She smiled reassuringly, but Hudson didn't look convinced.

"I've taken some painkillers and I'm sure I'll be fine by the time we land in Milan."

"No pressure to come to the office," Tom said, looking at Hudson who nodded in agreement.

"No, I'm sure I'll be fine. Probably too much wine last night." She saw Hudson's worried gaze and felt a surge of warmth inside her empty, knotted stomach. *Do you really care for me?* She was dying to know for sure.

"It was probably the dancing. Please, don't ever remind me of that," Tom said with a grimace, and they all laughed. Liz's good mood was returning but she swore it had nothing to do with Hudson's attentive behavior, it was because the painkillers she took were finally working.

Once they landed, the journey into Milan city center went smoother and faster than expected. Liz spent most of it discussing with Tom a few ideas she had for the new nursery. And by the time they checked into the color-coordinated curtains-cum-upholstery hotel, Liz was cheerful and re-energized.

She changed into her red dress and high heels, wrapped her hair in a classy bun and readied herself to take on the capital of fashion. As a bonus, Hudson gawked at her from the far side of the foyer, and she knew she looked better than good. Of course, she wanted to keep things professional but she saw him looking at her over and over again and she liked the way it made her feel. Maybe she had ignored that sensation for too long and now Hudson had awakened something inside her that didn't want to stay dormant anymore. *Maybe we could just be friends?* She told herself that was acceptable.

The refurbishment in Italy was complicated by the fact that the Milan office occupied the second floor of an historical building subject to several regulations and conservation restrictions. Liz had worked them into her plans and because of that she had to explain the whys and hows behind her decisions. The people were not quite as receptive as the team in Paris but in the end, everyone agreed on the plans and she accomplished what she had come here for.

"Everyone loved the plan," Tom said, squeezing her arm when they were alone, she knew he was putting a positive spin on things.

"Not really loved it, but liked it enough to go along with it."

"True," he agreed.

"I'm just glad they came around because when I started the presentation I thought I had no chance to convince them," she answered with a grin that quickly died on her lips when she saw a beautiful woman wrapped around Hudson. With no right to be jealous, Liz looked away.

"I'm starving! How about you?" Tom said. She couldn't tell if he had noticed the change of vibe and forced herself to be upbeat.

"Ah, yes," she answered but her stomach tightening even more told her she wasn't going to eat much.

As they walked towards Hudson, the woman kissed his cheek and then gently rubbed away the lipstick she had smudged on his skin. Her moves were obvious but Liz had to concede they were effective.

"That's Patrizia," Tom said to Liz. "I don't think their relationship is as intimate as she makes it look," he explained as they watched the exchange. "Hudson lived here for a while. They've known each other for a long time, nothing more."

"It's none of my business, really." Liz flattened her dress with the palm of her hand.

Tom looked at her with a raised eyebrow. "Sure about that?" he asked and stunned her into silence. "I don't mean to be nosey or anything, I leave that to my wife, she is a very talented meddler, but I couldn't help notice that you and Hudson were good together on the dance floor last night."

Liz laughed but nerves appeared under her dismissive façade. "I love dancing, haven't had the chance to stretch my legs in a while. Hudson is a good partner and I enjoyed myself, that's all. Plus, you are my clients and I wouldn't behave any other way than professionally."

"Of course! I wasn't suggesting otherwise," Tom said, and she hoped he was dropping the subject. Luckily, he did.

Only a few people were invited to the restaurant. Patrizia was one of them. Though Hudson acted as if she was nothing more than a friend, Liz noted that she had managed to touch his arm, or shoulder, or hand every few minutes for the entire duration of their dinner.

Coincidence in the seating plan put Hudson in front of Liz. However, she spent most of the time conversing with Tom while fiercely avoiding looking at Patrizia's constant fussing.

"Have you been to Milan before?" Hudson asked Liz, managing to claim her attention.

"A couple of times but never for long enough to appreciate the city," she answered.

Patrizia immediately jumped into the conversation. "Hudson used to live here," she said, red nails on Hudson's arm again. But he reached for his glass and she had to retract her claws. Liz knew it was petty but in her mind she smiled at that small victory.

"Yes, I studied for a master's degree in Milan," he said.

"That's how we met, on campus. Didn't we, *tesoro*?" Patrizia said, her voice stomach-turningly sweet with nostalgia, her eyes on him to prove they had a bond going back years.

"That's right," he confirmed too quickly, looking uncomfortable with her effusions and Liz wondered if his dismissive tone was trying to minimize the academic achievement or the involvement with the woman. If it was the latter, it didn't really work. Patrizia kept her smile firmly on her lips and her arm wrapped around Hudson's.

"Have you seen much of the city?" Patrizia asked and leaned heavily on Hudson's shoulder.

"Only some of it," said Liz. "I wish I'd seen more."

"Did you go inside the Castello Sforzesco?" Hudson asked, his attention turning fully on Liz. She saw Patrizia's smile dimming into a sneer and was glad the steak knives had been taken away.

"Ah, no. I've only seen it from the taxi. It looked magnificent." Liz realized her tone was dreamy but how could she resist a real castle? She was a dreamer at heart, someone who used to believe in magic until Sean broke her heart into a thousand shards.

"You have to go inside to appreciate its full glory," Hudson said.

"We have a few hours going spare before the flight tomorrow," Tom said, looking at Hudson. "You could take Liz for a tour: you know this city inside out, don't you?"

Liz felt Patrizia's icy-cold stare and tried to back out from the offer, the last thing she wanted was to cause a rift, she was going to deal with Patrizia in the next few weeks, and she needed their relationship to be friendly. "I'm sure Hudson has other plans," she said to give him an out.

"No, I don't, and I'd love to be your guide." Hudson's tone was resolute: there were no doubts he meant it.

"But, Hudson." Patrizia pouted, her voice whiny. "What about our plans?"

She could have whispered the words but Liz knew she said them loud enough for everyone at the table to hear.

"We didn't make any plans." Hudson's voice was polite but cold and Liz noticed Patrizia's shoulders stiffening.

"You know, I'm sure I'll be okay wandering around by myself. I can't really miss the giant castle in the middle of town," Liz said with a forced laugh.

But Hudson turned to her, his eyes as serious as his tone. "I'll be in the foyer at 9am waiting for you. Your move."

Liz's pulse accelerated and despite the menacing look Patrizia threw at her, Liz nodded.

"Mind if I join you?" Tom asked, probably to soften the blow for Patrizia and Liz was pleased about his attempt to lighten the mood. He was good at his role of peacekeeper.

"Of course not," Hudson said. "But be ready to walk without moaning."

"When do I ever?" Tom frowned.

"Every time we go anywhere on foot," someone heckled from the other side of the table, and everyone but Patrizia laughed.

CHAPTER 10

"Here, sir," said the man at the concierge desk, handing over to Hudson an envelope with the tickets and passes he had requested. "The weather is gorgeous. I'm sure you and your friends will have a wonderful time on the *guglia*," he added, referring to the top of the Duomo where the famous gold Madonnina watched over her beloved city.

"I'm sure we will," Hudson replied, trying to convince himself that it was the warm Italian weather and not nerves about spending the day with Liz that made his palms sweat. At least Tom would be there too, a chaperone to cut through the tension and stop him from getting carried away with the romance of the setting.

The concierge smiled and Hudson thanked him with a large tip, then turned to Tom who was standing a foot away wearing a three-piece suit. The formal attire took Hudson by surprise.

"What's this?" Hudson asked, pointing at Tom's tie.

"Last-minute breakfast meeting with a possible investor." His snort was enough to confirm that he was not happy about it.

"Why didn't you tell me? Should I be there too? Also, do we

need another investor?" Hudson asked, trying to keep the disappointment out of his voice.

"No, but it's good to have options. Anyway, not sure it's worth it, so no point wasting your time as well as mine."

"If you can handle that on your own, then thank you. I'll stick to my role of tour guide."

"Well, that's if Liz turns up. She didn't say yes to you, remember?"

"I remember, but something tells me that she'll come."

"Okay, wanna bet?" Tom was clearly enjoying himself.

"Depends on the wager."

"My kid's new room needs some furniture assembling. If Liz is not here by nine, then you'll be building."

"She'll be here," Hudson said, looking at his watch.

Tom did the same. "You have two minutes."

"Plenty of time."

"While we wait, I had to ask. What happened with Patrizia? She was so mad at you that at one point I even thought she was going to scratch your eyes out."

"Always so dramatic, Tom," Hudson said, and Tom laughed.

"From where I stood, it looked like a scene out of a soap opera."

"Nothing happened, I just had to remind her that we are not together and we never were. Gee, we had one date almost twenty years ago, and I'm flattered she is holding on to those feelings but we didn't click and we never will, it's as simple as that."

"Well, good luck, man, I don't think she's got the memo," Tom said, and Hudson shook his head thinking of Patrizia's irrational behavior. He looked up, and Liz was walking through reception. When his gaze locked on hers, he felt elation and despair in equal measure and realized he had never felt like this for anyone, not even for Candice Petroski in third grade. He felt foolish when a grin split his face as he watched her. He was happy and didn't care if it showed.

She was heading toward him with a bright smile, her eyes sparkling. Her ponytail bounced up and down with every step she took. She looked different from the sophisticated professional he had seen so far and the dramatic change made her even more interesting.

He wanted to know the real Liz, the person behind the mask. He wanted to know what she liked, what dreams she had, what worried her, what made her happy. This need to get deeply close to her scared him and motivated him. How could he feel so much for someone he had only just met? He didn't know but his romantic side provided him with the simplest option, something that he never thought possible: love at first sight.

Liz was wearing jeans and trainers and a stripy silk scarf casually around her neck over a loose blouse, and he almost sighed. She looked even more beautiful than she had yesterday in a tight red dress with stilettos.

Her skin radiated with a natural glow and her eyes were filled with anticipation for the adventure ahead. She looked young and he replayed in his head a conversation they had had the previous day: at forty they still had more than half of their life ahead of them. It hit him then that it was okay to be foolish and in love at their age, as much as it had been when they were in their twenties.

"She's here, I told you so," Hudson said.

"But it's 9:02," Tom whispered with a cheeky grin. "I still win the bet. You are helping with the furniture."

Hudson realized he'd been conned but Liz was a step away from them so he let it slide and focused on her.

"Hi," she said.

Tom answered first.

"Morning, Liz. Glad you decided for the guided tour: you would have broken Hudson's heart otherwise."

Hudson was unsure what to say to that, so said nothing.

Liz was the one who changed the subject. "Am I under-dressed?" Liz asked, looking at Tom's gray suit and skinny tie.

"No, you're fine. Something came up: you guys are on your own," Tom said, and Hudson noticed her jaw clenching. Was she bothered by that? He wondered why.

"Something happened?" she asked.

"Only a last-minute breakfast meeting with an investor that probably won't invest—but still, I'm not in the position to make assumptions."

"Oh, I see. I'm not keeping you from it, right?" Liz said, looking at Hudson.

"No, Tom never invites me to these things," he managed to say.

"For your own good," Tom said, patting Hudson on the back. "Anyway, have fun. I'll catch you later at the airport," Tom said already walking away.

Hudson shoved his hands in his pockets, then turned to Liz. "Still happy to go even if it's just us?" he asked, keeping his trepidation at bay.

"Absolutely, I really appreciate you taking the time to show me around." Her answer was polite and with awkwardness lingering between them, they stepped out of the hotel lobby.

"Do we have an itinerary?" Liz asked as they walked down Corso Magenta.

"Yes. First stop: Castello Sforzesco," he said, and she noticed he pronounced the z as tse like the Italians do. She grinned at him, impressed. He lifted the envelope he had been clutching and showed it to her. "I have tickets for the museum of the Castello: they have a temporary Renaissance exhibition that had fantastic reviews. A tour of Teatro alla Scala and the *Last Supper* to follow; but I built in time for us to explore the Duomo too."

They had been walking for a little while and Liz realized that Hudson ticked all the boxes on her wish list, everything was so perfect and she just wanted to tell him that and finally kiss him. Because that thought was disconcerting, she made a joke instead. "No allocated time for shopping?" she asked and his face fell.

"Sorry to disappoint," Hudson said not realizing it was a joke.

"I was just messing with you," she grinned. "Your plan is perfect!"

"Is it?" Hudson looked at her and when she nodded, she saw something in his eyes that made her pulse scramble. *Screw the rules*, she thought, leaning in for a kiss, but neither of them was ready for that and the moment hung until it was gone.

"Time's wasting," Hudson whispered to her ear and then, unexpectedly, he took her hand in his and pulled her down the long tree-lined avenue ahead of them. The shock of the contact made her stiffen, but her fingers curled so perfectly against his hand that she relaxed.

"Where are we going first?" Liz asked as Hudson jogged down Corso Magenta.

"To the Castello," he said, squeezing her hand.

Her heart leaped into her chest and she wondered, *Is this what love feels like?* She thought she had been in love before, but it was never like this, not even with Sean, the person she had thought she would marry. Hudson was something else, in a completely different league of feelings.

He pulled at her, then pointed to the massive needle with a giant multi-colored thread that emerged from the ground, passed through the needle's eye and disappeared again into the sidewalk. The sculpture was almost as big as the building behind it.

"It's incredible, isn't it?" Hudson asked, and she had to close her mouth that had dropped open.

"That's enormous!" She laughed at the absurdity of such a sculpture. Even if Milan was a fashion capital, a giant needle and thread coming out from the ground was a step too far.

"Yes." He laughed and started to walk again.

"Did you live here for long?" Liz's curiosity was trumping the fences she had erected.

"Just over a year. But I really loved this place. It feels like home." Hudson's voice was nostalgic, and a sharp twinge of jealousy pinched the soft spot in the pit of her stomach.

"Here it comes, the Castello Sforzesco," Hudson said.

When they reached the corner, she took in the enchantment of a fully preserved castle complete with a moat and a drawbridge. They grinned at each other. "It's so majestic." Liz almost squealed. Eyes wide, she needed all her strength not to admit she was falling for him. "Beautiful," she whispered in awe, turning her gaze from him to the Castello again.

"Indeed," he replied, and she knew he was talking about her as much as the building.

"Let's go in." Liz's voice carried the joyful note of discovery. The distance she was so desperate to hold on to was now gone and as Hudson held her hand, she felt happy, an emotion she had almost forgotten existed. "Thank you," she said.

"You are welcome," he answered with a smile, and they walked through the drawbridge and into the magic of the past together.

Almost three hours later, Hudson had to drag Liz out of the museum.

"Still so much to see, can't we stay a little longer?" she complained, but Hudson was irremovable.

"I have tickets for the *Last Supper*, and I want to show you the view from the top of the Duomo; we need to pay a visit to the Galleria and a check out La Scala too, so we need to get going." He delivered his speech while walking quickly down the road.

"Hudson, wait! Slow down." Liz laughed, trying to make him stop, pulling at his arm, she was breathless but mostly from laughter. "Wait! Wait… I'm getting a stitch," she panted, rubbing gently at the side of her stomach.

"You are way out of shape." He laughed but she had to agree with him, age was certainly catching up with her. She had a few aches and pains popping up here and there and she struggled to keep up with all the twenty-somethings at her spin class. "I'm not!" She tried to defend the indefensible.

"How come you are so unfit?" Hudson asked with a raise of his eyebrows. She could tell he was teasing and was ready to keep up the banter.

"I'm not unfit." She straightened up while gulping down another lungful of air. "I haven't had a stitch since I ran track in junior school."

"Is that because you haven't run since?"

They looked at each other. "Probably so." They both laughed and he wrapped his arm around her.

They walked into the Galleria. Hudson showed her the correct way to spin around the bull for good luck. Then hand in hand they climbed all the way up until they reached the top of the Duomo. They admired the rooftops of this magnificent city, feeling the life pulsing under them and Liz realized that it was true, she had been waiting instead of living, but maybe she had finally made the first step to change her life around.

The tour at the Teatro alla Scala was too quick and they left longing to discover more; but their slot at the Cenacolo was coming up and they had to go. They passed through the double doors, holding their breath, and looked up at the masterpiece until their neck hurt.

After spending all day together chatting, they sat in the taxi taking them to Linate Airport unable to say a word to each other. Liz knew real life was taking over from the blissful parenthesis they had had and now it was time to return to Earth. She wondered if Hudson felt the same way; but his eyes were unreadable and she had no idea what he was thinking.

They went through security and into the business lounge

without delays. Tom was already there, and they settled at his table.

"So, how was your tour?"

"Absolutely brilliant! Hudson was the perfect guide."

He smiled at her and Liz mouthed the words "Thank you" wanting to say how much the day had meant to her but knowing that she couldn't. *He's back to being the client*, she reminded herself and with the excuse of having to reply to Connor's email, she opened her laptop and buried her feelings under her workload. *Isn't that what I always do?*

CHAPTER 11

The taxi sped along the freeway. Liz watched the road ahead, reflecting on the fact that she was struggling to hide the truth: she liked Hudson more than she ever liked any other man who had crossed her path. Even Sean, who would always have a special place in her mind, was not a match. Hudson had no competition from the few others that over the years had run alongside her life for a while. None of them had had such an impact on her heart as Hudson.

She had loved spending time with him. She tried lying to herself but there was no point. She was attracted to him and it terrified her.

During the flight home she worried that the stability she had built so patiently for the past fifteen years was about to crumble. All she wanted was a stellar career, maybe one or two awards with her name on them and a corner office with windows. She didn't want to fall in love, not now and especially not with a client. *Why am I risking my heart again?*

When the taxi stopped in front of her building, she tipped the driver and without a word, she grabbed her stuff and walked to the door.

Pulling her luggage behind her, she was glad to be into the building before it started to rain any harder. She searched her purse's pocket for her keys. Euros jingled like bells when her fingers moved around in circles as she struggled to find them. Finally, the round shape of her key ring brushed against her fingertips just as Nick, the doorman, gave her a wave from behind his desk.

"How was Paris?" he asked.

Liz replied with a smile, knowing that Simone had been gossiping behind her back. "No comment, and whatever you heard is not true."

"Sure, sure," Nick replied, and Liz knew it was a lost battle to try to convince him otherwise, so she ignored his laughter and called the elevator.

The ride to her floor was quick and she was soon in her apartment. After closing the door behind her, she dropped her bag on the floor next to her luggage, and peeled off her sneakers. She was wired and exhausted, at the very same time.

Padding towards the kitchen she wondered if she should go to bed for a few hours even if it was only eight o'clock. She was exhausted but knew that with the mood she was in she wasn't going to be able to sleep anyway.

She opted for a cup of tea, putting the kettle on the stove and picking a fruit-flavored green tea.

"Liz?" Simone's voice made her jump. "Sorry, I didn't mean to scare you." Simone walked in and kissed her cheeks.

"I wasn't expecting you to be home so soon. Were you not on a date?" Liz asked too quickly with a too-cheerful smile.

"He was boring AF. So, when I saw your text from the airport, I used that as an excuse and left."

"Ah, glad to be of help," Liz said with a laugh, but she knew Simone would see through her façade.

"Would you like some company?" she asked, sitting down on one of the bar stools.

"Sure." Liz tried to relax. "Green tea?" she offered but Simone shook her head.

"I need wine," she said, and Liz turned to the fridge and passed her a bottle, then a glass. "So? Tell me everything, how did it go?" Simone filled her glass and took a sip.

"It went really well," Liz said, hoping that the topic would move to something else but Simone was heading straight to the contentious point.

"But most important, did you get to spend some more time with Hudson?"

"Yes." Liz tried to keep her tone neutral, she had not figured out yet what to say to Simone; even if she was her best friend and flatmate, she wasn't ready for her feelings to be dissected.

"I know you guys danced in Paris, but I want to know what else happened."

Liz knew Simone had no patience, so decided to throw her a bone. "He took me on a guided tour around Milan. We went to the Castello, the Galleria, I climbed to the top of the Duomo and even went to see the *Last Supper*."

"Wow! That man is a keeper, Liz, and he clearly cares. Don't be your usual self and let this one pass you by too."

Liz's head snapped up. "Why are you saying that?" Her tone was edgy.

"Because you always do. Opportunities, jobs, men… seen enough of those coming your way and you just ignore them."

"I wasn't interested, that's all." Liz looked down at the tea towel she was strangling with her bare hands.

"Sure? Because I've seen you interested a few times, yet you passed." Simone's eyes were soft and Liz knew she wasn't judging.

"I won't comment about the men, as for the job, you know my father is Connor's good friend and that makes it complicated for me to leave."

Simone rolled her eyes. "Even after fifteen years of loyalty? I think not but I understand where you are coming from."

Liz nodded. "Maybe you are right, I just need to work up the courage to cut the ties."

"And Hudson?"

"He's the client, as I said already that makes him off limits."

"There are other men," Simone suggested, but Liz knew there was no other man but Hudson. Unwilling to say that, she came up with an excuse. "It's hard for me to trust again after what happened with Sean. Also, it's bloody hard to get back into the dating game. I feel I don't belong on those dating apps where everyone is young and hot and I'm old enough to be their mom."

Simone laughed. "Stop that, you're gorgeous and I'm a year older than you and I'm all over all those dating apps—so I don't know what you are on about."

Liz wasn't convinced. She wasn't going to trust a stranger she met online nor was she going to date a client. She was stuck.

Simone drained her glass and poured herself another, while Liz took a first tentative sip of her tea that was still boiling hot.

Simone broke the silence. "I never really asked you about Sean. You rarely talk about him and then only in passing, but clearly whatever happened left you quite scarred."

Liz wrapped her fingers around her mug, looking for support. "Yes, it was a long time ago but it still stings." Liz took a deep breath. "Sean was my fiancé. Sounds ridiculous now, as we were barely twenty and back then I thought he was the only man for me."

"First love and all that. I get it, for me it was Richard Chapman. God, I still stalk him on Facebook. He's fat and bald now and I think he lives in a trailer park. I mean, I'm not judging, but I'm kind of glad that I've dodged that bullet."

Liz laughed and wished she had the same luck, but she had seen Sean's picture in the paper: he was still handsome. Her mother had reminded her so many times that losing him had been her own doing when she moved to Boston. *You should have stayed in Glasgow. Didn't he ask you to marry him? Instead of saying yes, you went galivanting in America.* She had heard the litany enough times.

"But he cheated on you?"

Liz sighed and decided to give Simone more info. "We were always in each other's pockets growing up, best friends, mischief buddies. But we never thought there was more between us. Then we hit puberty and we started to look at each other in a very different way."

"I bet, all those hormones flying," Simone said.

Liz found it hard to tell her the details. "Anyway, long story short, as always, we went to the movies, we shared popcorn but then he held my hand and we kissed in the dark. That night changed everything. We were together all the way through school, then we moved to Glasgow and studied there together at uni. He went for a master's degree after and I did a specialization in interior design. We were happy, settled. He asked me to marry him, I said yes. Then my father said his old pal Connor had an internship for me in his firm in Boston if I were interested. God knows how much I wanted to go, even if it meant time away from Sean. He was supportive about my dreams and aspirations, said it was an opportunity too good to miss, so I went. It was for two years, I tried to negotiate but Connor said any less and it wasn't worth the paperwork. My father pressured me and I signed on the dotted line. Sean and I were okay at the beginning; then he started to have scheduling conflicts with the time difference and his commitments. Our daily call became weekly, then monthly and when I couldn't take the frustration anymore, I bought a ticket to Glasgow to talk to him in person."

"Is that when you found out he was a liar and a cheat?"

Liz laughed. "Yes. I opened the door to my old apartment and realized he was living with another woman who was eight months pregnant."

"Gee…" Simone winced. "You should have kicked him in the nuts."

Liz had to laugh at that. Hadn't she thought the same? "I wish I had now. Back then I was too stunned to even speak. I just threw at him the shitty engagement ring he had given me and walked out."

"Well, good riddance to the scum that he was." Simone lifted her glass and Liz did the same with her cup of tea. "Cheers," she said. Then they sat quietly for a few seconds.

"You know, not all men are assholes," Simone said wisely.

"I know." Liz smiled. She knew that, of course she did, but it didn't make trusting someone with her heart any easier.

"Do you think Hudson is one of the good ones?"

"I don't know," Liz answered with a shrug. "Plus, it doesn't matter, I keep telling you, he's a client so these questions are pointless, really."

Simone raised an eyebrow. "He's not going to be a client forever. What then?"

"Who knows, we will have to wait and see," Liz said, unwilling to think about the possibility.

"True that, but I have a good feeling about you two."

Liz ignored the comment, she shouldn't get her hopes up. "I'm going to run a bath, then try to get some sleep." She stood up.

"Liz."

She turned to Simone.

"Don't pass on this one," her friend said with a wink, but her voice was solemn.

"All I'm going to do right now is run a bath," Liz answered, touching her friend's shoulder before leaving the room. She had a lot to think about while she soaked her tired limbs.

CHAPTER 12

"Ouch. Stupid piece of crap," Hudson swore after pinching the skin of his thumb in between two slats of wood. As he put the fingers in his mouth, hoping to stop the throbbing, Ava scolded him while covering Sam's ears with her hands, "Language! He's only four and I don't want him to go around saying bad words!" She cautiously lifted her hands away from her son's ears, keeping her gaze on Hudson as if he were about to blurt out a string of profanities.

"Sorry, I didn't think *stupid* and *crap* were bad words," Hudson apologized, only to be told off again.

"Language!" Ava shouted and holding Sam's hand, she walked with him out of the room, grumbling under her breath.

"Sorry!" Hudson called out to her, knowing that he'd have to find something better than a two-syllable word to earn her forgiveness. Tom chuckled and Hudson knew he was on his own on this battlefield.

"Man, you are in my wife's bad books now," Tom told him while hammering down the side of the new grown-up bed they'd bought for Sam. His cot would stay in the nursery, surrounded by all the new pieces of furniture as per Liz's design. Because he lost the bet in Milan, Hudson had to help get this stuff ready. Although, even without the wager, he would have helped Tom.

"DIY is not my forte." Annoyed, Hudson picked up a smaller Allen key, which still didn't fit neither. "Explain to me again why the godfather has to build the furniture?" Hudson asked with a cranky tone. "Can't I just be the cool uncle that takes the kids to watch a ball game or buys them ice cream?"

"No. That's what I do," Tom answered simply. "Also, you lost a bet, that's why you're here building."

"I didn't lose the bet, you cheated, but fine," Hudson answered, unwilling to argue with Tom. The task at hand was painful enough without a quarrel.

"Is the bad mood really because of this furniture?" Tom asked when Hudson mumbled under his breath.

"Yes, why?" He looked up at Tom who was kneeling a few feet away.

"You seem stressed. Are you sure there's nothing wrong?" Tom asked, encouraging.

"No. Everything's great." Hudson returned his attention to the drawer in his hand.

"Why don't I believe you?" Tom was clearly not satisfied with the answer.

"You are turning cynical?" Hudson suggested.

"Why don't you just tell me what's wrong..."

Hudson took a minute. He had spent the entire week denying that Liz had left an indelible mark in his heart. Was he ready to say that out loud? Maybe he needed to, but he didn't know how to start so he talked about work instead. "I didn't manage to get more info from the PR agency about our launch," he said.

Tom stared back, unsure what to answer. "Should we worry about that?"

"I don't know." Hudson picked up a screwdriver.

"Hudson, please, tell me there's nothing to worry about. I have enough on my plate without a bunch of guerilla marketeers from

London looking to make a name for themselves with something scandalous…"

"I wish I could," Hudson answered with a frown.

Tom stood up and the atmosphere in the room turned tense.

"I'm honestly nervous of not knowing what their idea is—especially because they are owned by Malone and I don't trust the man." Hudson placed the half-finished drawer on the carpet and stood too. They were facing each other, eye to eye, and Hudson felt the waves of concern pulsing out of his best friend.

Tom said, "We are about to invite that man into our house. He's going to own fifty-one percent of STYLE. He's going to have the final say in all major decisions."

"I know that."

"Is this how it's going to be from now on? If you don't trust him, why are we letting him in?"

Hudson shook his head. "We have no other choice: he's the one with the cash."

"There are other people with plenty of cash. The Italian investors I met in Milan, they were quite interested." Tom sounded positive.

"As soon as they find out that Malone is in the bid for us, they will all back off like all the other investors we had in the pipeline. You know Malone is powerful enough to make his competitors disappear." Hudson was resigned that they were in bed with him now and nothing could be done about it.

"Damn it." Tom dropped his screwdriver, then ran his fingers through his hair in frustration. "Why did we agree to get Malone involved in the first place? This is not us." Tom's words were sharp and true but Hudson didn't have a good answer. They were forced into accepting the deal.

"We didn't know who he really was until it was too late to back off," he almost whispered. "On paper he's such a great investor to have on your side. It was a choice that made sense."

Tom shook his head. "I wish we still had full control."

"He'll own fifty-one percent soon enough and that's us done for good," Hudson said in anger. They had too many debts to pay and Malone's money had been their lifeline, so they took it to save STYLE—even if it meant losing control of the company.

"Sorry, Hudson," Tom said, taking a step away.

"It's not your fault." Hudson looked at his friend with no resentment. They didn't waste the money; they provided good facilities and excellent benefits for their employees. That was where the money went, not on yachts, holidays or supercars, but into the company.

"It is. I'm the CFO and I should have been more ruthless with the numbers."

Hudson smiled; Tom was the best at self-deprecating. "Stop that. We pay people fairly, Tom. We agreed that we succeed together or we failed anyway. You just kept us afloat for longer than anyone expected."

"I'm just sorry that Malone had the power to make a vacuum around us to be the only investor left willing to give us the capital we needed."

"He's more a loan shark than an investor, Tom: he took fifty-one percent of our company when we were trying to raise money for twenty-five percent of its value."

Hudson sighed, then walking to the window, he watched Ava and Sam playing in the yard and knew they had done the right thing. They had ensured STYLE had a future.

Tom came next to him and in silence they watched his wife and his son. "I did my best: it just wasn't good enough," Tom admitted.

"I think Malone is the hill where people die. We were done when he set his eyes on us. You've done an incredible job at stopping him from taking the whole thing." Hudson placed one hand on Tom's shoulder. "I don't think there was anything either of us could have done differently. Malone decided that he wanted STYLE and did whatever was necessary to get it."

Tom exhaled and said, with tension in his voice, "I know you're right; it stings all the same."

"We saved the company. We kept our team from losing their jobs, we've done *good*," Hudson said sincerely. "I just wish I knew what he's planning for the launch—and for the future of STYLE."

"Do you have any inkling of what he'll do?"

"No idea." Hudson shook his head.

They stayed there for a minute longer before Tom broke the silence. "There's a silver lining at least. Malone led you to Liz."

Hudson turned to him. "What do you mean?"

Tom's eyebrows knotted. "You know what I mean. You're falling for her. I always thought that these love-at-first-sight stories only happen in the movies, not in real life," Tom said, sitting on the windowsill next to Hudson. "But I've seen you two, and I witnessed it with my own eyes. So, are you thinking of asking her out?"

"I… no." Hudson didn't know what else to say.

"You can't lie to me: I know you too well."

"I like her but I'm not sure she'll say yes if I ask her out."

Tom shook his head. "You don't know that."

"She was very clear about keeping things professional between us."

"But—" Tom was interrupted by the creaking of the door.

"Why is the bed still not done?" Ava walked into the room, looking disappointed.

Hudson quickly scampered back to the pieces of furniture he had abandoned on the floor, hoping that Ava was in a forgiving mood.

"Sorry," Tom said, kissing her cheek. "How did you even know that we were not working?"

"I saw you sitting on the windowsill, having a good natter like two old matrons," Ava said with a forced British accent. Tom chuckled, lightening the mood.

"What's going on?" she asked, looking straight at Hudson.

"Nothing. We were looking at the instruction booklet."

"I don't believe you." Ava turned her attention to her husband. "What's really going on?"

"Hudson's in love," Tom said, immediately caving under his wife's stare.

"Oh." Ava was taken by surprise. "I wasn't actually expecting you to say something like that." She pursed her lips. "Now I'll have to cancel all the blind dates I've already planned for you."

She said it with such a serious tone that Hudson knew she wasn't joking.

"Do I know her?" Ava asked.

"No." Hudson shrugged, hoping to be convincing enough. Ava looked at him for a second, trying to decide if he was telling her the truth, then changed the topic.

"Why don't we all go downstairs and eat the gingerbread cookies I made with Sam this morning?" Neither Tom nor Hudson replied until she added, "I also have beer and nuts." They both smiled.

"Thank you," Tom said, taking her face in his hands, he kissed her lips with a loud smack.

"Don't be too excited. This will be waiting for you tomorrow, when you'll be back to finish it," she said, and they all walked out the room, shutting the door on its chaos.

By eight o'clock, Sam was in bed, the kitchen was tidy and Hudson had left.

Ava sat on the sofa rubbing her belly while trying to decide if she wanted strawberries or black olives.

Tom went to sit next to her. "He's down," he said referring to Sam. "He was so tired after playing on the trampoline with Hudson, I think he was asleep before his head touched the pillow."

"Awww, bless. He had such a great time," she said, lifting her legs so her feet were now on Tom's lap.

He started to massage her ankles and Ava closed her eyes. "This is pure bliss," she said with a half-smile.

"Making a person is a tiring job," Tom said, and when she opened her eyes to look at him, he saw a flash of determination in her gaze and worried if he had said something wrong.

"Who's Hudson in love with?" she asked, taking him by surprise.

"Erm…" Tom wasn't sure if he should tell her about Liz.

"Tom, you know you can't hide things from me. I'll find out anyway, but you could save me some effort." Ava propped herself up so that he knew she meant business.

"I really don't know." Tom kept a straight face while rubbing her feet with more vigor. If Hudson was right and Liz was uncomfortable about dating a client, then getting Ava involved was only going to complicate things.

"I know you are lying. You always smile too much when you are lying." Ava looked at him with piercing eyes. "And the only reason for that must be that she's not right for him."

"Ava, stay out of Hudson's life," Tom warned her.

"You know that I love him too much to stop trying to find him the perfect match." Ava sighed at the pleasure of imagining Hudson happily coupled.

"How do you know who's perfect for him?" Tom asked with genuine curiosity.

"I just know. That's my talent, I'm a matchmaker."

"Ava, you shouldn't meddle in other people's lives, even if it's for their own good." There was a warning in Tom's eyes, but she was smiling her best plotting smile and he knew there was nothing he could say to change her mind.

CHAPTER 13

Liz sat in the back of a taxi watching the traffic jam spreading down the main road. The entire downtown was gridlocked and she was running late. She took her cell phone and made a call.

"Hello?"

"Ava, it's Liz. I'm stuck in traffic and I'm afraid I'll be late. We only moved a few blocks but we are not even moving anymore."

"Oh no. What's happening in Boston? Tom's been late home all week because of the traffic." Ava's petulant tone showed her annoyance.

"I'm not sure, to be honest. It looks like roadworks but I've been in the taxi for twenty minutes already and I'm starting to lose faith I'll ever make it to you." Liz watched as the taxi driver shook his head.

"If you don't mind catching the train, I can pick you up at the station," Ava offered, giving Liz an option she hadn't thought of.

"Anything's better than spending another second trapped here," Liz said.

"Ah, great. You need the Fitchburg Line from North Station."

"Sure, North Station is not far, I can walk there. Will text you from the train." Liz tapped the driver on the shoulder.

"I'm off. Sorry," she said to him, paying the fare plus a generous tip. He looked at the money and shrugged. The extra she gave him was enough to tame the frustration of losing the customer. She collected her belongings and jumped out of the car, happy to escape the mayhem.

One hour later, Liz was alighting at Concord.

She was nervous. She had checked her makeup, brushed her hair again, and chewed on several mints. From Tom's description of his wife and Hudson's almost reverential affection for the woman, Liz had pieced together the image of a fascinating creature, and now she felt the pressure of her approval. It was completely insane to feel this way, and yet, she was desperate for it.

Liz walked out the station and tried to spot Ava within the small crowd waiting.

"Liz!" She heard a voice calling her name and turned immediately to her left to see a beautiful woman hurrying in her direction. Dark hair was flowing down her back as she walked quickly despite the pregnant belly. "Hello." Ava panted slightly, then leaned in to kiss Liz's cheek. Liz had to move her portfolio out of the way.

"Ava, it's so nice to finally meet you. Tom and Hudson talked so much about you when we were in Europe, I feel like I've known you for years," Liz said genuinely.

"Same here. Tom kept singing your praises, and Hudson told me how brilliant you were with the team in Milan, but they had forgotten to mention that you are also stunning."

"Ah." Liz didn't really know what to reply but Ava's positive energy was contagious and they were now both grinning at each other.

"I'm just so glad you could make it. I loved the furniture you suggested for the nursery and Sam's room, the boys built it last weekend. It's brilliant." Ava rubbed her tummy, then stretching her arms out she pulled Liz into a bear hug, her bump squashed between them. "You are the answer to my prayers," Ava declared with a glint in her eyes, and Liz felt even more pressure added to her shoulders.

Ava patted Liz's arm softly. "Yes, definitely more beautiful than any of the descriptions I heard of you. They have been holding back." Ava's smile turned mischievous but Liz's heart was racing at the thought that Hudson had been talking about her.

Recovering from the frenetic blipping of her pulse, Liz returned the compliment with total sincerity. "I can say the same about you. You are glowing."

"Ah, stop it, I'm as big as a house already, and I still have months to go." Ava snorted. "With my first, Sam, I had the smallest, cutest baby bump. I managed to wear my skinny jeans until I was eight months; people didn't even notice I was pregnant until the last trimester, but with this one? Boom, I exploded the minute I peed on that stick."

She rubbed at her tummy again, and Liz felt a squeeze of softness for the woman, as if she was actually meeting up with an old friend she hadn't seen in a while.

"Anyway, let's go: we don't want to stand here all day. My feet hurt like hell." She chattered as they walked. "I didn't understand when my mum said that having kids in your twenties is so much easier. You know she comes from a very traditional Greek family, I thought she was just repeating what she heard."

"But?" Liz asked.

"No but, she was just spot on. I'm over forty, and I can tell you, it is hell," Ava said as they retraced her steps in the direction of the car park. "I don't want to put you off," she added as they walked. "Still magical of course." Ava smiled.

Liz nodded and for the first time in forever she felt a strange pull towards the idea of having a baby of her own. She didn't want to think of Hudson as the father but the connection came so naturally in her head she couldn't separate the two.

"Sam is having a playdate at his cousin's, so we have all afternoon free." Ava interrupted her musing.

"Perfect, although I was hoping to meet him. It helps when you can have a feel for the personality of the child that will use the room."

"Oh, that's so sweet," Ava said almost cooing. "Stay for dinner then, Sam will be back later: you can meet him."

"Thank you. I'd love to meet your little man but only if it doesn't add to the workload."

"Nah! I love to cook," Ava squealed, clapping her perfectly manicured hands together a few times. "I'm also quite good, so you are in for a treat."

"Great match then, I'm quite a good eater," Liz said with a cheeky grin.

"Sounds like we will get along swimmingly. I feel we are going to become friends." Ava winked, then pressed the button on her car key and the boot of a black SVU on the left of the parking lot popped open.

Liz put her portfolio carefully inside it, then walked to the front seat.

"Only a short ride."

It took them barely ten minutes to get from the station to Ava's home, but Ava managed to tell Liz her life story. Liz enjoyed every second.

"You live in such a nice village and I can't believe we are only forty minutes away from Boston."

"Yes, it's a good community. Small enough that we all know each other but big enough that we are not always nose deep into each other's business. There are lots of lovely walks and little quirky places to visit, so great to raise a family," Ava said. "Next time you come, I'll show you around."

"I'd love that," Liz said, realizing that it was the truth.

"Fall is my favorite season, the leaves changing colors and their reflection in the lake is an absolute glory so definitely worth it, although summer is just as gorgeous." Ava parked and looked at Liz. "I have a question."

"Sure, what is it?"

"Sorry to be nosey but that's who I am so better if we get this out of the way."

Liz waited, even more nervous now.

"Is there a Mister Right in your life?" Ava asked, looking at Liz's grandmother's ring on her finger.

Liz shook her head. "It's complicated, but no is the short answer. I'm not engaged, this ring is just symbolic and confusing, actually. Hudson also thought I had a fiancé, I don't," she said, and Ava smiled at her with empathy in her eyes.

"Everything will work out, you know." Ava's tone was filled with hope. "Always does in the end."

Liz nodded and got out of the car. After retrieving the port- folio from the boot, Ava linked her arm with Liz's and directed her towards a stunning white house.

"Oh, Ava. Your house is so beautiful, the picture I saw doesn't do it justice," Liz said, staring at the lovely colonial-style building in front of her. The patio ran across the front, two pale-blue Adirondack chairs faced each other on one side. There were plant pots around and the light-blue ceramic vases matched the color of the shutters that created a beautiful contrast with the white of the cladding wood.

"Thank you! A compliment from an expert isn't something I'm going to take lightly." Ava opened the door and they walked in. The interior was just as striking.

"Ava, your house is spectacular! It'd fit right into a magazine."

"Awwww, I'm flattered, it's all my doing but I used STYLE too." Ava was beaming with pride. "I have to give some credit to Hudson: he designed a great software, and so easy to use."

"You don't need an interior designer after all." Liz propped her portfolio against the wall and went for a little tour of the ground floor while she tried to find the right word to ask more about STYLE.

"So, you've used the software then?" Liz kept her tone casual.

"Yes, it's on the iPad. It's intuitive but accurate. Once it's out on the market everyone would be able to have an interior designer on tap for the cost of an app!"

Liz frowned. It sounded like democratization of technology—which was in general a good thing. She was just concerned about the health and safety aspect and the fact that major DIY work could damage a building's structure and make it dangerous.

Ava must have sensed her distress because she returned the subject to the house. "Tom wanted to buy a new house but I love my home and I don't want to move," Ava said, running her fingertips over the mantlepiece filled with family pictures. "He thinks that we'll need a bigger place with two kids. He wants more living space on the ground floor and there's been talk of a cinema room to do family movie nights. And also play video games."

"The four-year-old and the baby?" Liz asked and both women laughed.

"My thoughts exactly," Ava confirmed with a pout. "Although, I'm not against the extra space."

"But you don't want to move."

Ava shook her head. "I really love my home."

Liz took a minute to absorb the information. She then moved further into the room. Looked up and made a few mental calculations. "You could extend out here," Liz said, looking from the French doors opening over the massive garden at the back.

Ava walked next to her. "Hudson suggested the same when Tom mentioned he wanted a cinema room."

Liz smiled, it was silly to be happy about her idea aligning with Hudson's one, yet she was. "You have a large plot, a flat yard, and these are ideal conditions for an extension. You could do a one-floor extension and have a terrace upstairs, or you could extend upstairs too and add another bedroom or a bathroom or a study, or all of them," Liz said, knowing that Connor had pulled off beautiful extensions in more difficult positions, so this could be easily done.

"Do you think it'll be worth it, Liz?" Ava's eyes lit up.

"I do. I think you'll make the money back if you ever decide to sell. And the back garden is big enough to accommodate the extension and still have plenty of space for a patio, an outdoor kitchen area and lawn for the kids to play." Liz nodded.

Ava sighed. "I want everything you said. But is it really possible?"

Liz touched her arm. "I'm not an architect but I'm sure it's possible. Also, Hudson suggested the same and you trust him, right?"

Ava nodded.

"I could ask my boss to send someone to do a survey and draw the plans. I think it'll be easy to turn this house into Tom's dream home so you won't have to move."

Ava squeezed her in a hug. "You are a genius, Liz!"

"Only doing my job," Liz replied, pleased to be of assistance. After all, that was why she loved being an interior designer: she was passionate about turning people's houses into their ideal home.

Liz untangled herself from Ava's hug and took a step away. "It'll be stunning," she said.

"So, tell me about Hudson. Looks like you guys have a common vision. Are you getting along?"

"So far," Liz said, non-committal.

"He's smart, honest, loyal, and isn't he outrageously handsome with his brooding looks and the shaggy hair?"

"I don't usually rate the clients, only their projects." Liz wasn't taking the bait.

"Oh, you are very professional, I can see that. But let me tell you, Hudson's such a catch: don't wait too long to make your move or you could be missing out. He has plenty of women interested." If Ava intended to make Liz react, she succeeded.

"I'm not going to make any move on a client, plus I'm not interested," Liz said, hoping she had managed to hide her real feelings.

Ava walked towards her. "You are not a very good liar, you know."

"I-I—" Liz stammered, her mouth dry.

Ava laughed. "You are interested. And I know you like him because you have the answer written on your face."

Liz decided that saying nothing at this point was her best move. Ava laughed again, a heartwarming giggle that made Liz feel a tiny bit less awkward.

"Come on, this conversation requires some refreshments," Ava said, leading Liz into the kitchen. She took a jug of freshly-made lemonade and poured two glasses.

"What conversation?" Liz was stressing again.

"Have a seat," she said, then settled next to Liz on one of the stools at the kitchen counter. Without any preambles, Ava asked, "So, when did you fall in love with Hudson? Was it in Milan or Paris?"

"Excuse me?" Liz choked on her drink.

Ava laughed at her reaction. "Oh Boston, then. Love at first sight. So romantic," Ava said, fluttering her long lashes. "At least this explains Hudson's funny mood, he's been all over the shop since he came to your office. Worse even after Europe. At least now I know why and who's the mysterious woman he has fallen for."

At those words Liz's heart did a somersault in her chest. "Fallen for...?" Liz needed to make sure of what she had heard.

"I've known Hudson for twenty years. I know all his moods— and believe me the man has a collection of them—anyway, lately he had a new one, one that I haven't seen before. At first, I thought it was grumpy-but-pretending-not-to-be and I assumed that things didn't go well in Europe. But Tom swore to me that everything went great; and my husband knows better than to lie to me. Still, I knew something was off. Then last weekend I discovered Hudson is in love and now that I've met you, I've put two and two together and bingo, I figured it out. His new mood is his falling-in-love-with-Liz mood." She sounded like a professor giving a lecture, factual and precise, Liz was speechless. "Everything makes sense now," said Ava, pleased with herself.

Liz looked intently at the drink rippling inside the glass as she gently swirled it around. Ava's words had punched a massive hole into her defenses. She was worried that all her feelings would pour out on the kitchen floor and drown them both.

"Now that we've established that you guys like each other, I'd like to know what happens next?" Ava was expecting an answer.

Liz had none, so she used the same old adage as before. "Hudson's my client. Nothing happens." She tried her best to sound resolute.

"And you are okay with that?" Ava asked with a serious voice. "Your eyes soften every time I mention his name. I think we both know what your heart wants, and it's not professionalism."

Liz's cheeks flushed with embarrassment. "It's not only the appropriate thing to do; it's the only way I get to keep my job. My boss has a strict no-fraternization-with-clients policy and he's a stickler for rules." Liz looked Ava straight in the eye to underline that she was telling the truth even if really Connor was still out of action and the first who broke his own rules. Ava wasn't buying it, so Liz gave her something. "I admit it, Hudson is attractive, but this is not the right time." Liz took a massive gulp of lemonade to dislodge the lump in her throat.

"How long will this project last?"

"A few months. Although, it depends on approval from the Italian Beni Culturali," Liz answered.

Ava frowned. "I can't plot on an empty stomach." She walked

to the fridge to retrieve a fruit platter, which she placed on the counter before sitting down again. Liz waited for Ava to explain.

"I think Hudson has feelings for you, you are the woman he's been waiting for."

Liz's eyes widened at Ava's words.

"I'd like to see him happy." Ava took an apple slice and bit into it. "Some people are content to be alone but Hudson's not one of them." She took another bite, then dried her lips with a napkin. "He's also an incurable romantic and I know he's been waiting for 'the one', for 'the real thing' and that's you, Liz, and from what I can tell, you are just as smitten."

"Smitten…" Liz shook her head. "We only just met and we are not kids, so I concede there's physical attraction between us—but talking about 'the real thing' seems a bit premature."

"Look," Ava said, touching the back of Liz's hand, "I want Hudson to be happy and somehow, I think you will make each other happy; but waiting months to find out while pretending you don't feel anything for each other is not a good idea."

"There's no way around it, really," Liz said, too scared to think of the possibility of dating Hudson. She told herself she should prioritize her career, not a fling. She had her hands on a project that could change everything for her. She had waited more than a decade for that and she couldn't risk it. "When we were in Milan I saw Hudson pretty cozy with Patrizia, so maybe his loved-up mood is not for me at all. This is just guesswork and given the situation, it's safer to leave things as they are. I'd hate to make this awkward," Liz said.

Ava closed her eyes for a few seconds. "That's true, even if I know he doesn't love Patrizia. He has known her for years. If she mattered he would have done something about it by now. So, she's not it," Ava admitted, "but it's not a bad idea to find out for sure."

"And how are you planning to do that? Polygraph?" Liz's sarcasm was back in full swing, she used it to cover her tension.

"Simple, I'm inviting Hudson for dinner too. Once I see you together, I'll know," Ava said.

"For dinner? You mean tonight?"

"Yes, tonight. There is no time like the present!" Ava said already picking up her cell. Liz raised her arm as if to stop Ava, and then let it drop, resigned. She didn't think she could stop her; this lady was a force of nature.

CHAPTER 14

"Ava, I'm sorry, but I can't leave early today. The team is releasing some new features and I still have too much to do." Hudson's tone was firm but Ava's persistence was hard to fight off.

"You owe me, Hudson." Ava's sulky voice made him feel guilty even if he wasn't sure what he owed her and why. "I'm pregnant!" she moaned. "And I spent hours cooking for you: a mouth-watering thank-you dinner for helping with the furniture; and now you are not coming." She sounded teary and Hudson wondered how many more times Ava was going to use her state as a bargaining chip, or her tears. Knowing her, many, many more times.

"I should have put my feet up instead of straining my back with the effort." She grunted from down the line. He knew it would be quicker to just give in now; rather than arguing for an hour with her and then giving into what she wanted anyway. She carried on before Hudson could say anything. "Have you ever been pregnant? Eh? Do you know how sore your feet get when you stand for too long?" she asked sharply.

Hudson closed his eyes, exhausted. He loved her dearly, but Ava was one bossy lady.

"No? Well, let me tell you about the head of my unborn child pushing on my bladder while I was peeling a mountain of potatoes!"

"Fine! Fine, I'll be there at eight," he said quickly before she cranked up the melodrama.

"Make it seven and bring wine," Ava said, ending the conversation with those orders.

Hudson relaxed his shoulders and returned his attention to his laptop.

Looks like I'm coming for dinner, he typed into the chat opened in the corner of the screen.

So, I've been told, Tom replied immediately. I'm leaving now: I need to get dessert. DO NOT BE LATE!

Hudson checked the time and knew he had to go as well if he wanted to get a good bottle and be there on time. Begrudgingly, he closed his laptop and got ready to leave.

Luckily, the earlier standstill of traffic was gone, and he arrived in front of Tom and Ava's home with three minutes to spare. He walked down the path and knocked at the door. He looked around as he waited. He loved their house with its colonial style and well-kept yard. The perfect place for a family. He thought of his loft in Boston and wondered if he would be happy to trade that for a detached house and a white pitched fence. To swap his bachelor life for something like this. When the idea of wife and kids made him sigh, he shooed those thoughts away together with the image of Liz that immediately appeared in his mind. *Not the right time.* He told himself.

Tom opened the door. "You're late," he said.

"No, I'm not," Hudson answered defensively.

"Whatever, man. Ava said you're late; don't shoot the messenger." Tom seemed slightly nervous.

Hudson walked behind him trying to figure out what was wrong. Maybe Ava was having a really tough time keeping the hormones under control. Was that a misogynist bias or just a scientific fact? He wondered and promised himself to be extra nice to Ava. As he entered the kitchen, he was ready with a prepared compliment but he didn't have the time to deliver it because Sam, who was dressed as a pirate, jumped on him. "Uncle H! Uncle H!" Sam yelled putting his hands to Hudson's face and delivering a big sloppy kiss to his cheek. "Ouch! Spiky!" he said after rubbing his lips. He did that every time and Hudson laughed at Sam's short memory.

"Hey buddy," he said, placing on the counter the wine and the bunch of flowers to give Sam a better squeeze. The silver hook Sam wore over his left hand burrowed into his side while the corner of the black hat dug into his temple, and Hudson was glad when Sam loosened his embrace.

"You are late," Ava said after she finished checking on whatever was cooking in the oven.

"I'm not late," Hudson whispered into Sam's ear and made him giggle.

Tom came back into the kitchen to pick up a glass of white wine and a bowl of olives. He then hurried out again without a word.

"Give me a minute, buddy, I need to speak to your mommy," Hudson said, putting Sam back down. He watched him run out of the room at full throttle, then turned to Ava. "Why am I *really* here?" Hudson asked, stepping closer to her.

"For your thank-you dinner." Her innocent tone immediately confirmed to Hudson that she was up to something.

"Please tell me you didn't organize another blind date for me. We have been through this a dozen times before. It never worked; it only made it awkward for everyone." Hudson's voice was low but the annoyance was easy to detect.

"It's not a blind date, I promise," she answered, looking at him, mischief in her gaze, before returning her attention to the food. "You told me to butt out of your personal life, and I'm doing just that."

Hudson sighed. She was shoving some BS his way; he wasn't going to eat it. "If you haven't invited a date, then who's drinking the glass of white wine Tom has carried outside? I know it's not his." Before Ava could answer, he heard Liz's voice coming from the garden. His heart jumped into his throat at the unexpected emotions firing inside his chest. "Liz?" he whispered, turning his head towards the French doors leading to the garden.

"Oh, yes, did I forget to mention that?" Ava giggled. "Must be the hormones."

"Is she staying for dinner?" Hudson seemed to be struggling to put the words together.

"She came to discuss the kids' rooms. Then we talked about an extension—she agrees with your suggestion by the way, great minds and all that—and it was getting late so I asked her to stay given that I was cooking something special for you anyway."

Ava kept talking but Hudson was distracted. His attention was focused on the French doors. He felt unprepared for the encounter.

"Hudson? Hey, did you listen to a word I said?" Ava waved a wooden spoon in front of his face.

"No, sorry."

"I said, you should give those flowers to Liz," Ava repeated.

He picked them up from the counter, a little embarrassed. "I brought them for you," he said.

"I know, and you are very sweet but I still think you should give them to Liz."

"And you don't mind?"

"Not a bit," she answered just as Liz entered the kitchen.

She was carrying Sam and they were giggling together. It was a strange type of longing that hit Hudson's chest. Something that seemed to have a lot to do with a family and a house with white picket fences. The thought left him slightly shaken. *Not the right time*. It was getting harder to remember that.

"Hudson," Liz whispered when her eyes met his. His name on her lips turned his throat dry.

"Liz! Liz!" Sam was calling her, but her eyes were locked on Hudson's, as if she couldn't look away. To get her full attention, Sam placed his little hands on both sides of her face and turned her slightly so that she had to focus her gaze on him again.

"Tickle me again," he asked her, already giggling, but Ava stepped in, and with a smile she plucked her son away from Liz's arms. When he complained she offered him a bribe in the form of a pre-dinner treat and with a cookie in his hand, Ava took Sam into the garden.

Liz and Hudson stood in front of each other, with the counter between them and the silence surrounding them, tension was filling the space.

"Hi," Hudson said, taking a step closer.

"Hi," Liz answered, standing seemingly calm and at ease, but when he saw her hands shaking, he knew she was as nervous as he was.

"These are for you," he said, stepping closer to her. He offered her the bunch of flowers in his hand, glad to have something to say.

"Thank you." Her face buried into the fat pink peonies made him want to see her with that expression again and again. "They are so beautiful. I love them so much," she confessed candidly. That was something else he liked about her: she was genuine, there was no agenda behind her moves. If that was because they were not on an official date and the pressure was off, or because of their connection, he couldn't say.

"I'm going to remember that," Hudson promised, and saw the

change in her eyes. A shadow ran across them as if his words had triggered some worrisome thoughts.

"Were you stuck in the horrible traffic downtown?" she asked, playing with one of the petals.

"No, it had cleared by the time I left, but it lasted for hours. I could see the queue from the office. They better sort it out before the folks around here get their pitchforks out."

Liz laughed, holding the bouquet to her chest in a seriously disarming way. Hudson swallowed his needs.

"I don't know about pitchforks. Are they still a thing? Do they look good on social media?" she answered, making him laugh.

"Absolutely, I have a spare in case you ever need one," he said, then lifting one hand to his chin, he rubbed it, pretending to think about something important.

"What is it?" she asked.

"You have jelly on your face. I wasn't sure if I should tell you or not," Hudson said with a smile, and she immediately lifted her fingers to her cheek.

"Sam's sticky fingers." She sighed, rubbing her skin, hoping she was in the right spot.

"Whatever you say," he teased her, then watched her struggle.

"Am I even close to it?" she asked, and Hudson shook his head.

"Not really," he said.

She sighed in frustration.

"May I?" He waited for her consent.

"Please." She blushed when he traced her jaw with his thumb. She quivered when he reached the corner of her mouth. Her lips were full and parted and he wanted to kiss her more than he ever wanted anything in his life. *Who cares about timing?*

"Liz..." he said to her as Tom entered the room, clearly surprised at the sight of them. They turned to him and it was too late for him to duck out, so they all started to pretend this wasn't awkward.

"I came for another beer, would you like one, Hudson?" Tom asked.

"Erm... a beer. Yes, please, I'd like one," Hudson answered, shoving his hands in his pockets, his default go-to when he wanted to look casual.

Tom opened the fridge and passed Hudson a bottle. "Wanna sit outside?" Tom looked like someone who had lost the ability to think of anything more intelligent to say. Both Hudson and Liz were just as dazzled so they followed him to the back yard.

The evening was beautifully mild. The sky was painted with strokes of blues and pinks, wispy layers of cloud overlapped each other while the nearby river was a white-noise lullaby. But still, Liz was the one stealing the show. Hudson could not tear his gaze away from her. He could not get enough of her voice, her smile, her eyes. She had bewitched him in a way that he didn't think was possible. Never in his life had he been quite so taken by someone and it wasn't an easy feeling to handle.

The tension eventually eased off: Sam's enthusiasm for their duo trampoline antics helped with that and by the time dinner was served, he was relaxed and ready for some banter.

Liz seemed to have done the same and jokes were flowing effortlessly around the table, together with the wine.

Sam was in bed, and the house turned quiet around them. It was then that Hudson realized how easy it would be to get used to this life. An intimate group of friends, home-cooked dinner, kids in bed and the woman he loved laughing at his side. He had done the travel, the nightclubs, the casual dating, the building of a business that required burning the candle from both ends. This was what he wanted next.

He'd have to think about it later because Ava was digging up embarrassing stories from the past and he couldn't sit this one out.

"Tom used to have bleached white hair like a popstar when he was eighteen," Ava told Liz with a horrified expression on her face.

"Are we telling secrets now?" Tom said, pointing his dessert spoon in his wife's direction.

"More like horror stories, I'd say," she answered cheekily, earning herself a round of laughter.

"You loved it." Tom nudged his wife gently with his elbow.

She just shook her head. "I didn't," she said to Liz, making her laugh again.

Hudson turned his eyes on Liz, glad that she was enjoying herself. Didn't feel as if he was trying to push a square peg in a round hole, she fitted right in, with him, with his life.

"Ava punched Jimmy Tayler when she was eight and knocked one of his teeth out," Tom said, and silence descended at the table. They all turned to Ava.

"In my defense, it was just a milk tooth and was already wobbly."

"You still punched him," Tom added.

"I vaguely remember hearing about this. He was a bully, probably deserved that," Hudson said, high-fiving Ava when she lifted her hand to him.

"Well, he didn't bully anyone else after this one punched his teeth out," Tom said, patting his wife on the back.

"Tooth," she corrected him, "again, it was just a milk tooth. My knuckles, however, were sore for a week."

"Why did you do it?" Liz asked, looking at Ava.

"He called my cousin 'Miss Piggy,'" Ava answered. "My cousin Harold was quite—erm—large as a kid but he was a kind soul, always friendly, patient. People picked on him all the time because they knew he would sit and take it. Jimmy was the worst, so one day we were in the playground and six or seven older boys surrounded Harold and started to call him 'Miss Piggy.' They were doing horrible snorting noises and also implying that he was gay and teasing him for that. They threw food at him.

Suggested he wore a pink dress." Ava blinked, then continued. "As I walked up to them the rage mounted. I didn't even give them the chance to run. I marched straight up to Jimmy—he was the tallest and the meanest. I figured if I took him down, the others would run. I walked right up to him and punched him in the mouth." She laughed. "It wasn't planned, it was just the highest I could reach, but luck was on my side and the wobbly tooth fell out. Suddenly there was blood everywhere. Jimmy ran to the teacher; said I'd beat him up. The whole thing was blown out of proportion. He said I wanted to kill him, that I was a gypsy witch and Jimmy's mom demanded that I was suspended… it was a mess."

"Oh no," Liz said, reaching over to touch Ava's hand.

"It was stressful but Jimmy bullied almost everyone at school and people started to speak up, so in the end he was the one who got suspended."

"And Ava earned herself the nickname Rocky."

"You are Rocky?" Hudson was surprised. "How didn't I know that? Everyone talked about Rocky at my school, too, I didn't know your punching-the-bully story was the Rocky story. Why didn't you tell me before? We've been friends for almost twenty years."

Ava laughed but then she turned serious. "I'm not proud of it," Ava said. "Using my fist wasn't the best way to deal with Jimmy. I don't want Sam to learn that's how we deal with people, even the vermin like Jimmy."

"I get that," Hudson said with admiration.

"It worked though." Tom was swinging his fists in the air with a pretend uppercut. They all laughed.

"Right. Enough about me. Liz, you are up next," Ava said, keen to shift the attention away from her right hook.

"I—" Liz opened her mouth, then closed it again.

"Anything will do, but it needs to be embarrassing," Tom said with a wink.

Liz looked down at the empty dessert bowl in front of her and Hudson thought she was preparing herself to be teased.

"I'm scared of fireworks. I hate having to stay in my flat alone on July 4th when my flatmate goes to visit her family."

"Hey." Hudson stroked her arm, and she turned to him. "There's nothing to be ashamed of."

"Really?" She shook her head. "I'm a grown woman. A strong, confident woman. I shouldn't be scared of fireworks. They are pretty, people love them." Liz looked straight into his eyes.

"Fears are irrational," Hudson said. "Plus, confident and strong doesn't mean that you have to be alone or that you can't be frightened of fireworks." He smiled at her.

"Thank you," she whispered.

Ava chimed in. "Absolutely correct. I'm terrified of ants, even if I live the rest of my life like a boss, I'm freaked out by those tiny little innocent bugs."

Liz laughed and straightened her shoulders when Ava winked at her. "Also, you know what, Boston isn't that big, so you just give Hudson a call if there's a problem and I'm sure he'd be over in a flash." Ava's tone was determined and both Hudson and Liz turned to look at her, taken aback by the suggestion.

"Oh no, I wouldn't want to bother anyone," Liz said, turning her gaze to Hudson.

"It's no bother, really," he answered, reaching for her hand. Then feeling Tom's gaze on them he quickly let Liz's hand go.

The moment had turned slightly awkward and Hudson was grateful that Ava took charge of the conversation. "Do you like karaoke?" she asked Liz out of the blue.

"I love karaoke," Liz said. Her tone was excited, but it sounded a little forced.

"See? I told you people love karaoke." Ava clapped her hands, looking at Tom.

"Yes, you did," Tom answered.

"What's this all about?" Liz asked.

"I've been thinking of a big party to celebrate the acquisition, karaoke seems the right choice. Tom and Hudson are not convinced." She shot them a side glance. "I've been told the PR team in London is designing a launch with lots of publicity so a party over here would be a good way to amplify that."

Hudson knew she had started planning that anyway, and probably already chosen the new dress she would have to buy for the occasion. Stopping her was too much effort, Hudson didn't think he had the energy for it.

"We should aim for Labor Day. It's just perfect," Ava said, then turning to Liz, she asked, "The offices will be done by then, right?"

"Hopefully, if everything goes as scheduled," Liz said. "In my plans we will be done by 29 August so we can hand them over to the cleaning crew. But lots of it depends on the Italian Beni Culturali's approval."

"Beni Culturali?" Ava asked.

"Yes, it's for the protection of historical buildings. The Milan office is in one of them and there's lots of red tape I need to cut through to get the right approval."

"Sounds like a right pain, but I know you'll deliver." Ava gave Liz her vote of confidence. "And either way, the Boston office will be ready, right?"

"Absolutely," Liz said.

"I should start the planning on Monday then." Ava was determined and fired up.

"So, you are telling me you haven't started already?" Tom looked at Ava with incredulous eyes.

"I might have contacted a few catering firms, just to get a sense of their availability..." Ava answered with a grin, dipping the spoon in the tiramisu in front of her. "Maybe I've put together a mood board."

Hudson looked at Tom and laughed.

"Sure, go ahead, we need a party, karaoke is fun," he said with a resigned tone.

"Yes! You won't regret it." Ava looked at Hudson with a massive grin, then turning to Tom, she took his chin in between her fingers. "We can perform our duet," she said.

"Oh, no… no… no…" Tom said, shaking his head, but Ava nodded with a glint in her eyes that said she was going to have her way.

"I have a birthday coming up soon. Maybe we could have karaoke then too? I wasn't thinking of throwing a party but it's the big forty so maybe I should do something…" Liz said, and Ava turned to her.

"What! You have to do something, I'll help you… I know the perfect place and—" Then she stopped herself. "I mean, if you'd like some help organizing it, I'd love to be involved."

They laughed at Ava's poor attempt of disguising her nature.

"I'd love your help, Ava, I'm useless at parties. But only if you are up to it, I don't want you to strain yourself and the baby."

"No, I'll be fine!"

"In that case, you are hired," Liz said, and Hudson noticed that Ava looked very pleased.

The conversation moved on to other topics. Time went quickly and when Liz stifled another yawn, Hudson nudged her. "Tired?" he asked her.

"A little." She nodded, covering her mouth when another yawn caught her off guard. "Still a bit jet-lagged from Europe and I'm behind with other projects, so I've been spending most nights working and I'm exhausted," Liz explained.

"I should be apologizing for throwing you off your schedule. We gave Connor plenty of warning but until the morning of the meeting we didn't know he had put you on the project," Hudson said.

"If it's of any consolation, I only found out the day before. I had to pull an all-nighter because of his poor planning." Liz shrugged.

"Doesn't sound like Connor is a very nice boss," Tom said, inviting himself into the conversation.

"He's very protective of his clients and I think he wanted to be on STYLE, something to do with Malone and the friction they had in the past. But Connor was too unwell because of his hay fever, this year seemed to be worse than ever."

"Still, he didn't have to dump it on you."

"That's okay, I'm glad he did, it's a brilliant project." She looked at Hudson for a second and then turned her gaze on Tom. "Plus, I'm a night owl. I do my best work after midnight," Liz said before another yawn interrupted her. "See? Classic creature of the night." They all laughed at her joke. "I should call a cab, get some sleep," Liz suggested.

Ava shook her head. "Hudson will take you home. You guys live in Boston, makes sense he gives you a ride." Without waiting for Hudson to answer, Ava started to dispatch orders. "Tom, get Liz's portfolio, please, darling. It's in the sun room. Or should I say the soon-to-be cinema room?"

"I like the sound of that," Tom replied, standing up. He kissed the top of his wife's head before he went hunting for Liz's portfolio.

"I can't just leave without helping you with all this." Liz looked at the glasses and the dessert bowls that were still around the table. "I'll do some tidying up first: it's the least I can do after this gorgeous dinner," Liz added, already piling the cutlery into her empty bowl.

"Don't you dare." Ava pointed at her. "A guest in my house doesn't clean up. That's what a husband does." Ava looked at Hudson, he didn't know why he felt she was giving him pointers. "Marriage is a partnership. I cooked, Tom will take care of the dishes," she added with a sweet smile when Tom returned to his seat.

"That's right." Tom placed his palm on his wife's belly. "It's all under control. You go home and get some rest," he said, leaning against the back of his chair.

"But—" Liz started to argue.

Hudson interrupted mid-sentence. "You heard them, Lizzie. Better not quarrel with the homeowners; especially in this household: they are savages." He was looking forward to having some time alone with her, and he was itching to go. She looked at him for a moment, her cheeks were flushed but he wasn't sure what brought that on. She quickly turned to Ava.

"All right, you win," Liz said, reluctantly putting down the crockery she had already collected. She walked to Ava, bent over to kiss her cheek. "Please don't get up, you've been on your feet all day." Then she added, "Thank you for everything, you have a beautiful home and a beautiful family, and I felt really welcome."

"Aww…" Ava was almost in tears. "You are so sweet and you're going to make me cry," she said, fanning her hands in front of her nose.

"It's the hormones, don't worry." Tom offered Liz his hand.

She shook it and thanked him too.

Hudson bent to kiss an emotional Ava on both cheeks, thanking her for the delicious dinner.

"Look after my new friend," Ava instructed, and Hudson nodded.

"Night, pal," Hudson said, shaking Tom's hand.

"You know the way, right? I put Liz's portfolio near the door," Tom said without getting up, when Hudson nodded in reply.

After a few more back and forwards of goodnights and good-byes, Liz and Hudson headed out.

CHAPTER 15

Hudson opened the car door for her and Liz tried to remember the last time someone did that. "Thank you," she said, sitting on the front seat, holding in her lap the flowers that he had given her.

Hudson put her portfolio in the boot and walked to the driving side.

"It's a little chilly tonight," she said with a shiver.

"It's the woods: the temperature is always a few degrees lower than in town," Hudson said, strapping himself in. "What's the address?" he asked, tinkering with the satnav.

"Back Bay."

Hudson whistled. "That's a fancy postcode," he said, teasing her.

"My bedroom is as big as a closet."

He laughed.

"Where do you live?" she asked.

"South End."

She laughed. "Just as posh. So, we are neighbors after all."

"I'll be very quick when you call me," he said, starting the car.

"Excuse me?" Liz's voice sounded a little panicky.

"If you are scared of the fireworks." Hudson reminded her of their earlier conversation.

"Ah, yes. Thank you. I'll keep your number handy." She looked ahead but Hudson decided not to waste the opportunity to find out a little more about her personal life.

"I know it's none of my business, but I'd like to know what's going on between you and your boss."

She turned to look at him. "What do you mean?"

"I mean, does he treat you well? With the respect you deserve?" Hudson turned into the main road heading south. A few cars came in the opposite direction, lighting her face as they passed.

"Not always, but I owe him my career." Liz seemed to repeat that a lot lately. Was it because it didn't sound true?

"Were you with COBA a long time?"

"Yes, fifteen years."

"Why are you still working for him? I've seen your talent and your work ethic, I'm pretty sure you could get a job somewhere else."

"I could but there's a family tie keeping me at COBA. Connor and my dad are friends. They lived near each other and went to the same school, although Connor is a few years younger than my dad," she said, her tensed shoulders slightly hunched.

"Look, I get it. It's not my business and I shouldn't have asked." He shook his head. "I've just seen how good you are and it seems a shame that you have to live in the shadow of an unappreciative boss." He turned to her and their eyes met briefly.

"I value the concern, but I don't need rescuing," Liz said, and Hudson returned his eyes to the road. "I can deal with my boss and my career," she said, and saw a small smile tugging at his lips.

"Strong, confident woman. I dig that, but accepting help won't make you less so," Hudson said.

Liz laughed. "Not sure about that. It's a slippery slope." She looked down at the flowers, and Hudson felt her tension loosening.

"It's not. I can see how focused you are on your career. You have goals and ambitions, I can relate. And I'd be happy to have you in my team, if you ever decide to jump ship," he said. Liz felt her gaze on him. *From client to boss?* She couldn't think of anything worse.

"Thanks for the vote of confidence. What position do you have in mind?" Liz asked, trying not to reveal too much.

"I'd happily put you in charge of our product."

"Would you really?" She whispered the words, unsure if they were the truth.

"Yes, absolutely. You are great at what you do and having someone like you steering the features roadmap in the right direction would be priceless." She was flattered by the confidence he placed in her abilities.

"Well, that's an amazing offer and if I were not in love with the job I have, I would have jumped at the opportunity."

"So basically, a polite no?"

She nodded. "I'm sorry." Liz looked at him for a few seconds, then decided to open up. "I think your company is great, but I want to be an award-winning designer and I need to be on the frontline for that to happen. Despite his behavior, working for Connor is my best chance." Liz spat the words out really quickly.

"And you are sure about that?" Hudson thought back to what she had said about Connor dumping work on her without a proper handover.

"I am," she said.

"So why haven't you won any awards yet?" Hudson wasn't going to drop this. He cared too much.

"It takes time. Also, Connor is very protective of COBA's reputation and likes to keep an eye on every project, and then of course it's his name that goes on the trophy," she answered, evasive.

"Is that what you've been telling yourself?"

The tension returned. "I don't think you have any right to pass judgment on my career choices," she said.

"Ouch. Is that what you think I'm doing?" Hudson turned to the left and reduced the speed. They were almost home.

"That's what it sounds like," Liz answered, looking at him.

"Well, that's not what I'm doing." He reached for her hand. "You are talented, Liz, maybe it's time you took a risk and started flying solo. It doesn't make you less loyal."

"But that isn't true." She shook her head. "Leaving COBA for another firm is hardly a show of loyalty—" She sounded upset and Hudson hated himself for forcing her to talk about it.

He searched for a space near the curb, and parked.

"Why did we stop?" she asked, and her voice trembled. He could see she had clammed up and felt terrible about it.

"I'm sorry." He unfastened his seat belt and turned to her. "I am sorry, that was a step too far," he whispered, looking at her. "I shouldn't have said anything."

She was tense but let him take her hand in his.

"I was judging and it is unfair for me to do so. I know nothing about your relationship with Connor, in all honesty, I don't know him at all, so my assessment may be completely wrong. I just think that some people are not very good at sharing the glory. They are better at taking the credit for others' effort than they are in helping those very same people succeed."

She looked away. "I mean, part of what you said is true. Connor has used me and my work for more than a decade without giving me the recognition I deserve, but he also gave me an opportunity. I work for a very successful company and who knows if I would have gotten the job in the first place without my father's help and Connor's goodwill."

"Hey, don't say that. People like Connor are not generous. If he gave you the job it was because he saw your potential. So, maybe yes, he gave you a chance because he knew your father, but the rest is all you. People like him don't carry deadwood out of the kindness of their heart," he said sincerely.

"I know that I'm good at my job and yes, I've had people trying to recruit me." She said the words as if she was actually admitting that to herself for the first time.

He lifted her face to his. "I'd love to have you on my team. And you know I only hire the best."

Liz's heart had stopped when he said *I'd love to* even if she knew perfectly well he was talking about a business proposition, just a job offer, but still, her head had switched on selective hearing.

"COBA is more than just Connor, the guys there are like a family to me. I know I could leave, but I'm not sure I want to." She looked straight into Hudson's eyes. She was attracted to him and that was another reason why working for him wasn't a viable option.

"I understand," he said, and Liz moved back, putting as much distance as she could between them.

"But sometimes people do what they do because they feel forced to, not because they really want to," he said, returning his hands to the steering wheel. "I just want you to know there are options if you are looking for a change."

"I know." She sighed. "It doesn't always feel great but I'm sticking to it for a while longer," she said.

"Fair enough."

She smiled. "Thank you for caring and for the great offer, it's a real ego boost." She finally looked back at him.

After strapping himself in, he started the car and drove off. She wanted to say something but she couldn't find anything interesting.

"So you don't have any plans for July 4th?" he asked but it was more of a statement than a question.

Liz shook her head. "Nothing other than hiding under a blanket to escape the firecrackers." She grimaced at the idea.

"You should come to a party with me. Live music, great company, no pyrotechnics," Hudson said.

"Another great offer, but—" She stopped herself, took a deep breath. "But you are my client. We talked about not muddling the lines."

"Not on July 4th, I'm not. That's a public holiday and you won't be working on my project. You'll be a guest at a party I happen to attend as well."

She was quiet for a minute and he turned to her.

"So? What do you say? Better than being home alone."

"Just as friends?"

"Absolutely, no ulterior motive."

She loved the idea, still, she took a moderate approach. "Fine, I'll come but it's not a date."

"Sure, not a date." He smiled. "I'll pick you up at 7pm."

"No, that's too much like a date. Text me the address, I'll meet you there." She was determined to prove her point: they could be friends and enjoy each other's company but they were not crossing those annoying professional boundaries between them.

"Okay, I will send you the address, it gives me the chance to start the drinking earlier," he said, and she laughed at the smooth way he got to validate her concerns without making a big deal out of them.

CHAPTER 16

Liz's week had been as hectic as the last two. STYLE's project was an untamable beast.

She'd only just finished the fourth draft for the office in Milan and sent it to Michael's team that was drawing up plans for the structural modifications. She had never done this many sketches before, but the fact that the Milan office was in a conservation building made the entire process ten times more difficult.

To top this off, Connor was still at home, and his demands to be kept informed of the status of the project only added extra work to Liz's already packed to-do list. Another reason why she had to work overtime. At least her home office had everything she needed to get stuff done and that meant she didn't have to be at COBA by herself while everyone had the day off. *Today was supposed to be a holiday*, she thought, looking at the amount of completed paperwork on her desk. The Italians were masters at many things, and one of them was certainly the extended bureaucracy they required for even the smallest thing. She was sure the information she had supplied was correct but she worried that with the summer approaching the entire nation would grind to a halt and her application would be forgotten until September. She couldn't blame them for making the most of their glorious weather but she just wanted her plans signed off so they could start the work.

She sent a few more emails, then closed her computer, put some key files in her bag ready for Monday and decided it was time to get ready for Hudson's party.

She had Skyped her family in Dublin and with Simone gone she felt a bit nostalgic. Her life was filled by her job and it was in moments like this that she realized there was little else outside COBA. She tried not to think about it as she dressed in front of the mirror. Her legs were toned and she still had the same waist size as she did ten years earlier. Her boobs were fuller than they used to be but they were still perky which helped with this low-back dress she needed to wear without a bra. She knew she looked good, and this wasn't a date, yet the thought of seeing Hudson made her fuss over the details.

Liz was strapping her shoes on when her phone rang. Simone had promised to call. She took a deep breath hoping that her friend wouldn't noticed she was stressed about the party.

"Hey, girl," Simone said from the noisy street of New Orleans.

Liz lifted her phone to eye level. "Hello. Are you at the parade?"

Simone gave her a panoramic view of the marching band that was passing by, followed by a large mob of dancers and tourists.

"Looks amazing. How's the family?" Liz asked.

"My grandma is really well, keeps getting younger." Simone laughed. "My parents are good too and my little brother has finished his first year at uni. He looks so grown up; it makes me cry." Simone dabbed her cheeks pretending to dry her tears.

"What? Ritchie is already at uni? Oh, I feel old now," Liz said with the pout that rarely appeared on her lips.

"Ah, tell me about it. Janet is five years younger than me and she's married and pregnant with her second child! How's that for old?" Simone shook her head. Liz copied her expression.

"Anyway, enough about this, show me the dress," Simone said, raising an eyebrow.

"Right, here it is. What do you think?" Liz moved her phone so that Simone could see the full length.

"Gorgeous little number," Simone said, then whistled. "Come on, give us a spin."

Liz moved her phone to a different angle to give Simone the full view of her ensemble, showing off the neckline adorned with small rhinestones, the loose draped bodice with a deep V down her back and the fitted skirt hugging her hips. "Really?" Liz asked in confirmation.

"Absolutely," Simone said. "Show me the shoes. Are they Manolo's?" she asked.

"Yes." Liz giggled. "Is it too much?"

"No, they are perfect, you look fabulous! Hudson doesn't stand a chance," she squealed.

"It's not a date," Liz said.

"Okay… why go to so much effort then?"

Liz let out a sigh. "Blame Ava, Tom's wife. She is the bossiest shopping partner. I couldn't say no!" Liz joked, turning the screen up to her face again. "You'd love her."

"Yeah, I think so too. When will I get to meet her?"

"I'll organize lunch when you're back. We need to discuss my birthday party anyway. We can use that as an excuse to meet up— not that we need one," Liz said, looking forward to Ava and Simone meeting up.

"Okay, babe, I'm going to love you and leave you now. My family is expecting me back for dinner and I'm running late," Simone said, blowing a kiss into the camera. "But before I go, promise you'll have fun tonight?"

"I promise," Liz answered. "You have fun too."

"Of course I will. Just call me in the morning, I want to know all the details."

"Nothing is going to happen with Hudson, we are just friends," Liz said, slightly nervous about the evening ahead.

"He won't be able to resist that dress." Simone made a funny gesture with her hand and Liz laughed.

"Happy Fourth," they said to each other before disconnecting the call.

Liz threw the phone on her bed and ran off to finish her makeup.

As soon as she walked back into her bedroom, the sight of the peonies that Hudson gave her a week earlier at Ava's made her smile. She had spent the whole week thinking of him but she had kept a very professional façade.

She sent him emails with ideas or questions about colors and waited nervously for his reply, pretending that she wasn't. She would write back to him with a detached tone but then monitor her inbox like a hawk. They were flirting, they both knew that, but in such a subtle way that it was obvious only to them. She applied more lip gloss and looked at herself in the mirror.

"I'm just meeting a friend, not a big deal," she reminded herself, but her heart was beating fast in her chest. "Just friends," she told herself again. Then she took a deep breath, checked her dress, re-checked her makeup, ran her fingers through her hair and decided that she was ready. She was also late. So, she grabbed her purse and ran out to catch a taxi.

The streets were deserted, and she felt silly about not booking a car ahead. It was July 4th, after all—she should have thought about that. She squared her shoulders, crossed her fingers and marched down the main road. She hoped luck was on her side today.

A group of noisy teenagers were the only company she encountered before she spotted a taxi approaching. She waved at it and a massive grin split her face when she saw the car slowing down and parking a few feet away from her. She opened the door and clambered in.

"Hello, I'm going to Port Norfolk, Dorchester, and I'm running late," she said, strapping herself in.

"Sure thing, lady. The road's clear," the driver said, gunning the car into first and speeding away.

"Thank you." Liz rested her back against the seat and took a deep breath. After a few minutes, she noticed they were making good progress and she felt less stressed: she wasn't going to be too late.

"So, what's the address?" the driver asked.

Hudson had sent her a text with the address. "One sec, I have the details on my phone," she said, looking inside her handbag only to realize that her phone was not in there. "Oh, sugar!" she hissed, remembering precisely the spot on her bed where she threw it after she spoke to Simone. A surge of panic strangled her. What was she going to do now? She didn't remember the exact address and she didn't have her phone to call Hudson and ask him for it.

"Look, lady, I ain't got time to waste. Do you know where you are going or not?"

"I left my phone at home, could you please go back so I can get it?" Liz asked with a soft voice, but the expression on the man's face didn't look promising.

"Last ride, I have my kids waiting so I can take you back but I'm not going to wait and then take you to Port Norfolk. Choice is yours."

She didn't know what to do, maybe if she could get near enough to the road, she might recognize the name. She wracked her brain and remembered Hudson mentioning a park nearby.

"The house I'm going to, it's near a park, right on the Neponset River," she told the driver. "John Fenelon Park? Something like that…"

"Joseph Finnegan Park?"

"Yes! That's it. The house it's near there."

"Fine, I'll take you to the park but then I'm gonna split. I have stuff to do, so can't stick around, capisci?" he said, and she nodded.

In less than five minutes the taxi stopped in front of the park entrance. Liz paid the fare and took out twenty dollars from her purse and showed it to him.

"Please let me use your phone to make a call," she said, knowing it was a generous offer.

"Sorry, lady, I have no credit," he said, and Liz felt a sense of doom growing in her chest.

"You can send a text. They are free," he said, lifting his cell.

"Good enough." Liz passed him the money and took the phone.

She typed Hudson's number, immensely pleased she looked at his text so many times she had memorized the digits and with shaky fingers, she wrote a message to him.

EMERGENCY—stranded in front of Joseph Finnegan Park. Left my phone at home with the address. This is the taxi driver's cell but he's leaving now. Please come to get me. Liz x

She passed the phone back to the driver. "Thank you," she said, and clambered out of the car, looking around, unsettled by the deserted road.

"Hey, lady," the driver called out from the window. "This's a safe hood. You'll be fine."

"Thanks." She waved, slightly relieved, and he sped away.

She walked to the bus stop a few feet away and after cleaning up the bench with her palm, she sat down, hoping that Hudson had got her message and was on his way to her. She had no way of knowing that, so all she could do was wait. She kept looking in all directions, time went by painfully slowly. The evening was balmy and the air smelled of sizzling sausages and fireworks. She heard laughter coming from one of the houses on the opposite side of the road and there was jazz music lingering in the air.

Still, she was tense. She played with a sticking up cuticle on her finger, trying to concentrate on that funny feeling rather than the anxiety growing in her chest.

Bad memories were resurfacing, turning her sense of unease into fear. She hadn't thought about it in a long time but now, sitting alone in an empty road, in a part of town she didn't know brought to the surface a memory from a night in Dublin sixteen years earlier when she was followed home by someone who wanted to mug her, or maybe worse. She was lucky she never found out.

It was the graduation party of her best friend Louise whose parents had splashed out on it with a grand town-center venue and even an open bar. Liz, already a little tipsy, had mingled through the crowd to get another drink stopping to say a few words to friends keen to hear about her engagement to Sean, and the details about her apprenticeship in Boston. When she finally reached the counter there were lots of people waiting to be served.

While she waited for her turn, she gazed about her. The venue was a magnificent old building, a great example of late Victorian architecture. The walls were paneled with oak, the ceiling had beams across a perfect vault and two magnificent chandeliers were shining above her head.

A waiter who was making cocktails looked at her with a flirty smile, flattering her. She had had just the one boyfriend for most of her teens and the unexpected male attention gave her a strange boost, especially when added to the alcohol in her bloodstream. "Hello," she said in a friendly tone.

"Hello back," he answered with a wink, and she had giggled. This seemed silly behavior now, but then it felt like innocent fun.

"It's going to be a long wait to be served: why don't you take one of these?" he said, plucking one of the cocktails from the tray in front of him.

"As long as it's no trouble," she said, trying to look cool.

"No trouble. For pretty girls, this is allowed, one final touch," he answered with a smile and lowering the glass behind the counter, he sprinkled a few drops of something on it.

"Here it is," he passed it to her.

She looked at the pinkish color and the pungent smell of the liquid rippling in the triangular glass in her hand. Two olives speared by a cocktail stick were bathing in it.

"Hot dirty martini," he said with a hint of mischief in his tone.

She felt grown up and cosmopolitan. Was that the life waiting for her in Boston? Men paying attention to her and drinks she didn't know existed? She lifted the glass to her lips to take a sip. It was surprisingly salty and spiced by something she couldn't recognize.

"Tabasco," the waiter said, reading her thoughts.

She shivered when his breath washed over her shoulder. The cocktail tasted funny for someone used to cranberry or cola mixers but that only added to the appeal, it made her feel grown up and refined. "It's delicious." She smiled, trying too hard to finish it all to show him she liked it.

"I'll see you later," the waiter had said, lifting the tray and walking away but the look he gave her over his shoulder made her shiver.

At his words, her paranoia spiked and her pulse became erratic. Had she given him the impression she was looking for more than just a drink? Was she so tipsy that she had gone too far with her flirting without realizing? She was nauseous. The music was suddenly too loud; the lights were now piercingly bright and she had felt overwhelmed. She wanted to go home.

Without saying goodbye, she had walked outside, the cold of the evening cleared her head a little. She looked for a cab. The road was deserted and there were no cabs either. She had decided to cross the other side of the road, towards a bigger artery, she felt confused and when a motorbike came blazing by she had stopped for a second to catch her breath after the fright.

When she had reached the main road, she slowed down trying to get her bearings. She did not know this side of town well, she knew her parent's home was too far to walk there. She had tried a few more times to hail a cab but it was getting late. *Maybe I should try the train*, she thought and walked as fast as she could to the station. It was while she was waiting that she spotted the waiter who served her the martini walking down the platform towards her. He was wearing a blue jacket and a woolly hat and a scarf that covered most of his face, but she was sure it was him. She saw him staring, the menacing look she had noticed before in his eyes and she had panicked.

He walked in her direction then stopped a few meters away, she saw him glance up at the CCTV camera and pulling his scarf higher over his nose. Dark thoughts pervaded her. Had he spiked her drink? Was he now following her, waiting for the drugs to take effect?

The train arrived and when the door opened she boarded, keeping her eyes on him. He got onto the next carriage and sat down facing the other way. The train moved slowly, stopping and starting until it finally arrived at her station. She knew the area well, her home wasn't far, she was feeling reassured.

Liz remembered feeling cold and scared as she walked down the road, her head was still spinning but she knew her house was only a few minutes away.

The neighborhood was surprisingly quiet, with very few people around, and when she heard steps approaching the panic returned. Had the waiter followed her? She had seen him sitting on the train but she ran out the station so she couldn't be completely sure he was on it.

The footsteps were closing in and she looked around, hoping to spot someone she knew. There were rows of terraced houses on both sides of the road, lights were still on in most of them and she could hear the traffic from the main road ahead, but she was shaking with fear when a shadow fell on her. She turned, ready to scream. There was a figure lurking in the dark and she quickly stepped back stumbling over her own feet. Her high heel slipped down the pavement and cracked. That was when she fell and banged her head. Just before passing out she heard someone running beside her and saw a police car stopping near the curb. When she woke up there was a cop standing over her. She told them her story and they confirmed they saw a man following her, they reassured her he ran. They took her home safely, but that experience had traumatized her.

Still to this day, even now on a warm July evening, Liz felt the unease of that night creeping under her skin every time she found herself in an empty road.

When she heard the thumping of feet approaching, she felt her blood chilling, but when she looked over and saw Hudson coming to her rescue, she almost wept with relief.

CHAPTER 17

"Liz!" he called out to her and waved. She looked scared and he quickened his pace. "I'm here," he said, slowing down when he was near but when he saw her ashen face, he walked straight to her, and kissed her. She was shaking but responded to him with a passion that stunned him. He hadn't expected her to deepen the kiss but she had thrown her arms around his neck and he felt her feelings pouring out of her without restrain. He knew this was what he had wanted. Needed even.

He moved gently away and looked at her. Her eyes were soft, her cheeks flushed and he wished their situation wasn't complicated by their business relationship. She mattered to him.

"Sorry, I didn't mean to kiss you, but when I saw you... I couldn't resist." He swept his fingers through his hair.

"I kissed you back, so I guess we are even," she said, looking embarrassed and short of breath.

He wasn't quite ready to let go of her completely so he took her hand in his. "I came as soon as I saw your text but I had a few beers and I was over the limit, I couldn't drive," he explained.

"Thank you, I'm just an idiot. I left my phone at home and we were almost at destination when I noticed. I couldn't remember the address but you said it was near this park so I took a chance. I'm just really glad you came."

"Of course I came, Liz. I ran here," he said with a grin and squeezed her hand. He was in love, there was no other way to explain what he felt for her.

"I'm very impressed. You know how to make a woman feel special," she said.

"Really?" They started walking down the road.

"Top marks," she said, and Hudson could see the fear in her eyes was gone and their kiss had brought the color back to her cheeks.

"You haven't seen nothing yet. I'll make this your best ever date."

"It's not a date," she reminded him, but it looked like it cost her to put that fence back up. He didn't want it between them. He stopped and pulled her gently against him again.

"Hi," he said, looking straight into her eyes. The green was deep and mesmerizing.

"Hi," she replied, and when her voice trembled with emotion Hudson wanted to kiss her again. He restrained his impulses, sensing that slow and steady was the way to win this race.

"Ready to party?" Hudson asked, lifting her chin to him.

She opened her mouth but she was silenced by a loud blast in the sky. She jumped at the unexpected noise and her head bumped against his jaw.

"Ouch!" Hudson laughed, rubbing the side of his face while she did the same to the top of her head.

"Sorry. Bit jumpy still." She giggled, then look for the source of the noise. "What the hell was that?"

"It's a fog horn," Hudson said, placing a finger across her lips. "Listen."

Another blast exploded in the sky. The boom echoed around them. He could tell she didn't like it so he wrapped his arm around her waist. "They are celebrating," Hudson said.

want to lead?" Hudson asked her, and she laughed, ...head.

...proven yourself worthy," she said, and he took her

...Paris, they immediately found their rhythm. Their ...getting stronger, he knew she could feel it too. They ...pying the unusual moves of the old couple next to them. ...d Jacob were in their seventies and mocked the young-...ho halfway through the song were struggling to keep up ...e increasing speed.

...laughed, slightly breathless, as they moved from one song ...next. Finally, the band played a ballad.

...iz huffed. "My heart is beating crazy fast. Maybe I *am* unfit ...all," she said, leaning into him. The song was mellow, and ...atmosphere around them turned nostalgic and romantic.

"It's hard to tell from looking at you. I think to be sure I'd ...ed a closer inspection." He delivered the line running his hands ...ftly over her naked back and watched as his words sunk in.

He saw it in her eyes that she wanted him just as much, yet he ...was letting her choose the speed.

She pushed herself up and he felt her body brush against him. Bliss and torture.

"You are an architect, Hudson, not a doctor," she whispered in his ears, then nipped gently at his lobe. He tightened the grip on her, wishing desperately this was a date.

"Fine, I admit it, I'm not a doctor," he answered, looking into her eyes. "It's fair to say I'd still love to give you a closer inspection."

"Not a date, Hudson." Her tone was sexy and he knew she was intentionally making him suffer.

"Fine, let me take you on a proper date then?"

"I'll think about it," she said as they slowly swayed together. Her arms were knotted behind his neck, her body pressed against his, and he knew that his resolution of letting her set the pace

142

"Yes, well. They scared the shite out of me. Excuse my French."

He laughed. "Okay, I get it, loud noises are not your thing."

"No, I guess they are not."

"Shall we?" he whispered, and they started walking together.

"So, tell me something about this mysterious party."

"It's a family affair, an old tradition my grandfather started. We keep it going in his honor." Hudson's voice was mellow and nostalgic.

"Sounds lovely. Are you sure I'm not intruding?"

"I put in a good word for you with the host, she was glad to have an extra guest this year," he joked, trying to lighten the heaviness in his chest. This was a big deal, she was the first women he'd ever brought to this party.

"That's appreciated," she answered playfully.

"Come on then. Betty's waiting."

"Who's Betty then?" Liz asked, looking at him as they walked.

"She was my grandfather's girlfriend." The affection he felt for her dripped into his tone.

"She taught you how to tango, right?" Liz said, remembering what he told her in Paris.

"Yes." He was pleased that she had remembered that detail.

"Will you be dancing?" she asked with sincere excitement.

"Oh yes, but only with my new favorite partner," he answered, flicking her wrist making her twirl.

"I'm looking forward to it," she said, and he smiled.

"Betty's house is two minutes down this road." He took her hand again and they strode ahead.

The evening was mild, the birds were already asleep even if it was still light, the crickets and the cicadas were starting their serenades. He smelled the salt of the ocean mixed with Liz's scent and realized that this moment would stay with him forever.

Halfway down the road, she pulled at him. "Can we slow down," she said, pointing at her toothpick heels.

139

"Yes, well. They scared the shite out of me. Excuse my French."

He laughed. "Okay, I get it, loud noises are not your thing."

"No, I guess they are not."

"Shall we?" he whispered, and they started walking together.

"So, tell me something about this mysterious party."

"It's a family affair, an old tradition my grandfather started. We keep it going in his honor." Hudson's voice was mellow and nostalgic.

"Sounds lovely. Are you sure I'm not intruding?"

"I put in a good word for you with the host, she was glad to have an extra guest this year," he joked, trying to lighten the heaviness in his chest. This was a big deal, she was the first women he'd ever brought to this party.

"That's appreciated," she answered playfully.

"Come on then. Betty's waiting."

"Who's Betty then?" Liz asked, looking at him as they walked.

"She was my grandfather's girlfriend." The affection he felt for her dripped into his tone.

"She taught you how to tango, right?" Liz said, remembering what he told her in Paris.

"Yes." He was pleased that she had remembered that detail.

"Will you be dancing?" she asked with sincere excitement.

"Oh yes, but only with my new favorite partner," he answered, flicking her wrist making her twirl.

"I'm looking forward to it," she said, and he smiled.

"Betty's house is two minutes down this road." He took her hand again and they strode ahead.

The evening was mild, the birds were already asleep even if it was still light, the crickets and the cicadas were starting their serenades. He smelled the salt of the ocean mixed with Liz's scent and realized that this moment would stay with him forever.

Halfway down the road, she pulled at him. "Can we slow down," she said, pointing at her toothpick heels.

He dropped his gaze to her feet and was glad to have the excuse to look at her legs. She was really beautiful and he realized he liked everything about her. A compliment was on his lips but remembering his promise to take things slow, he cracked a joke instead. "Such a slow coach! You are out of shape. Hashtag fact."

She laughed out loud. "Nuh-uh. I told you already, I'm in great health and it's because of the shoes."

Hudson looked at her and then grinning, he scooped her up from the sidewalk with one smooth motion and held her in his arms.

"Hudson! What are doing? Just put me down! This is so embarrassing," she squeaked. Her tone was a mixture of surprise, outrage and reprimand all at once, but he could see her eyes were shining with laughter.

"Are you sure you want me to put you down? That means walking," he said.

She pulled a face and clasped her arms tightly around his neck. "No, you are right, I want to stay right here."

"Finally, something spontaneous."

"I'm too old and wise for unplanned fun!" she complained, but he noticed she was laughing.

"I'm not saying be reckless but maybe you could loosen up a little."

"Ah, a man telling a woman how to behave. How refreshing." Her tone was playful but he stopped walking for a moment.

"I'm not telling you what to do, Liz." Their eyes were locked and he could see that she was suspicious. "We don't really know each other yet, but I'm not that type of man."

She sighed and closed her eyes for a moment. "I know and you are right, I could loosen up a little. It's not easy for me but I could try," she answered, and that was more than he had hoped for.

"Great decision, Miss Walsh," he whispered solemnly. His heart thumped louder in his chest and he told himself it was because of the strain of carrying Liz and not because she was so near. Just for tonight, he was going to forget about everything else and just concentrate on enjoying her company. They would have tomorrow to worry about what next.

"Here we are, my lady," Hudson said, putting Liz down in front of Betty's door.

"Thank you." She skimmed her hands down her hips to adjust her dress, and he looked away with a sigh. Every move she made was so appealing too. He knew this impasse in their relationship was going to be painful.

"Ready?" He offered her his arm to match the old-fashioned music coming from inside. When she nodded, he opened the door and they walked in together.

The party was in full swing, which was an accurate description of what was going on inside, because the band, set on a raised stand in the large garden, was playing Glenn Miller's "In the Mood." Almost all the guests were dancing, Liz and Hudson were immediately catapulted back about eighty years into fascinating times.

The delight on Liz's face broke Hudson's composure. His stomach tightened and he realized he was powerless against his feelings.

"Let's dance," she said, looking at him with an excited smile.

"Sure," he agreed, moving towards the patio.

"Wait, stay still just for one second," she bid, and holding his arm with one hand, she balanced on one foot. "These are gorgeous but they are killing me." Then using her free hand, she took off her sandals one at a time. Hudson watched her amused. "Okay. Let's go dance," she declared, dropping her purse and her shoes near the chair in the corner of the room.

Speechless, he followed her outside. She looked free and relaxed as she headed straight for the middle of the dance floor laid on the grass. She turned to him, flirtatious.

"Do you want to lead?" Hudson asked her, and she laughed, shaking her head.

"You've proven yourself worthy," she said, and he took her hand.

Like in Paris, they immediately found their rhythm. Their bond was getting stronger, he knew she could feel it too. They jived, copying the unusual moves of the old couple next to them. Rosie and Jacob were in their seventies and mocked the youngsters who halfway through the song were struggling to keep up with the increasing speed.

Liz laughed, slightly breathless, as they moved from one song to the next. Finally, the band played a ballad.

Liz huffed. "My heart is beating crazy fast. Maybe I *am* unfit after all," she said, leaning into him. The song was mellow, and the atmosphere around them turned nostalgic and romantic.

"It's hard to tell from looking at you. I think to be sure I'd need a closer inspection." He delivered the line running his hands softly over her naked back and watched as his words sunk in.

He saw it in her eyes that she wanted him just as much, yet he was letting her choose the speed.

She pushed herself up and he felt her body brush against him. Bliss and torture.

"You are an architect, Hudson, not a doctor," she whispered in his ears, then nipped gently at his lobe. He tightened the grip on her, wishing desperately this was a date.

"Fine, I admit it, I'm not a doctor," he answered, looking into her eyes. "It's fair to say I'd still love to give you a closer inspection."

"Not a date, Hudson." Her tone was sexy and he knew she was intentionally making him suffer.

"Fine, let me take you on a proper date then?"

"I'll think about it," she said as they slowly swayed together. Her arms were knotted behind his neck, her body pressed against his, and he knew that his resolution of letting her set the pace was weakening fast. He had never had a serious relationship before, never needed or wanted one; but since he met Liz, everything had changed for him and he was suddenly impatient.

"I love this song but can't ever remember the words," she said, humming the melody.

Hudson lowered his lips to her ear and sang the lyrics, stressing the vowels and rolling the Rs as Frank Sinatra would.

"You are a great singer," she said. "So many hidden talents."

Her voice was too mellow to resist, and he had to tighten his grip on his emotions, lighten the mood with a joke, but all his head wanted was to speak words of love.

"Let me show you." He knew he was putting pressure on her but the attraction was too great, he wanted to be in a relationship with her.

"The dancing and the singing will have to do for now," she said, but the tone of her voice wasn't as convincing.

"Sure?"

"Not really," she said, and Hudson's pulse quickened and when she pushed herself up on the tips of her toes, he lowered his mouth to hers. The kiss was romantic, sweet even, but it burned with their needs.

"Hudson—" she looked at him and, in her gaze, he read her feelings.

"I know, me too," he answered, and she knotted her fingers in his hair. He was about to kiss her again when someone tapped his shoulder.

Hudson turned, slightly disoriented and his father's face filled his vision. "Dad?"

Jeff Moore was looking back at his son with a playful smile on his lips. When he turned his eyes to Liz, she broke away from Hudson and crossed her arms over her chest slightly embarrassed.

"First time my boy brings a date to this party, and he doesn't even make the introduction," he said, draping his arm around

Hudson's shoulders. "All I can say is it was worth the wait," he added, smiling at a blushing Liz.

"Dad, stop it." Hudson sounded like a sulky teenager.

Liz smiled politely.

"So who's your lady friend?" the older man asked.

"Sorry. This is Elizabeth Walsh. She is the interior designer refurbishing our offices." Hudson wished he could have introduced her as his girlfriend. "Liz, this is my dad, Jeff."

"Nice to meet you, Liz," Jeff said. "Hudson told me about the amazing work you are doing in Milan and Paris."

"Thank you." Liz looked embarrassed.

"Let's not talk about work tonight. It's a party," Hudson said, and Jeff caught his drift.

"Of course, you are right. I came to tell you that you are up next."

"What? No, not this year, Dad," Hudson said, shaking his head.

"But it's tradition," Jeff complained, then looked briefly at Liz. "Fine, you are here with a date, I understand; but you have to tell Betty yourself."

"Dad, come on." Hudson's voice was sulky, he couldn't help it. "You tell Betty, please."

Jeff shook his head, then turned to Liz. "It was very nice to meet you. I hope to see you again soon," he said with a sincere smile.

"Same here," Liz answered, but Hudson noticed that her smile didn't reach her eyes. *Trust issues*, he thought.

"What was that about?" Liz asked when Jeff was out of earshot.

Hudson took her hand in his, and gently guided her to the love seat in the far corner of the veranda. They sat.

"Every year, I sing for Betty her favorite song. My granddad used to do it so after he died, I took over from him." He turned his gaze to the couples that were now slow dancing to the notes of "Blue Moon."

"That's so sweet," she said, reaching for his hand. "What's the song?" Liz asked, dangling her legs back and forward.

"'Can't Help Falling in Love' by the King," Hudson said, turning his eyes to her. His words lingered in the air between them.

"I like that song too; it's romantic even though it's a little simplistic. I don't think destiny is responsible for happiness." She sounded cynical and maybe a little scared of the possibilities.

"What's the road to love, to happiness, then? A plan? Or avoiding the journey altogether?"

She looked hurt but Hudson wasn't ready to back down, their future together could depend on this. He said, "People met at inconvenient times, life happens and yes, destiny sometimes interferes or helps too. You can have the perfect plan but there are unpredictable elements that could change its course. Are you going to ignore those possibilities just because the timing is off?"

She pursed her lips and her eyes flared with contempt. "Are you talking about me or yourself? Because from what I've heard, you've been playing a waiting game too. Waiting for what, I wonder?"

"You." The word was out before he could stop it.

She widened her eyes. "Me?" There was irony in her tone. "You waited this long only to fall for someone you work with? Our situation is complicated, don't you think maybe that's part of the appeal?"

"I..." Things made no sense in his head either and that made it impossible to explain what he felt for her. All he knew was that his heart had taken over and he was in love with her. That was not complicated.

"I don't know." This wasn't the way he wanted to go but he'd made a mess of things and he didn't know how to fix it.

"Maybe you should have come alone to the party this year as well. This is not a date and the kissing, the dancing, are just confusing things." She straightened her shoulders. "You've been waiting for the one, the perfect woman. No one can handle such a pressure; no one can compete with an ideal. I put my career above everything and don't have time to practice for the role you ask me to play, so what are we even doing here?" She had said some truths but she was wrong about something: she was already perfect, just the way she was.

"Hudson!" Someone called his name but he didn't move.

"Hudson!" The caller was getting closer.

"You should go. They are calling you." Liz sounded upset, he didn't want to leave her now.

"I can hear," he answered dryly, his eyes still on hers. He didn't know what to do, they were at a stalemate and he had no idea how to get out of it.

"Hudson!" The caller was upon them and he had to turn, unable to avoid the teenage boy who was now standing a foot away. "Hey, I've been calling you! The band is ready, Betty's waiting," he said, completely oblivious to the tension he had cut through.

"Thanks, Rhys, I'll be there in a minute," Hudson answered, and Rhys reluctantly walked away. Hudson turned to Liz. Her eyes were deep and unreadable.

"You better go. They're waiting for you." Her voice wasn't stable but her tone was as sharp as a blade.

"We are not done," he said, that much he knew for sure.

"Aren't we?" Her tone carried the bitter taste of irony.

"We are barely started," Hudson said, then surprising them both, he took her face in his hands and kissed her until they were both breathless. She responded to him with passion and the ache this caused only made her worthier of his effort.

As he moved away, she kept her eyes on him. They were hard, just like the line of her mouth.

"Hudson. Come on!" Rhys had stopped only a few feet away, insistent. Hudson needed to go.

"We are barely started, and we are going to finish it," he repeated to Liz before walking on to the stage.

People cheered and clapped, someone wolf-whistled and the crowd laughed, but he kept his eyes on Liz. He reached for the microphone and nodded to the band that started playing.

He sang a song about the inevitability of love, keeping his gaze on Liz.

Couples danced, Betty listened, the few youngsters around kept their eyes on their phones, bored of this old-fashioned stuff. Liz watched him but before the song was over, she stood up and left.

Hudson ran after her with an angst he had not felt since the age of thirteen and that at forty-two was out of place. As she walked down the street ahead of him, the sky above exploded with fireworks. He imagined the fear twisting her stomach with every blast but she seemed determined to get away from him, she was heading for the main road.

Emotions were trumping over each other and he couldn't tell anymore what was stronger but one thing was clear, he wasn't letting her walk out of his life without a fight.

"Where are you going?" Hudson shouted when he was a few meters away from her. She was carrying her bag and her shoes and her feet were bare.

"Home," she replied without looking back.

"Liz, stop!" She didn't and Hudson swore under his breath, then sprinted to finally catch up with her. He grabbed her wrist and forced her to stop. A noisy cartwheel of green and blue colors lit up the dark sky.

"Let me go. I don't need the drama."

"Neither do I, but I'm not letting you walk away like this." He was breathing heavily from running after her but also from the tension fastening his diaphragm.

"I'll go if I want to, when I want to." She pulled her arm away from him.

He let her go. "And you want to go? Is that the truth?"

"Yes."

Her answer hurt. "Don't expect me to stand here and watch you leave."

"Why not?" The answer to that question meant he'd have to put himself out there. Meant serving her his heart on a silver plate and hoping she wouldn't just chew it and spit it out.

"So?"

"Because I care about you." This was as far as he was willing to go. For now.

"Why?" She was pushing harder than he had expected. Hudson didn't feel ready to answer.

"I just do, Liz." He raked his hair with his hand, a gesture of frustration he had performed many times in his life, but never for a woman.

"It's not good enough." She turned to leave and he panicked.

"I'm falling for you." He almost spat his heart out together with the words, still she didn't stop. He threw his arms out in despair. She was maddening, yet he loved her for it.

"Can't you stop and talk to me?" He followed her a few steps behind.

"What is there to say?" She kept walking, and Hudson was at total loss. Hadn't he kissed her with a passion that spoke louder than words, hadn't he run after her? Invited her to a family party that he had never taken anyone else to before? What else did she want from him? His signature on a contract? This was irrational.

"Fine. We are done then." He stopped. Maybe chasing after her wasn't a good idea. "If you want to walk away, to pretend there is nothing between us, then do. I've waited more than forty years for you but I guess you were right, I shouldn't have bothered."

She turned then, her eyes were filled with tears. "You are a hypocrite." She walked back to him with big powerful strides.

Her delicate feet walked quickly over the rough cement of the sidewalk but she didn't seem to care.

"A hypocrite? Why?" He met her anger with his own.

"Because you waited forty years to fall for someone and then you picked me. Someone you have to work with, someone with baggage, someone who is not that young anymore. Why? You could have anyone else, why me?"

His chest tightened. Her trust issues ran much deeper than he had thought. He needed the certainty he had been reluctant to give.

"I don't want anyone else, Lizzie." The time had come for him to be completely honest. He hadn't expected that time to come tonight, but nothing that involved her had been expected.

"Why me?" She pointed her fingers at her chest. "I want to know, why are you doing this to me?"

Hudson looked at her, completely lost for words. "I'm attracted to you."

"Oh, for fuck's sake. Why are you so obnoxious? You don't even know me!"

She almost stomped, he almost smiled.

"Lizzie, can you calm down a minute. I swear I have no idea why you are so angry at me just because I like you."

"I want to know exactly why you like me."

"I can tell you, but are you going to believe me?" He raised an eyebrow.

"I don't have issues with compliments, I have issues with lies."

He frowned. "You know what? I'm lost. I don't know what set this off, I don't know how to fix it and all these shades you are throwing at me are just making things more complicated."

"Shades? What are you, twelve?"

He laughed so genuinely, she smiled at him.

"This is childish," she said, and their antagonism dissolved as quickly as it came.

Hudson took advantage of the chink in her armor to push further into her defenses.

"Tell me what I'm doing wrong." He stepped closer but there was still plenty of distance between them.

"Everything, and nothing." She looked down, needing a respite from his gaze.

"Okay, well, that's very broad. Any way you could narrow that down a little?"

She sighed. "Let me try." Her tone was dripping with sarcasm. "You carried me in your arms like some sort of fairy-tale Prince Charming and a minute later you introduce me to your father as 'the interior designer who is refurbishing our offices'..."

She had a point. He had been blowing hot and cold since they met, and he couldn't fault her for feeling confused by his behavior. Still, she had been doing the same. "It's complicated, you know that."

She snorted and he knew he had to step up his game if he wanted her to listen.

"You've been doing exactly the same to me." He waited for her scorching reply, but she was silent so he continued. "You told me that we needed to keep things professional, then kissed me back as if those boundaries were all but forgotten." He saw her skin flush with the truth of his statement. "And the reason why I introduced you as 'the interior designer who is refurbishing our offices' is because I didn't think you wanted me to say 'date' given that you told me a million times this wasn't a date."

She took a deep breath then exhaled. "I'm sorry, Hudson. Everything you said is fair."

Her candid admission unlocked something inside him. He didn't want to hide his feelings anymore.

"I'm in love with you, Lizzie" he said, and her head snapped up. Her eyes were wide and he saw fear in them. He reached for her hand. "This is it. This is the truth. No more games, no more pretending I don't know my own feelings. This is it. I'm in love with you."

She was looking at him without saying a word. He spoke again. Now that the words were out, he felt courage coming from them, not fear. He stroked the back of her hand with his thumb and felt her pulse jumping.

"You don't even know me," she reminded him.

"I know, and yet, here I am, head over heels."

She closed her eyes at his words. "But we met only a few weeks ago."

"We did, but it's as if I've known you forever."

She shook her head. "I feel the same way." Her tone said that she couldn't believe her own words.

"Are you in love with me?" he asked her, nervous about her answer.

"Let's just say that I don't despise you."

He grinned and pulled her closer. "Do better," he said, lowering his forehead to hers.

"You are not as bad as I thought?" She whispered the words sweetly, and his mouth twitched.

"Almost there, try one more time." His lips fluttered near her jawline and he watched her swallowing her emotions.

"I'm in love with you too," she said, and the sky shattered with colors. The fireworks flew with a whistle then blasted into a myriad of falling stars.

"Great timing," Hudson said, pulling her into his arms. "Didn't I promise I'd keep you safe tonight?"

"You did."

"Are you scared?"

"Terrified," she said, but her eyes showed no fear.

He kissed her forehead. "Take a chance on me, Lizzie."

She dropped her shoes and her purse and after pushing herself on the tip of her toes, she wrapped her arms around his neck. "I might," she whispered.

Their lips touched while the sky above was lit by a rainbow of sparkles cascading around them. The kiss had deepened into a promise. Breathless, he looked at her. "I want a proper date with you."

She nodded.

"Let's have dinner. And I'm definitely picking you up this time."

She laughed. "I guess I deserve that."

He smiled.

"So, we are really doing this?"

"Looks like we are." She bit her lip in an excited smile.

"And you are not going to change your mind?"

She shook her head and he kissed her again.

CHAPTER 18

"Look, I don't know what to tell you, other than that he's been in a foul mood lately." Ava drank her smoothie as they sat on a bench watching Sam playing in the sandpit. Liz looked at the little boy with the affection of a godmother. Then pinched the top of her nose and exhaled the tension of the many sleepless nights she'd had spent thinking of Hudson.

"He's acting strange. I'm wondering if he banged his head and lost his memory."

Ava shrugged her shoulders.

"He only talks to me when strictly necessary, and even then, he answers my questions in monosyllables," Liz said. She wondered if she had dreamed their conversation the night of the party. Had she imagined him chasing after her and telling her he was in love. Maybe she was drunk, or hallucinating—but it felt so real. And yet he had not called her; nor had they gone on their proper first date as he promised. Something had happened but she had no idea what that was.

"He was mooning over you when you were over for dinner. This behavior makes no sense." Ava made a slurping noise when she finished her drink.

"Totally. I mean we were puffing hot and cold, forcing ourselves to keep things professional but we moved on from that —or at least that was my understanding when he said that he loved me…" Liz tried not to get herself too worked up over the frustration of his behavior.

"I'm sorry, but you are both miserable and the situation really sucks," Ava said eventually. "Maybe you should try to talk to him."

Liz shrugged. "Didn't I try?" Her tone showed her annoyance. "I called him earlier with the excuse of showing him the samples for the new carpet in the Boston office. I offered to pop by, but he just said he's happy with whatever I choose and literally ended the conversation. He's acting as if nothing happened between us. Or worse, as if he's changed his mind and doesn't have the balls to tell me."

Ava threw the empty smoothie container in the bin next to her and shook her head. "Sometimes people act in a funny way when they feel under pressure," she mused. "Hudson is caring, genuine, funny and charming in a way that makes you feel special because he's sincere. Maybe he's worried that he went too far too soon by saying that he loves you? I mean where do you go from there when you haven't even had a first proper date yet?"

Liz chewed on the inside of her mouth. Maybe Ava was right; maybe caught up in the heat of the moment he said too much. Maybe when the dust settled he realized that and didn't know how to handle her expectations. Was the explanation for his odd behavior really this simple?

"Remember that he has never had a serious relationship before. Just give him some time," Ava said. "He's a good guy and I think you are perfect for each other, so just cut him some slack— maybe this once," she said with a cheeky grin.

"Do you really think he hasn't changed his mind? He just needs time?" Liz asked, then watched Sam filling his bucket with sand.

"I do." Ava shook her head. "I bet he's stressing about how he came on too strong and what he should do next. He's probably wondering what your expectations are; and he's worried about not doing it right."

Liz kicked the gravel under her feet in irritation, then took off her sunglasses and gazed at Ava. "How do we get back on track? I hate this."

Ava tilted her head. "The old-fashioned way?"

"What's the old-fashioned way?" Liz asked, unsure.

"Sex, Liz. I'm talking about sex."

Liz looked at her and shook her head. "If I can be totally honest, this does not sound like the best advice. How's sex going to make this easier instead of complicating things even more?"

"Sex is only complicated because people make it so. Personally, I think it's the best way to get things moving. So apart from the fact that it's healthy and normal for two grown-ups who love each other to have sex, it also works well to make babies and settle arguments," she added, and Liz laughed, thinking of poor Tom who had to navigate life with this feisty woman at his side. He had no chance.

"Let's say I listen to your suggestion and give this a go," Liz said confiding her fears, "what if after... you know, what if we realize that the tension between us disappears with the release?"

"No, it won't. If this was about sex you would have done it the night of the party." Ava sounded completely confident in her assessment. "I know there's something between you guys that's deeper than physical attraction. You just need to work through this impasse. I mean, Hudson is not even talking to you at the moment so if you give this a try and it doesn't work, you won't be worse off than you are now, right?"

Liz shook her head. "I don't know, Ava, it feels manipulative to use sex to get Hudson to open up and tell me what's going on with him."

Ava laughed. "Okay, let's make this simpler. Would you like to have sex with Hudson?"

Liz couldn't deny the truth. "God, I really would," she said, and Ava gave her a sweet smile.

"There you go, you are not manipulative, you are just going after something that you really want." Ava rubbed at her tummy, then shifted her position on the bench. "Just be straightforward, his move next."

"Should I text him an eggplant and peach emojis combo? Or maybe I'd go straight for a booty call? See if he lets it go to voicemail?"

"Either of those, I'd say." They laughed but Liz's gaze turned serious.

"I don't know, Ava, it's a risk. What if you're wrong and he's actually regretting the little that has already happened between us? Suggesting sex will be the last nail in the coffin." She was worried. His behavior in the past week had been erratic and impossible to read. He said he loved her and then had hardly spoken more than five words to her since. He also called her Lizzie, no one had called her that in thirty years and her heart always melted a little when he did.

"That's not it, Liz."

"How do you know?"

"Taking you to Betty's party was a big deal, I can guarantee it was. Hudson is not a man who takes things lightly. If he kissed you, it was a decision he took after careful consideration. Same with using words like *love*."

"Well, for full disclosure we argued as much as we made out, so there you go. Maybe he didn't consider all the possibilities after all."

They were quiet for a minute, then Ava spoke like she was the oracle. "Make the first move. He will either take the bait or pass. It may hurt to be rejected, but at least you'll have your answer."

"Ava, I'm not going to play games, I told you already," Liz said, looking at her friend sideways.

"Really? Because it looks to me you've been playing this tug of war for a while now and it's time to end it."

Before Liz could say anything else, a squeal claimed their attention. Sam had poured an entire bucket of sand inside his trousers and he was now screaming at the top of his lungs.

Ava stood up. "I'm coming, baby," she said. She rubbed her bump as she walked to her son while taking a couple of deep breaths as if she was trying to ease some pain. Liz followed her. "Are you all right?" she asked, and Ava smiled.

"Baby's foot under my ribs, I think. It'll pass."

Liz nodded and bent down to take a closer look at Sam. "Hey, little man," she said, but he was crying so loud she wondered if he even heard her.

"Looks like we'll be here a while," Ava said, assessing the mess in Sam's shorts. "I've got this, baby." She crouched down in front of her son, drying his tears with her fingers.

"What should I do?" Liz asked, keeping her tone calm and reassuring.

"Go work things out with Hudson. We're doing just fine here. Aren't we?"

Sam nodded in between sniffles. Ava kissed his head and he finally stopped sobbing. He looked miserable; Liz bent down to kiss his cheek. "Your mommy is going to fix you up," she said, and he finally smiled.

"Have fun." Ava winked at Liz. "And let me know how it goes," she yelled as she walked away.

It took Liz a good few hours to build up the courage to follow Ava's advice and make the first move. She picked up her cell and phoned Hudson. It went straight to voicemail. She left a vague message asking him to call her back.

A day later, he hadn't yet returned his call. Impatient Liz called his office, only to be told Hudson wasn't around.

Hudson landed in London just as the clock struck midday. The heat of summer was coming from everywhere and his journey on the Piccadilly line made him feel claustrophobic.

Hudson entered the MediaOne's office and went straight to reception. "I'm here to see Jack Norton. It's Hudson Moore, I'm STYLE's CEO."

"One second, please, I don't have your name in my list of guests," the receptionist said as she typed something. "I'm sorry, but there's no meeting with you scheduled for today."

"I don't have an appointment but I need to see him now. I flew in from Boston to talk to him face to face. Can you please let him know I'm here?"

She looked reluctant but Hudson's patience was running low. "Either you get him now or I get Malone on the phone so you can explain to him directly why you are wasting my time." Hudson hated to throw his weight around.

"Erm, of course, one moment please."

"Thank you," Hudson said, stepping away from the desk. He didn't like to pressure people into doing what he wanted but this was a matter that outdid all niceties. Liz's career and reputation were on the line and he had no time for politeness.

After a few minutes waiting, Jack appeared at the end of the corridor. "Hudson, what a surprise!" he said, stretching his hand.

Hudson shook it, keeping his eyes on the man in front of him. He never particularly liked Jack, and he liked him even less now. "Can we talk?" Hudson's tone left no space for any answer other than yes.

Jack acknowledged that with a brief nod. "Right, let's find a meeting room." He led the way to a small room to the left. "So, what brings you here?"

"STYLE's launch." Hudson's hands fisted. "I want you to scrap it."

Jack looked confused. "Scrap it?"

"Yes." Hudson's voice was calm but underneath there was a

sharp edge. "The whole thing. I don't want anything currently planned to go ahead."

"Hudson, I don't understand. We booked the space already and the media planning team has worked out the entire integrated campaign already. We can't just *scrap it*." Jack laughed nervously.

"I'm not asking if it can be done, I'm telling you to do it." Hudson's tolerance was running low.

Jack shook his head. "I'm afraid it's more complicated than that. Malone has asked for full approval of this project and no changes are allowed unless he signs them off and I can already tell you, he loves what we've done, which was based on Malone's idea, he will not agree to scrap it."

"I'm STYLE's CEO. That's my company and you are working for me."

Jack shook his head again. "Malone owns fifty-one percent of the company, so you are one of my stakeholders but officially I'm working for him." Jack smirked. "Also, STYLE will get so much publicity from it, you are a fool for trying to stop it."

Hudson considered explaining to Jack the difference between right and wrong and the fact that nothing in the plan was actually ethical but he knew it would be just a waste of time.

"I have not signed on the dotted line yet." Hudson rose and without another word, he left.

§

Liz waited until the end of the week before walking to Hudson's apartment. Whatever his reason for not answering her calls, emails and messaging, it was not a good enough one and she was going to tell him just that. Right to his face. *There's aloof and there's rude, he has crossed the line.*

She walked fast but the sun was setting, and the colors in the sky were marvelous and she could not ignore the beauty. When she reached Hudson's building, she hesitated, paced back and forth a few times until she lost her nerve and decided that confronting him wasn't actually a good idea. But as she turned to leave, the sight of Hudson filled her vision. He was running right to her, so she tucked her hair behind her ear and stood her ground.

Hudson stopped in front of her. He was wearing a running top drenched with sweat. His hair was ruffled and his breath heavy with the strain of the exercise. Her achy heart told her that he looked even more handsome than she remembered him. She was determined to get things off her chest and leave but when his mouth curved into a smile, she felt her pulse accelerate. *Damn it.*

"Liz. What are you doing here?" he asked, still short of breath from the run.

She knew she was staring but she couldn't remember the reason why she wanted to see him, so she blinked to regain her balance. "I wanted to clear the air."

He raked his fingers through his hair. Droplets from it glistened in the sunset. His eyes took on a deep shade of blue and he was looking at her in that intense way that always left her breathless. She tried to ignore those feelings.

"Clear the air?" He seemed surprised.

"You never called me back. Nor did you reply to any of my messages, emails, voicemails."

"True." He said the word without apology, she waited but seconds went by and the world watched them as they stared at each other.

"I want to know why the radio silence."

He opened his mouth but Liz's phone pinged once and then again, then again before starting to buzz with insistence.

"Go ahead," Hudson said, but she didn't move.

"I'm sure it can wait." But as she said that, three more pings filled the silence and Hudson raised an eyebrow. When her cell buzzed again, she relented and fished it out of her handbag.

"Excuse me." She walked a few steps away to pick up the voicemail.

She listened to the message in shock and by the time the voicemail ended, she had started to shake. Hudson went to her. She looked at him but her eyes were not focusing.

"Hey, what's wrong?"

She opened her mouth but couldn't speak.

"Liz?" He called her name and took her wrists in his hands; she felt her skin turning icy cold.

"What happened?" he was asking her, but she shook her head.

"I can't breathe." Her voice was nothing more than a whisper.

"It's all right. Everything will be all right, just come with me," Hudson said, and wrapping an arm around her waist, he walked her into the building and up to his apartment.

CHAPTER 19

Liz was disoriented and let him guide her to the sofa in the middle of his living room. She closed her eyes, then opened them again but the haziness was still there. There was a buzzing in her ears and his voice was muffled. He said something she didn't understand, then disappeared from her peripheral vision. Her panic spiked. *Don't go, don't leave me here,* she wanted to shout, but there was no air in her lungs.

He returned with a glass, wrapped her fingers around it. "Drink," he ordered, but his tone was gentle.

"What is it?" Her voice shook.

He crouched in front of her. "Whisky."

"Not my favorite." Liz's complaint came spontaneously and she was pleased her mental faculties were coming back.

"Drink it anyway," Hudson said, then placed his hand lightly on her knees. She felt his warmth and the knot in her throat loosened. Sheepishly, she lifted the tumbler to her lips and took a sip. The whisky smelled strong and when she swallowed, it warmed her chest. She took another sip. "Thank you," she said.

Hudson lifted his fingers to tuck her hair gently behind her ear. When she had finished drinking, he took the glass back and placed it on the coffee table.

"I needed that," she said, noticing that her voice was steady again and her vision sharper.

"What happened?" Hudson asked.

"My father," she answered. "He's had a stroke."

"God, Lizzie. Is he okay?"

She swallowed then nodded. "My brother said he's at the hospital now, but he's out of danger. It was a very quick message, not many details other than what I've told you."

"But he's going to be okay?"

"I think so. Sorry, I've overreacted." She pressed her fingers against her eyelids and took a deep breath. "I've spent fifteen years on this side of the Atlantic worrying that something like this would happen and I'd not make it back in time to—" and with that thought she finally broke down. Tears came flooding, she couldn't do anything to stop them.

Hudson sat next to her and wrapped his arm around her shoulders.

When she finally managed to keep her sobs under control, she felt tired and empty.

"Call your brother, Lizzie. Have a good chat with your mom. It'll help."

"Yes, I should," she said.

He walked to the door. "I'm going to take a shower, give you some privacy."

She pulled herself together and called home.

Hudson let the cold water run over his head. With his eyes closed, he tried to flush away the image of Liz's distraught face from his mind. When he felt in control again, he turned off the water and toweled himself dry. Dressed in a dark shirt and a pair of jeans, he walked back to the lounge, unsure how he was going to tell Liz about the PR stunt organized by Malone to launch STYLE and explain that it would most likely end her career and damage her reputation. How could he say that to her now after what had happened to her father? He didn't think he could add to her worries and decided that the truth would need to wait for better times. When he entered the room, he saw Liz facing the window. When she turned, he saw her eyes were red and puffy, she smiled at him and he felt a sense of guilt weighing heavy on his chest.

"I don't usually cry," she justified herself.

"I do approve of a good cry." She laughed at his words, he took that as a good sign and he went to the wine cooler to choose a bottle. "Did you speak with your brother?" he asked, pouring the wine.

"Briefly, it's the middle of the night in Dublin and he sounded exhausted." She took the glass that Hudson offered her. "He'll call me tomorrow with an update but he reassured me. Looks like my dad was lucky." She took a sip of wine while holding the glass as if it was a buoy. "He had immediate treatment and he's going to fully recover. They are all a bit shaken up still, me included."

Hudson smiled. "I'm glad it's good news."

"Me too. And thank you for your support: not sure I would have coped alone." She leaned over the counter that was separating them.

"You are strong, Lizzie. I only offered you some whisky. And now a glass of wine," he said, lifting his glass.

"Are you trying to get me drunk?" she asked, and he smiled but there was a weight on him that wouldn't shift. He took a sip.

"Why didn't you call me?" Liz said, and he saw pain and disappointment.

He stepped away from the counter. He needed some distance. He needed the strength to lie to her. "I was away," he said.

"And you couldn't tell me?"

"It was a last-minute trip."

"To Mars?"

He frowned. "To London."

"Right, not so difficult to keep in touch then. Or at least you could have said you were away."

"I could have but I needed the distance."

She narrowed her eyes. "Why?"

"To think. To figure things out."

"And did you?"

"Not really."

She took a second. "I came to tell you that I was hurt by the way you behaved, but now I've lost the steam so I'm going to suggest that we pretend that nothing happened between us. Pretend we didn't say what we said or feel what we felt."

He drained his wine. The guilt was eating him up, he didn't want to lie to her but he couldn't share with her what Malone's PR team was planning without having a solution. No, it would only add to her worries. He needed to fix this without her knowing or involving her any further in this mess. "Is this what you want?" He walked to her. "To pretend?" he asked, and saw something dancing in her eyes.

"I can be professional, can you?" Her voice was mellow and her eyes calm but he noticed her fingers were running up and down the stem of the glass and realized that she was nervous.

"I can but I don't want to." He wanted her and a plan was hatching in his mind, if he didn't tell her about the PR stunt, he might have a chance to court her, win over her trust while trying to find a way to neutralize Malone's interference and stop his plans for the launch.

"What if we keep the two things separate?" he suggested.

"What do you mean?"

"I mean we play our roles as Moore and Walsh at work, and then we flip to Hudson and Lizzie, and that's our private life, we don't talk about STYLE or the color of my office's new carpet." It was a good option, the only one that could work.

"Totally separate. No crossover?"

"Two sealed compartments."

"It's easy to say that now, but what if there is an issue with the refurb. Are you sure the two streams won't get muddled up?"

"I can separate the woman from the designer. Can you do the same?" Would she hear the warning in his words?

"I think I can but I guess we'll have to take the risk, there's no other way of knowing," she said, finishing her wine.

"I'm game," he said, knowing that he would have to use the next few weeks to stop Malone while making sure Liz loved him enough to forgive him if he didn't succeed.

"Sounds like we have a deal, should we shake on it?" she said.

He put his glass down on the counter. "I have one condition."

"What condition?" She looked at him with amused suspicion.

"We are not allowed to talk about work outside work," he said, determined to put as much space as he could between their relationship and Malone's plan.

"Fine by me," she said.

"Okay then, let's shake on it." He offered her his hand.

"Deal." She shook it.

The moment dragged, the tension intensified and Hudson wondered if he actually had enough willpower to lie to the woman he loved.

"Are you hungry?" he asked, keeping her hand in his.

"Yes, actually." She sounded surprised.

"Then let me take you to dinner."

"Well, you owe me a date, so it's only fair." Liz's tone was playful. He was glad she was recovering from the shock.

"Any requests?"

"Impress me," she challenged him.

"So much pressure already?" He pulled her toward the door. She grabbed her handbag on the way.

"Only a little bit." Her tone was sarcastic and he felt things between them were back on track.

He turned to her. "I'll do my best to deliver." He kissed her lips softly, sealing a promise that went way beyond dinner.

They left the house and walked for a few blocks, talking about the warm weather and their plans for the summer.

"I want to take two weeks off," Hudson said with a wishful tone.

"Really?" Liz looked up at him but he kept his gaze straight ahead.

"No, not really. I just wish I could. Two weeks is not really possible, but after the launch I'll take a break."

"And do what? Think about work?"

"Ah!" He elbowed her gently. "You think you have me all figured out, eh?"

"Yes. You are a workaholic," Liz said with confidence. "It takes one to know one."

He laughed and she stopped walking. He turned to her.

"When is last time you took time off? A proper holiday with no interruptions, no emails, no worries." Her gaze was as direct as her question.

"Spring break."

She frowned. "Really?" The suspicion in her eyes told him she didn't believe him.

He had to own up. "It was spring break, twenty years ago. Final year of uni, I think."

She laughed. "That I believe."

"Okay, then. What about you?"

"My last holiday?" she asked even if really there was no need for confirmation.

He nodded and they started to walk again.

"I went to Dublin for Easter," she said, her eyes moistened. He knew she was thinking of her father and tried to distract her.

"I mean a holiday where you get soft sand under your feet,

scuba diving on the reef, and lazy afternoons sleeping in a hammock."

"I'd be bored out of my mind in a place like that." She laughed out loud.

"Maybe not with the right company," he said, squeezing her hand. She looked at him with a smile full of possibilities and he hoped that maybe, just maybe, things were going to work out for them.

They crossed the road and Hudson pointed at the café in the corner. "They make the best waffles. You need to try their hazelnut and banana combo."

"All right, I'm a sucker for overly-sweet decadent treats but is that what we are having for dinner?"

"No, we'll keep that for breakfast." He let the implication of that linger between them.

"One date at a time."

He laughed: her witty replies always delighted him. "Slow and steady, I'm okay with that." Hudson led her into a small alley.

"Where are we going?" she asked, looking around.

"It's a gem of a place, well-hidden and only known by a few lucky people. Worth the trek, trust me." He directed her into a small shop.

"Oh, it smells so nice! Is this a Chinese grocery store?" she asked as they moved through the aisles bursting with colorful noodle packets and many products she had never seen before.

"No, it's Korean," he answered as they reached the back of the shop.

"Gosh, I'm sorry, I hope you don't think I'm racist." She was genuinely embarrassed and he stroked her arm in reassurance.

"I'll point out the differences for you and you won't get confused again."

"Thanks." She smiled and he focused on her lips, he loved how they turned up in an uneven way. He was planning on kissing her again, but not just yet. When they stopped before a man sitting on a rickety chair Hudson addressed him politely, bowing his head to show his respect. *"Annyeonghaseyo."* Hudson said.

Without a word, the man lifted his cane and tapped at the door behind him with its round head.

The door opened and a young girl, probably not older than twelve, welcomed them.

"Annyeonghaseyo," Hudson said again.

"Follow me please," she said, and they walked down the narrow corridor.

"Where are we going?" Liz asked.

He took her hand. "My favorite restaurant." He watched Liz's eyes widening as they entered a large room. Across both sides there were rows of low tables. Intricate room dividers gave privacy to the dining guests.

"Oh, wow, this is so unexpected," Liz said, looking around.

"It's a great little place, and the food… it's simply the best Korean in town," he said as they walked further in.

"Hudson!" One of the waiters waved at him from the back of the room.

"Dae, I was hoping to find you here," Hudson said when he reached them. They shook hands.

"Yes, Friday night is my shift. My cousin plays bowling, so I cover for him."

"Dae, this is Liz, my date," Hudson said, then turned to her. "Liz, meet the traitor who left my company to be a waiter."

"Nice to meet you," Liz said, shaking Dae's hand.

"I'm not a traitor, and not a waiter," he whispered to Liz but loud enough for Hudson to hear.

"You were my best developer and you left me when I needed you the most," Hudson complained.

"I gave you three years notice!" Dae laughed.

"Three years?" Liz asked.

"Yes, and still he resents me." Dae punched Hudson softly on his upper arm.

"Why so long?" Liz looked intrigued.

"Let's sit down and I'll tell you all about it," Dae said, escorting them to a table in the corner.

"Don't you have to work? Serve the customers? Wash dishes?" Hudson teased him.

"Are you trying to get rid of me?" Dae asked, looking from Liz to Hudson and back again.

"Yes," Hudson said seriously.

"Really?" Dae asked.

"Yes," Hudson said, keeping up the farce.

"Fine, I'll leave you guys to it then," Dae said, patting Hudson's shoulder. "Sorry, Liz, this very *interesting* story will have to wait until next time," he said when they reached their table.

"Disappointing," Liz commented, and Dae laughed.

Hudson sat down and took Liz's hand. "She'll survive. We are not talking about work, it's the rule." She smiled at him and the knot in his throat tightened.

"The usual?" Dae asked, breaking their romantic moment.

"Yes, but I think Liz would probably like to see the menu," Hudson said.

"You know, I'll take *the usual* too, sounds perfect. Thanks, Dae."

"Won't be long. Plus my mom is in the kitchen tonight and she's the best." Dae's tone was dripping with pride.

"Give her a kiss from me, would you?" Hudson said, and Dae nodded before disappearing through a small door.

"I hope you were not expecting a two-Michelin star restaurant on the seafront," Hudson said, realizing that he was nervous and he was seeking her approval.

"Are you kidding me?" She squeezed his hand. "This place is fantastic and I feel so privileged that you have brought me here."

Emotions bubbled inside his chest and they were becoming too strong to control. He entwined his fingers with hers and looked straight into her eyes. He had to lie to her but he didn't want to.

"I'm glad you like it," he said, trying to push his troubling thoughts away for now.

Dae returned with their drinks.

"Soju," Dae said, filling two shot glasses.

Liz looked at the clear liquid with curiosity.

"It's like vodka but weaker and sweeter. Hold the glass with two hands, then down in one," he said to Liz, then placed the bottle in front of Hudson. "You know what to do, right? Drink up, fill up, shoot."

"Thanks," Hudson said, lifting his glass to Liz. "Ready?" When she nodded, they drank it together.

"So, what do you think?" Dae asked.

Liz coughed a little. "It's... warm," she said, and both men laughed.

"Well, you keep enjoying that. Food is on its way, Mom says hello, she is glad you brought a date." Dae winked at them before disappearing again. The restaurant was busy and he was rushed off his feet.

"You okay?" Hudson asked, filling her glass again.

"Yes, but if we don't slow down with the shots, I'll pass out under the table before the main course arrives."

Hudson laughed. "You don't want to miss out on the food."

"If it's as good as the smell, I'm in for a treat," she agreed, and took only a small sip this time. "What are we eating?" she asked.

Hudson saw her shoulders relax and decided that getting a little tipsy and loosened up would do her some good after the upset of earlier on.

"Dolsot bibimbap," he said.

She frowned. "I have no idea what that is. I travelled around South East Asia for a few months when I was at uni but never stretched further east than Thailand."

He stared at her, curious to hear about her past, this was nice.

"I've never been to Korea either. I'd love to go to Seoul one day, that's where Dae's family is from originally." He drunk from his glass. "Anyway, dolsot bibimbap is rice and vegetables topped with a fried egg. It's served in a hot stone bowl. I think it's delicious, I just hope you'll like it."

"I'm sure I will." She smiled.

"How come you are so confident that you will?"

"We have lots more in common than I originally thought," she admitted.

"I was thinking the same." He had noticed that too.

They were quiet for a while, looking at each other without the need to speak.

He broke the silence with an apology. "Sorry, it was rude not to call. I had lots on and the London trip wrecked my schedule but they are just excuses. I should have called you back or at least answered your text."

"All true, it was despicable behavior," she said, but he saw laughter in her eyes and he knew she wasn't grumpy.

"Am I forgiven then?" he asked.

"You are." She looked down for a few seconds, then returned her gaze to him.

"Thank you. Won't go off the grid like that again, I promise." He reached for her hand again.

"You do and you'll see my nasty side."

They both laughed.

"I'm glad you came to see me tonight." He knew he would have avoided her otherwise.

"Me too." She looked pensive.

"What is it?"

"I was thinking that I'm struggling to figure you out."

"I'm not that complicated," he said.

"Okay, humble is definitely on the list."

He was flattered, modesty was a trait he respected. "What else?"

"I only scratched the surface but you have the soul of an artist and the brain of a mathematician. You are caring without being patronizing, and logical but with a flamboyant edge that makes you surprising and unpredictable. You are an intriguing mix, Hudson."

"You'll have to stick around to see if that's true," he said, and she laughed.

"Maybe I will."

"Cheers to that." He lifted his glass to her and they drank at the same time.

"Okay, my turn."

"Do you have to?"

"Yes."

"Go on, then, let's hear it."

"You are creative. But you are also a meticulous planner. You are caring and tough, and strong, and gentle, and funny, and beautiful, and just overwhelmingly sexy."

"I—" She said nothing else and color rose to her cheeks.

"I'm so attracted to you it almost hurts, I never felt this way for anyone before, Lizzie. I've never told someone that I love them and I've never been more scared about messing something up than right now with you." He had so much more that he wanted to say but words were not going to be enough to properly explain his feelings. He lifted her hand to his lips and softly kissed her fingers.

"I don't want to mess this up either, but I have trust issues, you should know," she said.

"We won't mess it up and if you let me, I'll work hard to earn your trust, I promise," he whispered, knowing he was going to do his best to keep it.

Dae arrived with their food.

"Do you have time to sit with us?" Hudson asked him.

"I thought you'd never ask." They laughed and Dae sat with them for a while. He told Liz a few stories about Hudson and

Tom in the early days of STYLE, as well as enlightening her on interesting Korean traditions and culinary quirks.

"This was the best food and the best date I've had in ages," Liz said to Hudson as they walked back to his place hand in hand.

As they kissed under the starry sky, Hudson swore that he'd find a way to get Malone to back off and save Liz's career. Whatever it took.

CHAPTER 20

Liz woke up with the warmth of Hudson's body wrapped around her and smiled. God, she was in love with this man and it felt so good but when she moved her head, she realized that she was also hurting. She had drunk way too much soju and now her brain was pounding inside her skull. Slightly confused, she couldn't quite remember all the details of what happened the night before, there was just a glow of happiness coating her memories of the time she spent with Hudson.

She looked around the room, trying to focus. Hudson was lying on the sofa next to her. She was curled up against his shoulder and they were both fully dressed, she was sure their clothes never came off. There was a slight regret at that but also some relief. The flat screen TV was on stand-by and on the coffee table she spotted the remains of their midnight feast: a half-full bowl of popcorn, a tub with melted ice cream at the bottom, two spoons, two wine glasses and an empty bottle of Chablis.

The full picture was slowly returning. The Korean restaurant and Dae. The shots—she blinked—way too many shots. Then the walk home. She smiled at the memory of Hudson's romantic little gestures. Once back in his flat, they watched old movies and talked about their childhood while they munched on junk food and then they kissed until exhaustion set them apart.

Then her heart ached at the memory of her brother's voicemail telling her their father had had a stroke. She felt her chest caving in with the pressure of her worries and leaned on Hudson's shoulder for some stability. He was there, real and steady, and she felt her feelings pouring out of her after a decade of entrapment. She sighed and curled back next to him. His scent was now both familiar and exciting and she realized that she wanted this and a lot more.

She closed her eyes and gently leaned further into him. The firmness of his chest against her palms made her pulse jump, the emotions battering her like a relentless storm. She looked at him sleeping and that was the moment she knew. She wanted everything that she had given up when Sean betrayed her, and she wanted it with Hudson who seemed to have restarted her heart.

Too emotional to stay still, she slowly moved away but he stirred and wrapped his arms tighter around her. When she was against him again, he turned his face to her and kissed her forehead.

"Morning, beautiful." His husky voice made her shiver.

"Sorry I woke you," she whispered, holding on to the last few moments of intimacy before the light brought the distance of a new day between them.

"Is it morning already?" Hudson asked, and she smiled.

"Yes. It's… eight o'clock," she said after checking her watch. He loosened his embrace and sat up. She combed through her hair with her fingers, a little self-conscious.

"It's still early. Let's go to bed," he said, pulling her to him again.

She laughed when he kissed her neck but wriggled away.

He opened his eyes then and looked at her. "Sorry I wasn't trying to pressure you."

"I know."

He looked so cute as he tried not to come on too strong, while she sensed that his needs were as demanding as hers. She leaned over and kissed him.

"It may be easier if I go," she whispered against his lips, but he only tightened the grip on her.

"I don't want you to go. Spend the day with me and I don't mean in bed."

She laughed. "What do you have in mind then?" She settled next to him again.

He rubbed his face with both hands. She was enjoying seeing him flustered. "It's a beautiful day." He was fully awake now. "We could go sailing."

"Sailing?" she said, and saw the laughter on his face.

"Is it weird?"

"No, it's great. Do you have a boat?" she asked.

"Yes, it was my grandfather's boat." He pushed himself up.

"I love boats." She sighed at the idea, then realized she had neither the right clothes nor the right shoes for sailing.

"I need to go home first."

"Why?"

"To shower."

"You could shower here."

Her breath was caught in the tightening of her chest. She was nervous and tried to find another excuse. "Still, I can't go around in this dress, I slept in it, it's all creased and I think I spilled chocolate ice cream on it and on my arm," she said, her tone incredulous.

"Really?" He took her arm and turned it to check. There was a dry line running from her elbow all the way down her wrist. He traced it with his fingertips and made her quiver. "You are a messy eater," he whispered in her ear, then munched gently on the lobe, she remembered her doing the same to him.

"Stop it!" She jumped off the sofa with a giggle. This was silly, they were grown-ups, healthy and unattached adults who were *apparently* in love with each other—and like Ava had said, maybe sex was the answer.

Hudson walked to her and placed his hands on her waist. Maybe it was time she stopped running away from the inevitable. "You can take a shower here, borrow a T-shirt, I'm sure I can find something that fits, or I'll go to your place and pick up anything you want. I just don't want you leaving." She felt his fingers running lower on her hips. She shivered again under his touch, her pulse jumping with every word he spoke.

"You know you sound like one of those psychopaths from the movies who keep women trapped in their apartment, right?" A joke was all she had.

"We don't have to stay in. We can go sailing, we can have a decadent waffle breakfast and go for a walk on the beach, we can watch another film noir, read or cook." He lowered his forehead to hers.

Or make love. She closed her eyes for a moment, collected her strength. "And then what?"

"I don't know, Lizzie. Maybe lunch on the seafront, a drive somewhere remote?" He held her closer, their bodies pressed against each other. "You choose, I don't really care what we do as long as you stay."

"I'm staying." She didn't want to think or resist anymore.

He smiled, then turned serious as he slowly lowered his lips to hers. The kiss started gently but she was wired and running her fingers on the back of his head she deepened it, trying to fill her need for him.

"I know what I'd like to do, and it doesn't involve boats... or clothes," she murmured, then her fingers reached his shirt and she started unbuttoning it. He closed his eyes and when she used her fingertips to trace the lines of his stomach he took a deep breath. She went for the button of his slacks and he encircled her wrists.

"Are you sure about this?" he asked.

"Yes, absolutely sure."

He took her hand and they walked into his bedroom. They made love, letting their passion finally run free. She felt happy for the first time in a very long time.

They spent the weekend doing nothing in particular and yet it meant everything to her. The easy way he took her hand, the soft words he spoke in her ears, the laugher and the teasing and the budding of a relationship made the need to win an award less pressing.

Her focus had been narrow so far, but Hudson had pushed himself into her life that dominated by her career was quickly giving up some of its space to something more, something exciting.

They had taken a break from reality and as promised neither of them mentioned work, but she knew they were on borrowed time so when Sunday night came, she was prepared to say goodbye. She insisted on walking home alone but after an exhausting battle of wills she let Hudson accompany her. Outside her building, they kissed like teenagers, like no one was watching, like they never kissed before and when he eventually walked away— after a million goodbyes—Liz felt a deep ache right under her ribs.

She waited until his silhouette had disappeared, then ran in. She waved at the doorman, rushed into the elevator and held her breath the entire way. When she exhaled the reality of what had happened to her father dragged her back down to Earth like a lead balloon.

When she opened the door of her apartment, Simone was waiting for her. "Hey, girl, new clothes?" Simone said in her usual upbeat tone. "They are way too big and way too manly to be the result of a shopping spree."

"I had to borrow something from a friend after I spilled ice cream on my dress. I couldn't come home to get changed…

Anyway, it's a boring story." Liz knew that her evasive tone wasn't going to get her housemate off her back.

"Unplanned weekend away?"

"Erm, yes, something like that."

"Are you gonna tell me the details, or do I need to pull it out of you?"

"Okay, fine. I'm wearing Hudson's clothes," Liz answered, kicking off her shoes.

"Ohhhh." Simone sat up, crossed her legs on the sofa to make space for Liz. "Do tell, don't leave anything out."

"Nothing to tell really." Liz wasn't trying to minimize what happened also, with Hudson gone, she couldn't get the worries about her father out of her head.

"Okay, just one question."

"Fine," she said and leaned back against the cushions.

"Did you guys kiss?"

Liz rolled her eyes at Simone. "We are not five," she said with an annoyed tone but then she smiled.

"Okay, I'll take that as a yes. What else? First base? Second?"

Liz felt her cheeks turning hot. "Simone, I won't give you the details."

"Was it good? Great?"

"It was mind-blowing." Liz giggled, but the memory of what had happened back home hit her mood again.

Simone looked at her. "What's wrong? Something happened?"

Liz knew she couldn't keep the news about her father a secret. "My dad had a stroke on Friday, but he's fine," she added quickly.

Simone's mouth opened in a shocked O-shape and Liz reassured her. "He's out of danger. They are keeping him in hospital for monitoring but he'll be out soon. He had no permanent damage, so you don't have to worry."

"Liz, oh my God, you must be so scared. Why didn't you text me?"

"I was in shock and I didn't want you to worry."

Simone leaned over to hug Liz. They stayed there a few minutes, then Simone spoke again. "Did Hudson know what happened?"

"Yes, he was there when I got the call. He was great and having him there made me realize I want him to be in my life." Liz looked at her friend. "I want to be with Hudson. I want to be in a relationship with him. A proper one."

"Of course, babe."

Liz shook her head. "You don't understand." She looked down at her hand. She had removed her grandmother's ring and her finger felt naked without it. "I don't want to 'date' him. I don't want to wait until we go through the courting stages. I want to be with him now, to get married, to start a family. My father's stroke showed me that our life can change on a dime and I don't want to waste any more time. I love him." She shook her head, thinking that it seemed impossible to fall for someone this fast. "And I don't want to wait, I want our life together to start." Liz threw her arms up in exasperation. "It sounds so crazy."

Simone took Liz's hands in hers. "It does not. The heart wants what the hearts wants. And also, love doesn't come with a prescribed timeline. Four dates before sex, six months before you move in with me. That's just BS you read in a magazine, because what works for some people is totally wrong for others. Look at you and Sean for example. You were together since forever, lived together, got engaged and yet it went all tits up—'scuse my British." Simone squeezed her hands when Liz smiled. "You know your own heart and if you think Hudson is the one, then just trust your guts."

Liz chewed the inside of her mouth, reflecting on that. "I love him, that much I'm sure of."

"And what did Hudson say?" Simone asked.

"To what?"

"To your let's-make-a-family proposal?"

Liz knew this was the sticky point. "He doesn't really know

what I want. It was all a bit crazy and we went from 'keeping it professional' to 'sleeping together' in a very short space. We didn't have the time to discuss the details."

"But you are going to talk to him about it, right?"

"I really don't know how to say that to him. What if he doesn't feel the same way? What if part of the appeal is that I'm forty and still single and he assumed I don't want a family? What if he runs a mile when I tell him that I want to have a baby?"

Simone looked serious, then smiled. "I bet he'll love the 'making the baby' part of your plan." She waggled her eyebrows and Liz burst out laughing.

"Yeah, well, I'm looking forward to that part myself," Liz said and they laughed again. She felt a bit lighter now, the worries for her father's health dissipating and the possibilities of a future shared with Hudson made her believe that her happily ever after was finally here.

CHAPTER 21

Hudson spent every second he had to spare trying to speak to Malone about the launch but his PA had so far managed to keep him away from her boss. Unhappy to just sit and wait for a call back, Hudson had contacted every senior manager he knew in Malone's team and tried every other possible avenue. It had been almost a week and Hudson was running out of patience.

"If the mountain will not come to me, then I'll have to go to it. I'm not afraid of a little climb." And with that resolution, Hudson checked the train times. If Malone wasn't going to be rational and compromise, then Hudson was going to find the way to limit some of Malone's decision-making powers.

Hudson looked around Carter Smith's large office for a moment. There was a floor-to-ceiling window behind him. The Manhattan skyscrapers were looking at them, judging. He didn't care: he was here on a mission and wasn't going to leave without success.

"Mr. Moore, I'm afraid we cannot renegotiate the terms of STYLE acquisition at this stage. The launch is less than a month away and there's nothing I can do to push through an amendment now. Also, everything in the contract is an integral part of our agreement, and I'm sure Mr. Malone would not want to change that," said Smith, with a pleasant smile. He was Malone's lawyer, the one who handled their account since the very first meeting eighteen months ago.

"I'm sorry you wasted your time but, in my defense, I thought my assistant reminded you of our terms over the phone.'

"Yes, he did," Hudson said. "I don't want to be reminded of the terms. I want to change them."

"Well, that's not going to happen just because you came here in person." Smith stressed the words with an annoying gesture of his fingers.

Hudson tried to keep his anger under control. "What other options are there because I'm not happy with your boss taking over the management of my company? That's my job, I'm the CEO." His hands clenched into fists as the anger built with every second of this passive-aggressive charade of politeness.

"I'm not sure you have any options to be honest." The lawyer's placating tone was absolutely maddening.

"Look, what I want is very simple, and I'm going to spell it out for you, so there are no misunderstandings. I want Malone to stay out of my company management as that was never part of our agreement," Hudson said, trying not to choke on the anger that was filling his throat.

Smith looked at him with a duplicitous smile. "Mr. Moore, the documents we sent you clearly state that Terry Malone will become the major stakeholder of STYLE as soon as the contracts are signed, which they will be shortly. Meanwhile, as per our agreement, he's entitled to make any arrangement he sees fit to ensure STYLE is a commercially viable venture. I recommend that you go back home and have a chat with your own lawyer, who is definitely better placed to give you advice than I am."

"Yes, thank you for the insightful suggestion." Hudson's tone was sharpened by sarcasm. "I've already done that and I didn't like what my lawyer had to say. That's why I'm here."

Carter laughed and this only aggravated Hudson's bad mood. He wanted to shout his frustration but shifted in his chair instead, keeping his emotions under control knowing that Liz's career was on the line.

"Mr. Moore. Hudson, if I may," Smith said, warily friendly, "the publicity that you'll get from this PR stunt is second to none. This will put you on the map. Why this sudden need to turn your back on a very lucrative plan?"

"Because it will ruin someone's reputation and I don't care how much my company would benefit from it: it's unethical as well as unfair."

"If the designer in question was better than the software, we wouldn't be having this discussion."

"You don't know anything about *the designer in question* who happens to be a professional with a sterling rep and heaps of talent. I don't know how MediaOne got those results from the software or who from my team helped them with it but I'm sure there's a mistake."

"Oh, I see. This is personal then," Carter said dryly. "Unfortunately, you've signed an agreement that gives Malone access to the assets as well as the operations the moment the acquisition is finalized. That will happen an hour before the launch which means Malone has the right to plan whatever he wants."

The idea was making Hudson's blood boil. "I know that!" Hudson said, slamming his open hands on the glass table. "I didn't come here to listen to more bureaucratic bullshit. I came to cut a new deal. He can have more of my shares but I want him to relinquish the operational control."

"Malone has no interest in doing so. He bought the majority shares for this reason, to have control. I'm afraid you've just wasted your time. The time for negotiation is long gone," Carter said, standing. "Have a safe journey back, Mr. Moore," he added, leaving the room.

It took all of Hudson's restraint to walk out without breaking anything. On the train he cursed himself for failing. With his head in his hands the reality dawned on him, he had exhausted all options. All had turned out to be dead ends. He had been trying to think of something that would make Malone change his mind, he had offered him more shares and that really was all he had. Anger grew at the idea that the launch would go ahead as planned and Liz's career would be ruined. His biggest fear was that when that happened, she would not be able to separate their working relationship from their personal one. She had promised him that she would but he knew she could not ignore that he was the one who had cost her everything she had worked so hard for.

He arrived in Boston at ten to midnight. The city was quiet and sleepy but he was too wired up and knew he wouldn't be able to sleep, so he went to the office.

He sat at his desk and hoping that it would calm his nerves, he reached for a bottle of whisky. *The irony*, he thought. That was the bottle Tom had opened to celebrate Malone's offer. He poured himself a double and drained the glass in one gulp. As soon as the alcohol hit his empty stomach, Hudson felt the warmth radiating from his core to his extremities and he hoped it would quench his anger. He knocked back a second glass, then poured himself another. When that was empty too, Hudson took the bottle and went to sit on the sofa. Leaning all the way back, he stared at the ceiling, waiting for his heartbeat to slow down. Sipping the whisky, he waited for his head to switch off. He finally felt mellow and sluggish. When the tiredness that had accumulated over the past few days caught up with him, he closed his eyes and slept.

He woke up when the lights of dawn started to filter through the skylight. He had stretched out on the sofa in his office and his head was now exploding. He sat up from the couch and his body seemed to ache and throb absolutely everywhere. He rubbed his stiff neck but that brought him no relief at all. He needed to go home but he felt too lousy to go anywhere without having some coffee and some strong painkillers first. When he stood, he felt queasy, so he leaned back and closed his eyes. After a while, he fell asleep again.

"Hudson."

Someone was calling his name.

"Hudson. Wake up…"

The noise was almost unbearable. He blinked several times until he could keep his eyes open and focus.

Tom's face was a few millimeters away from him. He was frowning. "Hudson? Are you okay?" Tom asked, giving his partner a hand up.

"Just tired."

"Tired? You are drunk!" Tom said, lifting the empty bottle from the floor. "And on my whisky," Tom snorted.

"Stop shouting, would you." Hudson shrugged and his brain imploded.

"I'm not shouting." Tom lowered his volume anyway. "What's wrong with you, man? It's Thursday morning and you are sleeping off a hangover in the office."

"Nothing's wrong, apart from your shouting," he said, sitting on the sofa and rubbing his stiff neck again. He remembered that he still hadn't taken any painkillers.

"I'm not shouting," Tom hissed in annoyance. "What the fuck is going on with you? You've been manic lately. You went to London, yesterday to New York, yet I check your diary and there were no scheduled meetings. Are you going to tell me what's going on?"

"I'm just exhausted, I've got a migraine and I don't have to answer any of your questions."

"Oh, I really think you do, pal." Tom frowned at him in concern. "You get drunk in the office, you are making this my

187

business. Is it because of Liz?" Tom said, shifting to his side to face Hudson.

"No, we are good."

"So? What is it?"

"Nothing, it's nothing." Hudson pressed his fingertips against his eyes hoping he could reach some sort of migraine-switch inside his skull and turn the pain off.

"Bullshit." Tom was angry but Hudson didn't have the strength to tell his partner how devastating it was to have your balls caught between a rock and a hard place.

"I'm just having a few operational issues with the PR team and Malone not playing nicely. I got back from the meeting in New York really wired and I needed to unwind."

"So, this is really just work stuff?"

"Yes, why?"

Tom paced the room.

"Please can you sit down you are making my headache worse."

Tom sat. "It's only because your odd behavior started after you started out with Liz and I thought this may have something to do with her."

"Things with her are great, in fact, I love her and I want to marry her."

"You—" Tom was shocked. "You are getting married?"

"I haven't asked her yet."

Tom blinked. "Sorry, trying to get my head around it. You met Liz less than a month ago and you are planning a proposal. I'm just taken aback by how fast things are moving for someone that never even had a long-term relationship before."

Hudson rubbed his temples. He really needed some medication. "Do you think she'd say yes?"

"I don't know but I hope so."

Hudson held his head in his hands but nothing seemed to offer any relief. Tom's relentless round of questions was not helping either.

"Look, I don't have any answers yet but you'll be the first to know, I promise."

"Well, congratulations—" Tom said, but a knock at the door interrupted him.

"Yes?" Hudson said, feeling his head exploding at the noise.

Jay stepped through the door. "We are waiting for you to start the Ops meeting, guys."

"I'm coming, give me a second to grab my laptop. Hudson is going to skip today, can you cover for him?"

"Sure. No problem." Jay left, closing the door behind him.

"Thanks." Hudson pinched his nose.

"Go home, take a shower, eat something greasy and get some sleep, okay?"

"Yes, that's a plan. Maybe I should check my emails first." Hudson was feeling too sorry for himself to be embarrassed.

"No, just go. You look like shit," Tom said, slapping Hudson's back intentionally hard.

❧

Friday night was finally here. Five days without seeing Hudson had taken its toll and it was ridiculous how excited she was at the idea of finally seeing him.

She looked at herself in the mirror, checking the final result of an hour spent on makeup and general beautification. She took a deep breath as she flattened the creases out of her dress and adjusted the neckline. When the phone rang, she swallowed the nerves that were making her hands shake and went to answer.

"Hi, Nick. Yes, let him up," she said to the doorman who'd rang.

When she heard the knock, she opened the door and Hudson was standing there with a massive bunch of flowers. "Hey, beautiful," he said, and the words she had prepared were swallowed by her feelings.

"Hi," was all she managed.

He leaned over to her and kissed her lips. The light contact amplified the tenderness.

"Come in," she said and then closed the door behind him with a sigh.

"I love the dress but you need to change."

"Why?" She blinked at the unexpected remark.

"Because we are going sailing and I need a first mate. Also, you need clothes for a couple of days too."

"But—" She was a bit dazzled by the news.

"I know I should have told you, but I wanted to surprise you. We're spending the night in the bay and we will set off at first light. Candlelit dinner on board first, I hope that's okay."

Liz was still catching up with what he was saying. Not just dinner, like she imagined, but a weekend of sailing. With Hudson. Three days together. Just the two of them. On a boat. At sea. She felt the excitement bubbling inside her stomach, and it wasn't just a few butterflies fluttering about but a swarm filling her chest with the anticipation of a life that was about to turn upside down. She was quiet and he took her hand.

"Bad surprise?" Hudson seemed to be worried so she smiled at him in reply.

"Good surprise." She couldn't stop grinning. "So exciting. I better go and pack a bag. Come with me." She ran quickly to the kitchen to put the flowers in a vase, then took his hand again and led him into her bedroom.

"Nice boudoir," he said, and Liz was pleased now that she had taken a few minutes to make the place extra tidy. Hudson took off his blazer and went to sit on her bed while she opened her closet to get her overnight bag.

"So, where are we going?" she asked, busying herself trying to find the perfect trousers and T-shirt combo.

"Maine. I was thinking we would head north and then when you see a place you like, we stop."

"Sounds brilliant," she said, stuffing a jumper at the bottom of her bag. When she turned, Hudson was looking at her intently and she sensed the change in the air.

"How soon do we need to leave here?" she asked with a flirty smile, the insinuation behind her question brazenly clear.

"As soon as possible really, dinner's waiting, we wouldn't want to spoil it." He grinned as he delivered his challenge. She took the hint and ran with it. Sailing to Maine sounded great but maybe staying in her bedroom for three days sounded even better.

"Sure, won't be long, I just need to get some underwear." She sauntered to her chest of drawers and intentionally picked her sexiest black G-string, then chose a lace bra that was so skimpy it'd barely cover anything when she wore it. She turned to him and pouted. "Will this do?" She fluttered her eyelashes and saw him tense. Now that they had started playing, she wasn't going to spoil the moment.

"Yes." He sighed, but she knew he was watching her as she grabbed more alluring lingerie from her drawer.

"Maybe I should try this on? Just to be sure it fits."

"We don't have time." He smiled at her and she was quite impressed by his control given she was aching for him and all she wanted was for them to get naked.

To have it her way, she needed to take this up a notch. "Okay, my bag is ready, I just need to change now." She walked to him and after moving her hair to one side, she turned. She had seen this move in many movies and it always worked, so she went full on Hollywood rom-com on him.

"Mind undoing my dress please?" She giggled quietly as he stood up to reach the top of the zip. She felt his breath on her neck and the tickle of his fingertips on her skin and she quivered.

When the zip was all the way down, his hands returned to her shoulders and slid the fabric off till the dress pooled at her feet. She was working on her next move when he ran his hands over her back, up her stomach and cupped her breasts. She took a sharp breath and felt her body melting against his touch. *This move really works!*

"Make love to me," she whispered when he lowered his lips to her neck.

"Dinner's waiting," he murmured, and she shivered.

"Please make love to me, I don't want to wait another minute. I missed you so much." Liz closed her eyes and he turned her around to face him.

"I missed you too." And with those words they fell onto her bed, dinner plans and sailing trip all but forgotten. The night had fallen and snuggled against him, Liz was starting to feel sleepy.

"Shame for dinner," she said.

"It'll keep." Hudson kissed her forehead.

"We will go sailing tomorrow," Liz whispered before she grew too tired to keep her eyes open.

"Yes, we'll go tomorrow." He kissed her again and Liz nestled herself to his side and slept.

❦

Hudson pulled her closer and spent the night awake, thinking of Malone's plan that was threatening to destroy their future.

CHAPTER 22

I t was six on the dot when Ava arrived; Simone and Liz were already sitting at Gino's waiting for her. Her presence immediately lit the place up. She was radiant and Liz had an immediate surge of affection for her new friend.

"Ladies," Ava said, shimmying herself into the booth with some difficulties. "I think this is how Santa feels coming down the chimneys at Christmas." Her tone was bitter.

"Ava, you look great, honestly. Pregnancy really suits you," Simone said sincerely.

"Oh, good! Because I don't feel suitable for anything at all at the minute. I feel like a giant whale stranded on the beach and I still have two months of this to bear." Ava put her purse to her side and shook her head. "Maybe even longer if the little lady here decides to keep us waiting."

"It's all worth it, you know that." Liz didn't mean for her words to drip with longing but her emotions were so close to the surface these days it was hard to keep them hidden.

"It is worth it, honey. One day soon it will be your turn to waddle," Ava said, touching her hand with a gesture that said she understood that broody feeling perfectly well.

The moment dragged and Liz opened her mouth to say something, then closed it again. She had been thinking of babies a lot lately and she wasn't sure she could speak without her voice breaking.

Simone stepped in. "Right, shall we discuss the arrangements for the party then?"

"Yes, this is so exciting. I have lots of ideas," Ava said, looking at Simone. "I hope you don't think I'm being bossy."

"Nah, I still have the maid of honor's spot so I don't mind you taking the lead on this one."

Ava turned immediately to Liz. "Maid of honor?" Her eyes were wide. "Did Hudson pop the question?" She held her breath and Liz's cheeks flushed red.

"No, not officially." Liz shook her head.

"But he mentioned it?" Ava asked, her voice eager.

"Well, he just kept talking about how he loves his apartment but he had been looking at houses with a swing on the porch and how nice those are, especially if they have a back yard and white picket fences." Liz felt her face and her neck was engulfed with a blush.

"That's not a hint, it's a ton of bricks," said Ava, rolling her eyes. "So, when was it?" she asked, clearly keen to get the whole picture.

"Last weekend on his boat."

"What?" Ava seemed surprised. "He took you on his boat?"

"Yes, why?"

"That boat has been off limits since forever. He has never taken anyone sailing with him, not Tom, not even me!" Ava was speechless for a moment. "He took you to Betty's party as well... OMG, Liz, you are the one. He's really going to propose. Are you going to say yes?"

"Of course she will," Simone said. "Look at her, she's poached."

"Poached!" Ava laughed. "Love that expression."

"Okay, have you two quite finished making fun of me?"

Though she tried to sound annoyed, Liz had to give in and join her friends in their laughter.

"I think we should plan Liz's birthday party in a way that it could double up as an engagement party," Ava said, picking up the menu.

"That's a fantastic idea." Simone passed a menu to Liz before taking one for herself.

"He hasn't asked me yet, so don't get ahead of yourself, ladies," Liz warned as she read the specials, even though she knew she was going to order exactly what she always did.

"You could ask him, right? That's what I did with Tom," Ava said, looking at Liz sideways. "I mean, he did the one-knee thing but I organized the setting and the timing and everything else around it."

"That's sensible. If I ever find someone I want to marry I'll just say that straight up. I'm not much into the marriage thing, but you know, never say never." Simone closed her menu. She also always ordered the same pizza at Gino's; Liz didn't know why she bothered to look.

"I'm not going to ask him to marry me because it's way too early, and in all honesty, if he proposes, I'll suggest he takes some time to really make sure it's what he really wants before I even give him my answer."

Ava frowned.

"Because the waiting game went so well last time, right?" Simone said. Her tone wasn't mean, it wasn't a judgment, but still Liz felt a dull ache piercing her heart.

"Oh no, were you engaged before?" Ava asked, but Liz only nodded.

"I'll tell you what happened," Simone wedged in. "Liz was in Boston doing her apprenticeship at COBA and instead of pining for her, Sean, her fiancé, couldn't keep it in his pants and got another woman pregnant." Simone's voice carried the anger that

Liz saw in her friend's eyes and once again she was reminded that Simone was big on loyalty.

"Dafuq!" Ava hissed, slamming the menu shut. "What earthworm does that?"

Liz took a deep breath before she spoke. "Look, we were young and clearly it wasn't the real thing. Sean has been with *the other woman* for the past fifteen years now, they have three kids and I think they are happy, so I'm not holding a grudge." She sighed. "Who knows if what at the time felt like a tragedy was actually a blessing in disguise? If I were Sean's wife, mother of three, living in Glasgow, I wouldn't be here with the two of you discussing if I should or should not ask Hudson to marry me." It felt good to say those words out loud, it felt right.

"True that." Ava opened her menu again. "First round of mocktails on me," she said, breaking the tension. While Ava and Simone discussed the best venue for the party, Liz hid her nose in the menu and wondered if she was actually ready to put her heart on the line again.

❧

Just a few blocks away, Hudson was on the phone with Media-One. "Jack, I know we already discussed this but I need you to listen to me. You have to change the launch campaign. I am your client, STYLE is my company and I'm still the CEO and I don't want to be linked to this defamatory campaign you are planning."

There was silence from the other side of the line. Hudson tapped his fingers to the metal edge of the computer, waiting for Jack's answer.

"Look, man, I appreciate your position but you have to understand that Malone is my boss and he wants this to happen. He specifically demanded that COBA takes a hit, the harder on them the better and I'm doing my best to deliver. I won't repeat this to anyone else but I agree it's not the most dignified way to ensure publicity, yet this is what I'm going to do because if this campaign fails Malone will ensure that I will never get a job in media again." Jack went quiet. Then he said, "I'm really sorry, Hudson, but I can't help you."

When the line went dead, Hudson looked at his cell, wondering if throwing it against the wall would make him feel any better. He decided it wasn't going to help so he grabbed his blazer and headed for his lawyer's office. There was one more option to explore.

❧

"I'm here to see Aaron Alterman. Before you ask: no, I don't have an appointment but I need to see him. It's urgent," Hudson told the receptionist.

She must have read the determination in his eyes because she decided to make the call.

"And your name is?" Her voice was soft with understanding. She had probably seen many people in trouble standing in this very same spot and developed some empathy for their predicaments.

"Hudson Moore."

"Please take a seat, I'll let Mr. Alterman know that you are here."

Hudson didn't sit, he paced the hall instead, too nervous to actually stay still and accept that the success of STYLE would come with a price he was unwilling to pay.

"Mr. Moore?" The receptionist claimed his attention. "You can go up now. Mr. Alterman is waiting for you."

"Thank you," Hudson said, heading for the elevator.

Aaron was waiting for him outside his office. "Hudson." They shook hands. "Come in, let's sit down."

"Aaron, thank you for seeing me without an appointment. I need your help."

Aaron closed the laptop and moved it to one side. "Of course, but please tell me that it's not about the launch again."

Hudson's mouth twisted in a grimace.

"We've already looked at all the possible options, Hudson. I'm afraid I have no more suggestions." Aaron seemed sincerely apologetic about the situation. "I wish now that I had pushed back harder about the operational control. However, we are dealing with Malone and you know better than I do there's nothing that can stop that man getting what he wants. He will force us into a corner and you'll lose."

Hudson placed his hand on the table in need of a firm grip as he pushed the boundaries toward an irrational solution. "Can we withdraw from the acquisition?" He spoke the words as if they were unwilling to leave his throat.

"I don't understand."

"Are we still in time to break the agreement we have with Malone?"

"The short answer is yes. Although it's not going to be simple," Aaron said, and the two men stared at each other in silence. The desk separating them was like a raft they were both holding on to in the tempest of what could happen next. "Also, I strongly advise against it. It would be a suicidal move." Aaron sat back. "The backlash you and STYLE would suffer by going against Malone..." He shook his head, "I don't think your business would recover from it."

Hudson swallowed. "I understand that. Talk me through the details anyway."

Aaron stood up and walked to the door, with a resigned voice he asked his secretary for STYLE's file. She was back a moment later with a green folder.

"See here?" Aaron passed the document to Hudson who quickly read the footnote. "When we were drafting the agreement, Malone's lawyers insisted on a number of clauses that were designed as deterrents. They are famous for their stick and carrot methods. Anyhow, they put this footnote here to make sure you felt them breathing down your neck. This paragraph stipulates that either party can rescind the contract with no reason or notice period up to a week before the acquisition is final. The thing is you could use this to your advantage now."

Hudson rubbed his chin as he thought of the implications of using this clause.

"I know these people, they like to reign with fear. They put this in the small print because they like the idea of giving you no certainty until the very last minute. What they haven't thought about is the fact that we can use this as well. They know, however, that it's a suicidal move so they are not worried."

Hudson's cell buzzed in his pocket but he let it go to voicemail. "What are the implications of us pulling out of the deal?"

"Legally, none. Thanks to Malone's arrogance you can walk away today with no repercussions." Aaron folded his arms. "Economically, however, I think you are most likely to become insolvent and very quickly as I'm expecting Malone to release his dogs on you."

Hudson nodded. "What's your worst-case scenario?"

Aaron took a deep sigh. "Hard to tell but I'd say you may lose a few clients, may not win any more tenders, probably no investors in their sane mind will touch you. I wouldn't be surprised if your creditors started knocking at your door, too, calling in their loans."

Hudson knew all of that, he knew it meant willingly walking into Armageddon, yet if that was the only way to save Liz's career and reputation, he was happy to do it.

"Also, you will no longer get a payout, so no cash will be coming your way any time soon."

Hudson remembered the many plans Tom and Ava had already made counting on that bonus and dread filled his throat. For the first time he saw his situation with clarity. He was stuck between saving Liz's reputation and crashing his partner's dream and possibly destroying STYLE's future. The other option was to send Liz to the slaughterhouse.

"I don't like Malone and I would love nothing better than to take him on, but, Hudson, is it really worth it?" Aaron asked.

The silence was heavy, Hudson clenched his fists. "I don't know. This is a lose–lose situation for me." He stood up and shook Aaron's hand. "Thanks for your help."

Aaron squeezed in solidarity. "You don't have long to decide. If you want to go ahead with this, we better hurry."

Hudson nodded, then left the office with the pressure on his chest choking him.

As soon as he stepped on the sidewalk his phone rang again. It was Tom and he picked up.

"Hey, where are you? We said we were going together?"

Hudson frowned. "Going where?"

"Senior leader pre-acquisition party."

Hudson swore under his breath. "Sure, I'm on my way." Hudson was distracted; he was letting things slip.

"We are at the Eclectic," Tom reminded him, but the pause that followed was charged with questions.

"I'll be there in ten minutes," Hudson said, already hailing a taxi.

"Cool. But let's talk when you get here, okay?" Tom was asking, but his tone left no doubt that he meant they needed to discuss what was going on.

CHAPTER 23

Hudson had to run out of the club. His head was still throbbing from the stress he was under as well as Patrizia's incessant hounding. He took a deep breath, gulping down the cool evening air, hoping that it would cleanse his system.

Patrizia had been around him all evening. Her sensual looks had followed his every move, her tight jeans and her see-through top had filled his vision, leaving nothing to the imagination. She had turned her flirting to full-power and he had felt suffocated. When she came to sit on his lap, he knew it was time to leave. "I'll be in the bathroom," she had whispered in his ear, before sashaying down the corridor. Hudson knew it was time to flee and this was his one chance to escape. He stood up and when she disappeared behind a double door he walked in the opposite direction. He didn't want to be cruel to Patrizia who had been chasing after him since the day they met but she needed to back off, he was going to propose to Liz as soon as this mess was over. Taking the stairs two at a time, he walked outside.

When he spotted Tom's silhouette in the dark, he trudged to

him. He knew he couldn't avoid this discussion any longer and now was just as good as any other time to share his burden.

"Hey," said Tom, taking a drag from his cigarette.

"Smoking again?" Hudson asked, unimpressed.

"Give me a break," Tom answered, taking another deep puff. "I've been under so much stress: nicotine is the only thing that keeps me going." He took another drag and the smell made Hudson desperate for a smoke too. "You've been avoiding me," Tom said, frowning.

"I know." Hudson had an unsettling feeling in the pit of his stomach.

"I wanted to chat with you but Patrizia cranked up her flirting and I really didn't want to get in the middle of that." Tom laughed but Hudson only managed a half-hearted smile.

"She sure did, I even told her I'm dating Liz. She completely ignored me." Hudson rubbed the back of his neck.

"Well, you're safe now." Tom emphasized his words with a raised eyebrow. "Let's talk."

"We have a problem, Tom, a big one," Hudson said, kicking a stone. "It's about the launch. Malone has planned a PR stunt that will give us a ton of publicity."

"How's that a problem?" Tom crushed the cigarette against the wall and then threw the stub in the bin.

"He's going to use Liz's plan for the Milan office and pitch it against STYLE's plans showing our software is much better. Cheaper, better laid out, faster timeline. The intention is to make STYLE's software look better than the professional, the problem is that it portrays Liz as completely incompetent."

"I don't understand?" Tom turned to face Hudson. "We were the ones who suggested using STYLE software and getting contractors in as it would have been cheaper, but Malone insisted on using COBA for the office refurbishment. He was so keen on hiring a high-profile firm. I was surprised—" Tom's jaw fell open at the realization that Malone had been planning this from the very beginning. "He wanted a renowned firm on purpose. He needed their plans so that he could show how much more efficient our AI is in comparison!"

"That's right. If that goes to press, Liz's reputation will be ruined together with COBA's and Malone will just amplify the message that using our technology is better than any professional."

"But—" Tom frowned. "How did Liz get this so wrong?"

Hudson shook his head. "She didn't. Whoever used STYLE for the plans they sent to Jack at MediaOne has purposely ignored the fact that the Milan office is in a listed building in a conservation area. Removing that, the AI plans are better in delivery, more cost-effective with a few weeks turnaround versus a few months."

"Well, we just need to tell that to the PR agency and show Malone the error," Tom said.

"That's what I've done. I spoke with anyone who would listen. But they are going ahead with it anyway. I threatened to go to the press, but they are planning to publish an amendment apologizing for the 'human error' that caused the issue." Hudson choked on the words.

"That's not good enough!" Tom shouted, his shoulders tensing. "By then the damage is done and by the time we send out a corrigendum of the press release, COBA and Liz's reputation will be tainted."

Hudson nodded. "Precisely."

"How long have you known?"

"Tom, I just didn't—"

"How long?" Tom got closer.

"A few weeks."

"Weeks?" Tom's angry voice cut straight through all the bull-shit that Hudson was about to use to justify his behavior. "I cannot believe you kept this from me. I'm not only your best friend, I'm your partner."

"I know," Hudson said.

"I know—I don't know. Classic Hudson response for everything."

The city fell quiet around them. "I hoped that I could fix it, find a solution. I spoke with everyone I could get hold of, reasoned, threatened them, begged even," Hudson said, shaking his head.

"Is that why you went to London and New York?"

"Yes." Hudson had nothing else to offer but the whole truth. "He won't stop, Tom. I tried everything. Our lawyer, their lawyer. I even offered Malone all my shares in exchange."

"You offered Malone your shares?" Tom said in disbelief.

"He said no."

"For fuck's sake, Hudson." Tom walked away, then came back. "This is a mess."

Hudson tried to keep his balance, what was coming next was going to be even harder.

"Why are you telling me now?" Tom asked.

"Because there is a way to stop Malone."

"So, let's do it." Tom frowned.

"It's not that simple." Hudson needed to tell his friend and business partner, but it was hard to find the right way.

"Doesn't matter how complicated it is, Liz's career is on the line. We need to do it."

Hudson waited a beat, then delivered the blow. "We have to withdraw from the acquisition. That's the only way to stop Malone from controlling the narrative."

He saw awareness dawning on Tom's face as he realized what the consequences were of doing it.

"We are fucked," Tom said, and Hudson knew he was right.

The sun was shining high in the clear blue sky as Liz sat out on the terrace of COBA's offices enjoying the beautiful weather and the smell of the lavender blooming. She thought of poor Connor, who was inside sneezing and scratching his itchy eyes.

It was quite nice not to have him breathing down her neck for once and standing by ready to take credit for her work. STYLE's offices were at the final stage and she now had the time to go back to her other projects. On the terrace she was doing some sketching while trying not to think of Hudson. She was scheduled to show the complete Boston refurb to him and Tom in a couple of days and she could hardly wait for their feedback. She knew they were going to love it: it was her best work yet.

Concentrating on the kitchen she was planning for the Jonas family, she didn't hear the steps approaching until she looked up. The sun blinded her and she had to squint until the silhouette in front of her took a recognizable shape. "Patrizia?" Liz closed the drawing pad on her lap. "What a surprise. I didn't know you were in Boston."

Patrizia sat on the chair next to her and crossed her legs. "Yes, been here a couple of days. Last night's party was wild, shame you were not invited." She laughed. "Hudson and I danced so much I'm exhausted by the performance, you know what I mean, right?" she said, but Liz intentionally ignored the insinuations.

"How can I help you?" Liz held her notepad with both hands as Patrizia's eyes glowed malevolently.

"Oh, you've got this backwards." Patrizia almost hissed the words. "I'm here to help you."

Liz swallowed. "Okay, how?"

Patrizia took her phone and pressed a few keys, then looked at her again. "In your inbox. I think you should know what's coming, see the real Hudson at work."

Liz stood up. "Wait, I don't understand. What should I know? And what do you mean with 'the real Hudson.'"

Patrizia looked over her shoulder as she walked away. "Email," she said.

Liz just stood there for a few seconds, dazzled by the encounter, then picked up the rest of her stuff and marched to her desk. Her hands were shaking as she opened the laptop and logged into her account.

She couldn't see any email from Patrizia and for a second, she wondered if she had misunderstood the meaning of her words. Still, she decided to check her spam inbox. Amongst the usual offers of bitcoins an email from A.Friend@gmail.com attracted her attention. She opened it with wary suspicion.

The email was empty apart from two attachments. Liz knew it was silly to open stuff from an unknown sender in her spam but Patrizia had left her unsettled, she needed to know. She pressed on the first PDF. The title at the top of the press release read:

STYLE AI BETTER THAN THE HIGH-PAID PROFESSIONALS

The article that followed described some basic facts about STYLE, its founders, the acquisition and COBA appointment to complete the refurb of STYLE's offices. Her name appeared right after. Her plans for the office in Milan followed. Parts of it were highlighted, other figures were circled in red.

Her stomach flipped as she went through paragraph after paragraph of harsh criticisms of her choices. Below the fold there was another plan designed by STYLE's software.

Her jaw dropped as she looked at it.

The plan itself was great, the fluidity of the connection between the areas was better than in her design; the cost was almost half and the full refurb could be achieved in a third of the time she had allocated for it.

She didn't understand. How had she managed to be so wrong about this project?

A sense of doom descended on her as she finished reading the damning piece which shredded her work and handed it to the world so that everyone would know of her failure.

The shock made her eyes water but she blinked the upset away and looked again at the details. She had checked and rechecked: the paperwork required by the Beni Culturali alone took her weeks of work, and that was without considering the many follow-ups. She still remembered the many letters she had exchanged with the officer assigned to that case, the delays it had caused and the many compromises she had made to appease the concerns about modifying the historical building. How was it possible? Then something pinged.

She scrolled back and enlarged the document. She read it again and it confirmed her supposition, she hadn't got it wrong at all. Her plans included *all* the requirements from the Beni Culturali, while STYLE's layout had completely ignored them. None of the specific requirements she had to adhere to had been included in this report which meant the criticisms of her plan and her slow execution and higher budget had no real foundations. The plan designed by STYLE software was beautiful and cheaper but would have never passed the Beni Culturali approval.

She was relieved—but only minimally. Who had drafted the press release? Why would anyone want to publish such a damaging piece in the first place, especially when the information was actually wrong?

She returned to the email and clicked on the second attachment.

It looked like a video clip. A dark street, then two shadows appeared. Liz recognized Hudson immediately, then Tom came into full view before they turned to face the other way.

They were talking quietly. Most of the words were muffled but then there was a clear sentence spoken by Hudson that left her shaken.

"…the AI plans are better in delivery, more cost-effective with a few weeks turnaround versus a few months … Liz … totally incompetent…"

Her heart sunk. Was that what Hudson thought of her and her work? Or had he orchestrated all of this to use her for his own gain? Was the man she loved really this callous and duplicitous? But why? None of it made any sense.

She stared at her screen for a few minutes before she took her cell. Hudson's number was at the top of her list and her finger hovered on it ready to make the call. She hesitated, then dropped the cell into her purse and rushed out of her office.

She swept the tears from her cheeks with her fingers, then headed for the elevator. She walked out of the building and almost jumped in the middle of the road to hail a taxi. She gave the driver Hudson's address, knowing that his office was out of bounds and that he was probably working from home. She was hurt but she was also angry and the nearer she got, the more the resentment grew.

When the taxi stopped a few steps away from his building she alighted almost in a trance.

The weather was glorious, but the heat and the light from the midday sun were suffocating. One uncertain step after another, Liz passed Hudson's place but instead of stopping she continued on the sidewalk. One block, then two. Her heart was growing from within now and with the weight of the world on her shoulders she reached her flat. She walked into her bedroom with her heart broken. She dropped onto her bed and stared at the ceiling, regretting having trusted again. She had believed in him, in their relationship, in a shared future. Wasn't this exactly what happened last time? She called herself an idiot while trying to decide what to do next.

She ran options in her head. Connor's name was not on the plans or the correspondence, she was the only one of COBA responsible for this project, she was the one losing out in all of this.

CHAPTER 24

Liz had promised herself not to sulk, not to fall into depression, not to let what had happened affect her in the same way that Sean's betrayal had fifteen years earlier, but it was easier said than done. This time she didn't just lose the man, she lost her career too. But she woke up in the trance-like state she had fallen into after seeing the draft of the press release Patrizia had sent her. Simone had already left for the office and Liz was unable to think of what to do with herself other than sink into a bath and let the warm water soothe her. She stared at the bubbles filling the tub while Hudson's face appeared in her head. A million different expressions, a million little memories burst by painful shards. She undressed slowly, dropping her PJs on the floor, and then she immersed herself till the water covered her shoulders. She stayed in that same position for a long time, staring at the tiles in front of her, running her eyes over the grouting as if it were a maze she needed to escape from. Too overwhelmed to deal with her feelings, she emptied her head of everything and everyone, thinking of absolutely nothing. When the water turned cold, she got out.

She dressed slowly, taking her time and once she was done, she realized that without her job or Hudson there was nothing she wanted to do. She meticulously organized her laundry by shade. When that was done, she looked for more mindless work that wasn't needed. She cleaned the kitchen cupboards, dusted off the book shelves and rearranged the books by size and color.

She also spent a great deal of time avoiding calls. From Hudson. From Ava. From Simone. With a cup of coffee in her hand, she sat in front of the TV watching whatever programs came on. She didn't move for hours, nor changed the channel nor drink her coffee. The celebrity cooking line-up made space for a family movie, followed by a talk show and then quizzes with shouty presenters. When her eyes stung from the hours in front of the screen, she decided to read a book. But she ended up staring at the pages open in front of her, reading the same sentence over and over again until in frustration she put it back on the shelf.

The phone buzzed insistently. Ava, again. She had called so many times Liz felt terrible about avoiding her once again. Willing herself to sound cheerful, she picked up. "Hey, Ava."

"Liz, why are you avoiding me?"

"I've been avoiding everyone." Liz was trying not to fall apart.

"I've got the message but after what happened you need your friends more than ever. Why are you shutting us out? Simone said that Connor had rescinded your contract and denied all affiliation with you. Hudson is beside himself with worry and told me you won't speak to him. What's really going on here?"

Liz held her cell with shaky hands. She tried to process Ava's question, but her brain was filled with rage. "Connor is the coward that he has always been. When I went to ask him for help, he did the opposite and said I was on my own so COBA wouldn't be dragged down with me when the press release is published."

"I don't understand," she said.

"Ask Hudson. Ask him to tell you about the press release." Hearing her own voice saying his name out loud for the first time since she discovered what he had done was more painful than she had imagined.

"What press release? For the launch? Hudson said ages ago that Malone's PR was working on that."

Liz was quiet for a few uncomfortable seconds. Hudson used Malone's power, Connor's cowardice and her own naïveté to orchestrate the perfect publicity for himself and his company. Amplified by the lies, this PR stunt was going to make a strong ripple. "I went to Connor for help because he's supposed to be my mentor, Ava, but when I told him that the STYLE press release was going to end my career, all he cared about was saving himself and COBA."

"Again, I don't understand." Ava sounded worried, distressed. "What has STYLE got to do with any of this? And what's in the press release?"

"Lies." Liz's voice trembled.

"Please explain, Liz. I'm struggling to follow."

Liz could no longer speak: her throat had gone dry. "I can't, sorry, I have to go." Liz cut the call. She had broken into pieces and she wasn't sure how to glue them back together. She closed her eyes and hugged herself but then someone called her name. She looked around the room, unable to locate where the noise was coming from. The shouting seemed to be outside so she walked to her window. On the sidewalk, Hudson was looking up. "Liz! Let me in."

She swallowed the feelings that were crushing her chest. She had given the doorman clear instructions about not letting Hudson in. She had not expected him to make a scene in the middle of the street. Angry, she took her cell and texted him. 'GO AWAY' were the two words she wrote. She watched him read them, then drew the curtains and turned her phone off. They were done.

❧

Hudson kept looking at her window even though he was clear she didn't want to talk to him. He realized that being fired had been a shock, but why was she avoiding him? Why was she angry at him? He couldn't understand. Connor hadn't given him any more clarity and he was out of his depth.

His cell rang, he knew without looking that it was Ava again. She had been calling him nonstop for the past hour. He had kept ignoring her, focusing on finding a way to reach Liz, but he knew she wasn't going to leave him alone so he picked up. "Ava, I'm in the middle of something. Can I call you back?"

"Absolutely not!" She sounded angry, no, more than that, she was furious.

"What's wrong?"

"I just spoke to Liz and she told me about the press release!" Ava was shouting so loud Hudson had to move his cell away from his ear.

"How does she know?" he asked almost to himself.

"Never mind that. You just come over to this house immediately because you and Tom have a lot of explaining to do."

"I'm at Liz's. I need to talk to her, to explain. All I need is to convince her to let me in and—"

"You won't get through to her like that. Also, Tom said that you don't have a solution yet so we need to sort that too and the time is ticking, so get your ass over here right now!"

Before Hudson could decide whether to agree or argue, Ava disconnected the call. With one last glance at Liz's drawn curtains, he walked back to his car and drove off knowing that he would have to tell Ava the whole truth, but first he needed to piece things together. The monotonous roaring of the engine matched the tortuosity of his thoughts. He didn't want to dwell on it yet, but the hollow inside his chest resounded with the fear he had lost Liz already. He couldn't breathe at the idea that she might decide never to talk to him again. She knew about the press release and it hurt him to think that she thought he was responsible for this. That he was a calculating man who would destroy someone else's career for his own gain. Didn't she believe him when he told her that he loved her? How she could think he could do something this despicable?

He parked the car in front of Ava and Tom's house and walked up the drive. The door opened before he could knock. Tom, with concern in his eyes, invited him in. "How are you holding up?" he asked, but Hudson only shook his head.

"Come on in, coffee is ready."

Hudson sat down at the table under Ava's scrutiny. Tom poured some coffee in the cup in front of Hudson, then topped up his own.

"Why haven't you resolved this situation yet?" Ava's tone was bitter.

"Because it's not that simple." He looked down at his hands. "I can't believe Liz thinks I have something to do with this."

"That's not our main focus, but I'd say that given the situation her behavior is justified," Ava bit back.

"But I haven't betrayed her. I was trying to protect her."

"But you could have told her." Ava pursed her lips. "This involved her and you knew it, yet you didn't say anything to her."

"But—" Tom opened his mouth to speak, then closed it again when Ava shot him a side glance. She rubbed the side of her bump before shifting the weight to a more comfortable position.

"After talking to Liz, I called Simone, this is what she knows, maybe we can try to get the full picture. Patrizia dropped in to see Liz and sent her an email with the press release that crucified her for the Milan office and a short video clip of you two in a dark alley talking about Liz and the press release." Ava turned to Tom. "Apparently, you were smoking, but I'll deal with you later."

Tom swallowed.

"Apparently you said that Liz is incompetent. Simone watched the video. It's not the best quality but those two words were clear enough."

"This makes no sense." Hudson shook his head. "Plus, I never said the word incompetent in connection to Liz."

"You did," Tom said, turning to him. "Outside the nightclub, a few days ago."

"What are you talking about?" Hudson's expression was exasperated.

"You said that if the press release came out Liz would look incompetent." Tom lifted an eyebrow. "Not that hard to manipulate the video and pivot the entire meaning of your sentence."

Hudson looked at them, unsure. It sounded like corporate espionage, he had heard of worse, but why? "I can't believe Patrizia would do that. I mean, we are assuming this was her doing, right?"

Ava tensed her shoulders. "She wanted to get in between you two. Classic bitch move. I bet she hoped that by the time you got around to explaining to Liz that the video had been manipulated, that you've been trying to stop the press release and are not the instigator of it, the damage to your relationship would be done," she explained. Her tone was assertive, but Hudson wasn't convinced.

"But to what end? Even if Liz and I don't recover from this, I'm not just going to date Patrizia, especially after finding out she orchestrated all of it."

"Oh, she knows that. She knows she doesn't stand a chance."

"Seems so petty," Tom said.

Ava sighed. "It is but we are not here to judge; we are here to find a solution." Ava rubbed her tummy with some vigor, Hudson noticed she was getting more uncomfortable. "Any ideas?"

"I've talked to Connor to see if he was willing to stand up to Malone but he's unwilling to help. He has already prepared a press release of his own that explains Liz was a freelancer and that COBA has no affiliation with her. He claims STYLE was one of *her* clients and she was the only one in his firm involved in this project," Hudson said.

"Son of a bitch," Tom said, and Ava stood up. She rubbed her back and went to get some water.

"There must be a way to show Liz didn't make a mistake."

"I reviewed the plan designed by our software and it's cheaper because it doesn't consider the requirement for the conservation of some of the building features. Liz did extensive work on this, she is right and the software is wrong but people won't bother to look for the truth, they will read the headlines and make up their minds."

"We could do another press release and tell the truth?"

"Yes, I thought of that, but even if we admit to the mistake, it's risky for Liz's reputation. Once the perception is out there, it's hard to change people's minds." Hudson sighed, then looked at Tom. There was a quiet exchange between them but Ava didn't miss it. "Plus, we are going against Malone. He owns several media and publishing companies, he'll easily drown our message."

"What's left then?" Ava's tone was demanding an explanation. "I sense there's something else that can be done. What is it?"

"We could pull out of the acquisition. That way Malone won't have any control over the communication channels or anything else. He won't be able to send the press release," Hudson explained.

"But without the acquisition STYLE will still be carrying a debt and we won't be getting any cash from selling the shares to Malone, right?" Ava finished for him.

Hudson nodded. "I'm afraid so."

There was a moment of silence, then Tom pushed his hand across the table to touch Ava's arm. "I don't need a bigger house, or a cinema room. I'd rather be poorer but in control of STYLE instead of richer and working for a man without principles. This is bigger than just Liz. This is just the beginning."

Ava thought for a minute before speaking. "I guess this is it then?"

Tom looked at her. "Are you sure? We may never recover from this. STYLE may not even survive. Malone won't let this go easily, he will come after us. We won't know how bad it is going to be until it's too late to change our decision. Our lawyer thinks it's a mistake and has advised us against it."

Ava nodded. "I understand that, but we cannot in all conscience keep the deal with Malone knowing it will ruin Liz."

"We have a few days to pull out from the deal without penalties. Just talk about this, sleep on it to make sure it's really what you want," Hudson said.

But Ava's eyes were fixed on him. "I've already decided. Get your lawyer now, Hudson, and stop that horrible man from hurting our girl," she said.

Hudson sighed. "STYLE may not survive this," he said, looking at Tom, "but the idea of sticking it to Malone is invigorating." Tom laughed in agreement.

"Okay, you get this done, meanwhile, I'll find the way to ensure you get the chance to explain everything to Liz," Ava said to Hudson.

"How are you planning to do that?" he asked.

She shrugged in reply. "I don't know yet, but don't worry, I'll find the way." She waved her hand in front of her. "Now chop-chop, we have no time to waste."

Hudson drove back into town with a silent Tom at his side. He felt dread as he parked outside their lawyer's office; he also felt excitement bubbling in his chest. He was about to lose a payout of five million dollars and a deal with a media mogul that could cost him everything and yet he was strangely ecstatic about the idea of staying independent.

"You know what's funny?" Tom spoke, looking at the traffic ahead.

"What's funny?"

"I don't remember wanting to be in business with Malone, I only remember being forced into business with Malone."

Hudson's jaw tightened when he felt Tom's eyes on him.

Tom continued. "Not by you, by the circumstances," he clarified. "We were looking for investors, we had so many people interested and then suddenly Malone arrived and all the others disappeared, gone." He clicked his fingers. "Do you remember when we spent the entire week contacting our suitors, trying to find a new one but no one wanted to touch our business in fear of competing with Malone?" Tom shook his head. "Even the guy I met in Milan told me he didn't know we were in bed with Malone, otherwise he wouldn't have asked me for a meeting." Tom looked ahead again. "Malone made a vacuum around us, Hudson, and we were coerced into this deal."

The traffic thickened as they reached downtown and as they crawled, Hudson started to laugh.

"What is it?"

"We are on a suicide mission, you know?" Hudson was almost snorting and Tom just had to join in. "Malone is going to make our life impossible. He'll put us on our knees and yet I never felt more pumped about the future."

Tom had tears in his eyes as a hysterical mirth seemed to have taken over their self-control. "We are royally fucked!" he said in between gasps.

Hudson was laughing so much the car swerved and the horn of a lorry coming by sobered them up.

Hudson returned his attention to the road, lifting his hand in apologies to the lorry's driver. A middle finger out of the window was the other man's reply.

"We will survive this, Tom. We did great for ten years without anyone's help, we will go another ten."

"Agreed, partner." Tom placed his hand on Hudson's shoulder and squeezed. "Also, I can't wait to see Malone's face when we use one of his tricks against him!"

Hudson parked the car in front of their lawyer's office. "Let's do it, man. Let's pull the pin," he said, looking at Tom as they entered the building. They both knew this was probably the hill they would die on. Still, it felt right.

CHAPTER 25

Liz was finishing off her makeup but when she looked in the mirror her eyes were still red and dull and her expression carried the sadness she felt deep inside.

She had spent last week doing everything she could to stop thinking about her ruined career; how her reputation was about to be shredded by the media; and how her love for Hudson had turned into pure hatred. It didn't work, in fact she thought of little less. Her father being the exception. She even thought of cancelling the party as she was hardly in the mood to celebrate but Simone and Ava had been so insistent that she felt too guilty to pull the plug after all the work that had gone into it. Her only condition, a non-negotiable one, was for Hudson not to be on the guest list. She had been suspicious of Ava's agreeable mood but when she said that Hudson was in Milan, Liz felt reassured.

"It's a party not a funeral," Liz told herself, even if, actually, the latter was a better match for the mood she was in. With no more excuses to procrastinate in front of the mirror, she left her bedroom and called an Uber.

After a quick taxi ride, Liz walked through the double doors of the up-and-coming cocktail bar selected by Simone called

Linee Verticali. Forcing a smile onto her lips, she tried to remember how seriously Ava and Simone had taken their roles as party organizers, keeping her away from the preparation, and making her feel special. They didn't relent until they had found the perfect dress, the perfect shoes, and the perfect bag to go with it and credit to them, the ensemble they had put together looked absolutely fantastic. She thought it was all too much for a party but they insisted and they were almost teary, holding each other's hands as they looked at her trying on outfits. They had been acting strange and she wondered if they were up to something, but she was so stressed about the press release that would soon be out, and about Hudson's betrayal, that she put the questions about her friends' odd behavior aside and concentrated on keeping herself from falling apart.

The place was so crammed already Liz felt instantly claustrophobic as anxiety got hold of her. A week of self-isolation had made her senses hyper-perceptive. Her head was spinning as she entered the crowded space. When she was finally over the threshold, she started to subtly push and gently shove to get through the sea of people that filled the place. She looked through the strangers' faces trying to spot Ava or any of her colleagues on the guest list. Nothing.

She had expected Ava to be at the door to greet her, at her absence a frown appeared on Liz's forehead. Was Ava all right? She wondered. Simone had said that Ava had to go to the hospital the other day as she started to have some contractions. Apparently, it was something called Braxton Hicks and everything was fine. Still, Liz felt unsettled and hoped to see Ava's smiley face appear in the crowd.

She took a few more steps towards the main area only to discover that there were several small lounges spinning off the central hall. She had no idea which of them Simone had booked.

"Where are you guys?" she whispered, hoping to see someone she knew in the crowd. A few minutes later, she turned and headed to the bar, knowing they would have the booking on the system. Liz tried to get the barman's attention, but he was too busy. He looked her way a few times, even smiled but the relentless flow of customers was unforgiving and he couldn't stop mixing and pouring, not even for a second. Feeling the pressure of being late to her own party she waved at one of the waiters who was piling a tray with freshly-made cocktails, hoping he may be able to help.

"Hi," she said with the most charming smile she could pull off. "Do you have an area reserved by a Simone?"

"One moment." He glanced at a printout taped to the side of the till, then asked, "Birthday party?"

She nodded.

"Are you Liz?"

"Yes, that's me." She smiled back.

"You're booked downstairs." He tilted his head to one side, and pointed at a staircase near the entrance. It was where she had come from.

"You've got to be kidding me!" She swore under her breath, realizing that she literally came from over there.

"Sorry," he said, then walked away.

"Great! I'm definitely going to be late for my own party now." She sighed, realizing that she'd have to sail through the crowd again to get down there.

With determination, she started the trek back through the horde of cheerful people. She made very slow progress, and trapped in the crowd she started to feel hot, uncomfortably so. The music seemed too loud, the lights piercingly bright and for a second, she worried she was going to faint. *I shouldn't have skipped lunch, or breakfast or almost every meal for the past week*, she admonished herself just as someone knocking into her made her wobble. Trying to regain her balance, she bumped into the person who was standing behind her.

"I'm sorry!" she apologized, then turning slightly to the right, she spotted a less busy passage and sprang in that direction only to collide with someone who was coming from the opposite side.

"Sorry, I didn't—" she said, lifting her eyes. The rest of the sentence died on her lips. She didn't have to see his face to know it was Hudson. As soon as his hands were on her arms to stabilize her, she had *felt* him. He was supporting her weight as gravity pressed her body against his. Her blood rushed to her head, to be immediately drained away by her fast-beating heart.

"Hudson," she whispered his name while staring at him. "Why are you here?" she mumbled, confused.

"We need to talk." He stared into her eyes and no reply came to her lips. Wearing a perfectly tailored suit, he was even more handsome than an asshole had the right to be. His hair was styled for once and she had to admit her traitor of a heart was still his. Her pulse was erratic in response to his vicinity, and she was annoyed about the power that he had over her. She hated him even more because of that.

"Can we talk?" He almost begged, but she was resolute.

"Not a chance," she answered bitterly as her rage spiked.

"Please," he said.

"We have nothing to say to each other." Her tone was icy.

"I have plenty to say. But I'm going to start with a compliment: you look stunning," he said, studying her.

With his eyes roaming all over her, she found it impossible to catch her breath. *We are done*, she reminded herself, straightening her back, trying to put some distance between them but when he moved with her they ended up being even closer than before. Their bodies fit perfectly.

"You need to go, I don't want you here," she said, but he didn't budge.

"I owe you an explanation and an apology."

"Bit late now. Thanks to you Connor has kicked me out of COBA and I'm about to become a joke for the entire industry!" She spat out the words. She stepped away from him but he lifted his hands from her waist to her arms, and moving nearer again he held her even closer. His vicinity was intoxicating, and she cursed her heart for being so weak, so malleable. She cursed Hudson, too, for everything he had done.

"Liz," he took a deep breath, "if you let me, I can explain everything. I swear the press release wasn't my idea, it was Malone's." His voice was softer now and filled the small space that was separating them. All around them the chit-chatting of hundreds of strangers was loud and chaotic but when his breathing deepened, she found herself caught in an intimate bubble that made her dizzy. She had promised she would ignore her feelings for him and she tried so desperately to keep that promise, but now that she was wrapped in his arms again, she realized that indifference wasn't going to be enough. She'd have to hate him if she wanted to succeed.

"I don't want to hear what you have to say. You are the CEO of STYLE and I'm sure if you were against it, you could have said so and stop it. Yet, you didn't do a damn thing." She was mad. "I trusted you, that's on me, but there are only so many times someone can take a betrayal and move past it, I guess I've reached my limit." She needed to kick him out of her life once and for all, before he wormed his way back with his lies. "It's better for everyone if you go now."

Instead of leaving, he leaned closer to her. "I should have told you what was going on, that mistake is on me. But please believe me, I just wanted to protect you."

"Protect me? That press release is a death sentence for my career. Did you think that I'd just marry you and be happy with the role of housewife? So that my career didn't matter anymore? That it could be sacrificed for the good of STYLE?"

"Damn it, Lizzie, don't be absurd. It was Malone's idea, I was trying to stop him."

Her snort was meant to be dismissive. "Don't call me Lizzie," she said, "actually don't call me at all. I don't want to see you ever again."

His eyes flared with anger, then cooled down again. "It took me more than forty years to fall in love with someone and it happens to be you." He swallowed. "I was scared, Liz. Scared of losing you, so I tried to convince Malone to change his plans, and I kept it a secret because I didn't want anyone to read that press release and get the wrong idea."

"But you told Patrizia," Liz said.

Hudson glared. "I didn't, she was the one who helped the PR agency with the comparison of the two plans."

"Well, how convenient that she forgot to point out the implication of refurbishing a building protected by the Beni Culturali."

Hudson took a deep breath. "I'm sorry, Liz. She meant to punish me but ended up sabotaging you."

Liz closed her eyes, her brain refusing to believe a word.

"Please, Liz, this has nothing to do with us. You promised me we would keep our careers out of our private lives," he said.

"You put me out of business, nothing we said back then still stands."

"That's not fair." He was trying to keep his temper in check.

"Really? You have the guts to talk about fair?"

"I can fix this, Liz, if you let me," he almost begged.

A chain reaction started in her body when his breath washed over her skin and in the hottest bar in Boston she started to shiver. He held her closer, his hands touching the skin on her naked back, painful memories of their lost love.

"You're shaking." He stroked her back gently, soothingly, but his touch made the quivers worse. "Please, give me another chance, give us another chance. I've given up everything for you, if you let me explain you'll see there is a future for us," he pleaded.

She felt her will weakening. She needed her defenses back up. "No," she hissed, stepping back. This time he let her go. "There is nothing you can say or do to get me my job back. There's nothing you can say that will make me trust you again. You knew that press release would destroy me, yet you kept it a secret. And even if you did that with the best intentions, it's patronizing that you thought I couldn't handle it, that I couldn't help. Is that how you think of me? A helpless woman who needs protecting and saving? That's not the type of partnership I want."

He was quiet for a few seconds, then looked at her in the eyes. "Maybe I should have told you but this impacted you as much as it impacted Tom and me. It wasn't just an easy black-and-white choice. I was in a lose–lose situation and I didn't want to pitch you against him."

"So you kept us both in the dark? Maybe it's you who has trust issues." She spat out the words with resentment.

"Maybe."

His answer made her stomach twist. "Maybe." She moved further away. The distance was helping, made her feel stronger, resilient enough to walk away from him without breaking into pieces.

He raked his fingers through his hair. The gesture was pure frustration but his eyes were soft. "I want you back, Liz. Tell me how to fix it?"

She shrugged his words off quickly before they reached her heart. His gaze was sincere and she could feel her armor creaking.

He reached for her, and finding her wrists he pulled her back to him. "I want to be with you, Liz. Can't you see that this, us, is all that matters to me?"

"God, Hudson, this might be what you want, but what I want is my career back, can you do that?"

"If you let me explain—"

"No." She almost shouted that one syllable.

He took her hand and pushed her palm against his chest, she felt his heart beating. "I love you, Liz. Is this really nothing to you?"

She jerked her hand away and despite feeling lost without the contact, she pretended to be in control. She closed her eyes to collect herself, and when she opened them again they were dry of all emotions. "We are done, if there was ever a choice to make, Hudson, it would be my career over you, I'm sure of that," she lied. Her tone an octave lower than usual to ensure he believed them. "Now, I have a party to go to," she said, taking another step away.

"Wait." He sounded desperate, his lips drawn in a straight line.

Her heart broke a little at that sight and she realized she was more in love with him than she wanted to admit.

"Do you love me?" he asked, tightening his hold on her while searching her eyes for the answer she didn't want to give him.

"No," she lied again, but at that word he let her go. Without even breathing she walked away. She turned when she felt at a safe distance. He was staring at her through the crowd. Disappointment was written in the curve of his lips. She headed downstairs.

The basement was a big open-plan area with a low ceiling and low lights. The walls were exposed bricks and the furniture and furnishing had an eclectic ethnic feel. Soft music played in the background, there were candles lit everywhere, and pink peonies in vases on every coffee table. There were fairy lights hanging from the ceiling and it looked like stars were raining down on her.

The place was completely deserted. She looked around wondering if the guests were hiding, waiting for the right moment to jump out shouting "Surprise" but there was nowhere to hide. Simply no one was here. The music was so romantic her heart squeezed painfully inside her chest.

When she turned, Hudson was walking down the last few steps. "Where's everyone?" she asked as he reached her.

"No one is coming." Hudson's voice was deep with a sad note that dampened her anger.

"Why not?"

"Because I told them not to; because I needed to talk to you and this seemed the only way to reach you."

This explained Ava and Simone's odd behavior.

"There's nothing to say." She was about to walk away but he stepped in front of her.

"I don't want to lose you, Liz," he said. "I've waited all my life for you, and I don't want to lose you over a misunderstanding." He took another step towards her. When he lifted his fingers to caress her cheek her body responded to his touch, engulfing her skin with flames.

"We've pulled out of the acquisition," he said, and she stiffened.

"I don't understand."

"Tom and I went to Malone and told him where to shove his offer."

She stared at him, her brain slow at catching up. "You what?" Her jaw felt lax.

"We pulled out of the deal. We are staying independent. We will still launch the new offices but no nasty press releases to go with it. We are taking back control."

"I—" she shook her head. "This is absurd. It makes no sense." She shook her head, thinking of what Ava told her, all the projects they had for when the payout came in. All gone now, she needed to sit down, yet she couldn't move. She stared at him. "You've lost millions."

"Yes, about five each, but who's counting?" His attempt at a joke fell flat.

She was too confused about the revelation to say anything.

"It was the only way to stop Malone." He lowered his forehead to her. "I did it for you, Liz."

She shook her head and the tip of her nose rubbed gently

against his. "You shouldn't have," she said, feeling a deep sense of guilt replacing her anger and the confusion.

"Yes, I had to. Malone would have ruined your career. I couldn't let him. Ava and Tom agreed with me, I didn't even have to convince them."

"You gave up ten million to protect me?" It wasn't quite a question.

Hudson smiled, then entwined his fingers with hers and pulled her into the middle of the empty room. "I would have done it for a hundred million. You are worth everything, Liz. Plus, I didn't want to be associated with someone like Malone. He's a bully without morals. Being in business with him is not what success looks like to me or to Tom."

They danced slowly, in silence, looking into each other's eyes and listening to the song. Hudson pulled her against him, lowered his lips to her ear. "Marry me, Liz," he said, and her heart stopped.

She wasn't prepared for a proposal. She wasn't prepared for the beautiful engagement ring he was holding between his fingers and her heart that had slowed down to a flatline was now speeding up so fast she was light-headed.

He took a step away. "Do you want me on one knee?"

No, she was not prepared for any of this and completely lost, she grabbed on to logic.

"Are you out of your mind?" she asked him, feeling as shaken as if she had been taken out from a washing machine drum after a full hot cycle.

"No," he said with a light tone. "I've never been more certain. This is the right way to happiness."

At those words, she started to cry.

CHAPTER 26

The magnificence of the tropical flora of the island added a magical atmosphere. She quivered at the idea of spending her honeymoon in a place this beautiful.

The stars were gleaming bright in the dark of the sky and she felt as if a lifetime of wishes had come true.

"Thank you for bringing me here," she said, turning her eyes to Hudson. "I love it."

He kissed her and circled her shoulders with his arm before turning to admire the view. "Do you really like it?"

"Absolutely," she answered, watching the reflection of the torches in his eyes, thinking that it was like watching fire burning on ice. "Magical," she said directing the word at him as much as the garden.

"Yes, that's the perfect description."

There was a sweetness in his eyes that tasted of Christmas Days and summer holidays and a puppy and children and the promise of growing old together.

"Shall we?" He opened the imposing inlaid wooden door of their villa. They stepped into a foyer that was as spectacular as the garden.

She looked at the large open space in awe. This was an interior designer's dream home.

"Dinner?" he asked, grazing over her lips.

"Later," she whispered, pushing herself up to deepen the kiss.

"That's exactly what I was hoping you'd say.' Hudson's sexy grin made her shiver. Then without giving her the time to realize what he had in mind, he plucked her from the floor and put her over his shoulder. The surprise got a squeal out of her.

"Put me down!" she complained through the giggles.

"Not a chance." He walked along the corridor.

"What are you going to do? Hold me like this forever?"

"Forever," he answered, and she laughed but something didn't feel right and the room was getting smaller and Hudson was fading away.

Noises and voices were pushing their way into her dreams.

"Miss? Excuse me, Miss." Liz felt a hand on her shoulder and she knew immediately it wasn't Hudson talking to her.

"Miss?"

She opened her eyes; a flight assistant was bending over her. "Excuse me, miss, we are landing. Could you please reset your seat to a vertical position?"

She nodded, disoriented by a reality so different from what had been in her dream. She was on a flight home. She was going back to Dublin. She pushed her fingertips against her closed eyes until all she could see was static. After fifteen years, she was leaving Boston and her entire life behind, to start again.

Hudson had hijacked her birthday party and made it into the most romantic marriage proposal she could think of. He offered her an engagement ring that was worth as much as a ten-million-dollar acquisition and did that to save her career. But despite wanting so desperately to say yes to him, Liz had run. Too many emotions had surged into her chest. She couldn't manage them with any real clarity so she had taken off and left him, and Boston.

Despite her reputation being intact, thanks to Hudson and Tom's sacrifice, she was broken. She needed some distance, she needed to heal. In an odd way, her father's stroke had given her the perfect excuse to go home without anyone trying too hard to stop her.

Hudson had begged her not to go, of course. Ava had called, trying to dissuade her from leaving, and Simone had poured the wine as they drowned their sorrows. Still, Liz had booked a flight and gone, leaving her life behind and even if they knew she was using her father as an excuse, they didn't say that to her face.

In the taxi from Dublin airport, Liz emptied her head and made a resolution to not dwell on the past or the future. She was home to visit her father who was still recovering and that was the official line, one she had started to believe herself.

When the car stopped in front of the Victorian terrace she grew up in she took a deep breath. She went to the door and turned the handle. She knew she would find it open. The house was quiet, so she tiptoed down the hall. "Ma?" she called out softly.

A muffled cry came from the next room. "Liz, my darling." Her mother came running and they almost collided. Laughter mixed with tears as they hugged in a vice-like embrace. "You are here," her mother croaked, just loud enough for her to hear.

"I know he didn't want me to come." She held her mother's hands.

"He's a grumpy old goat. He doesn't mean it, he's just proud."

Liz nodded. If someone asked her to define her father in just one word, she would definitely say *proud*. "How is he?" she asked her under her breath.

"He gave us a scare, that's for sure and I think he's scared himself. He won't say but it shows. But he's good, almost completely recovered. Come, he's asleep."

In the front room her father was dozing in his favorite armchair, the cat was asleep on his lap. She noticed the gray stubble on his chin, the outgrown hair sticking up on the side of his head and his dull complexion made him look older.

"He looks pale."

"He is better, Liz, I promise. He just needs a few more weeks of rest to regain his full strength. Sometimes he forgets the right word, he gets muddled up with numbers but it's only temporary. We just need to be patient."

Liz knew patience wasn't one of her father's strengths.

"Would you like a cup of tea?" her mother asked.

Liz smiled. "Yes, please. I miss your special brew."

Her mother smiled too, and kissed the top of her head making her feel like a child again.

Tears threatened to spill, so she yawned to cover up her emotions. "Sorry, jet lag."

"You sit here for a minute, I'll make the tea, then we will have a good catch-up, okay?"

"Sure," Liz said, smiling. Her mother looked exhausted and she felt guilty for not coming home sooner. It was true her father would have hated the fuss but she also realized that her mother could have done with her help.

"It's so nice to have you home," she said, then stood there for a little longer, reluctant to leave the room as if something bad would happen if she did. Then she straightened her skirt, adjusted her blouse and left.

Liz took a deep calming breath, shrugged off her jacket and peeled off her shoes. She checked that her phone was off and curled up on the sofa.

Her father's soft snoring and the cat's purring were a soothing mix. The kettle whistled in the other room and Liz tried not to think of Hudson but found it impossible. She looked up and followed the intricate Victorian covings on the ceiling until her eyelids turned heavy. Slowly, she fell asleep.

She had been back two days, and she had to agree with the doctor's prognosis, her father was going to make a full recovery. She watched him devouring his breakfast and felt reassured.

Her mom, however, was the one who worried her this morning. She looked as if she hadn't slept a wink. She was wearing a dressing gown over her PJs. Its collar was slightly twisted and the pockets were overflowing with tissues, Liz wondered if she was getting a cold or if she had been crying. She hadn't yet said a word, nor eaten anything on the plate in front of her. All she had done was sit at the table nursing a cup of tea that was still half full and now, probably, stone cold.

Liz looked at her parents with a sudden worry. They were getting older, it was inevitable things were going to be more difficult with time and maybe she should consider moving back to Dublin for good so that she could take care of them. Her brother always said he had it covered and that was only fair given the fifteen years of help he had received from them as well as their undivided attention. She accepted that before but now it was as if the ground had shifted under her feet, and maybe she needed someone to focus on to forget her troubles. Without her job at COBA she didn't have to go back to Massachusetts, and the further away she was from Hudson, the easier it was to forget him and move on.

"I took some time off work, and I was thinking of exploring new options here in Dublin, you know, maybe I could move back." Liz picked at the food on her plate.

Her mother's head snapped up. "But this is wonderful! How long do I get to keep you?"

Liz slid her hand over the table to lay it on her mother's. "As long as you want me."

Her mom was delighted but she saw a dark look in her father's gaze. "Did Connor fire you?"

"Dad!" Liz shook her head, embarrassed he could see through her so easily. "I'm a freelancer. I decide my schedule, take holidays when I want to." Liz smiled "I'm taking a break. I'm not sure Boston is for me, I want to see what's on offer here. Maybe it's time I came home."

"I thought you loved America." His speech was slightly slurred but she picked up the meanness in it. "Plus, I can't have the two of you fussing over me every minute of the day, it'll drive me crazy. One woman is enough in this house." He watched Liz over the rim of his mug.

"Do you want me to go?" she asked, surprised by his odd reaction.

"There's no need to move back to Dublin for me. I'm fine!" he said, putting down his mug in the exact same spot he had picked it up from. *What a fastidious man*, Liz thought, then glanced at her mother who was pretending to clean some imaginary crumbs from her placemat.

Liz turned to her father again.

"Dad, you had a stroke. You were also diagnosed with diabetes. This is serious," she said, trying to be patient and understanding. But when his mouth stayed set in a straight line with his chin sticking out, she knew that his reticence was a much bigger obstacle in his recovery than his other ailments.

"I don't need looking after," he said coldly. "I'm not an invalid, and your mother is not hopeless. So, we don't need you to play hero. You should go back to your life in Boston. Connor was so good to give you a chance. You don't want to be ungrateful."

There it was again, his pride coloring all his decision. *Stubborn old man*, she thought, then saw herself in him and felt deep regret for how she had left things with Hudson. Hadn't she acted the same way? Too proud and too stubborn to see Hudson's intentions? Also, maybe it was time she told her father what type of person Connor really was. She wanted them to understand how lonely life had been, how she repaid Connor's kindness with fifteen years of loyal servitude, and the fact that it was subjugation she felt most of the time, given the way he treated her, the way he pushed her away when for the first time she asked for his help. Somehow, she knew her father wouldn't have believed her, that he would have taken Connor's side.

"If I moved back, I'd get my own place, Dad, I wasn't expecting to move back in," she said.

She wanted to tell them about Hudson too, but her mother spoke first.

"Your dad is right, sweetheart," her mother declared, standing up. She picked up her mug and the teapot. "We will be just fine on our own. Your life is not here anymore, I've accepted that." She took the china to the sink.

Liz blinked twice trying to dissipate the tears burning at the back of her eyes. "Let me help with the washing up," she said, and went with her into the kitchen. She tried to restart the conversation but her mother had changed the subject several times and Liz knew it was better to leave it for now.

The atmosphere in the house was thick and as soon as the dishes were done, Liz withdrew to her bedroom with a flimsy excuse. She took the stairs two at a time as if she were still a child and as soon as she reached her room, she closed the door behind her and pressed her back against it. She waited there a few seconds hoping for a revelation of what she should do next, but when nothing came, she sat on the bed, and started to laugh. Holding her head with both hands, shaking with loud unpleasant snorts, Liz worried that she was on the verge of a breakdown.

CHAPTER 27

Hudson entered the hospital room forcing a smile on his face.

A chubby newborn was sleeping in the clear basinet next to her mother's bed. Her round fingers were wrapped into even plumper fists while her mouth was busy imbibing air with a consistent suckling sound. Tom and Ava were chatting softly, holding hands, and Hudson suddenly felt as if he was invading their privacy.

Ava spotted him hovering awkwardly near the door and smiled. "Are they for me?" she asked, looking at the enormous bunch of flowers in his arms. A pink balloon floated above his head every so often, grazing his hair.

"For the little lady actually." He stepped closer to Ava and gave her a gentle hug.

She took the bouquet in her lap when he offered it and smiled at the colorful blooms. She poked the balloon and laughed softly. "Thank you on her behalf."

Hudson turned to Tom. "Congratulations," he said. "She is a beauty," he added, returning his gaze to the baby. She had given them a scare, arriving a good few weeks earlier than expected but she was strong and determined and it looked like she was going to be just fine.

"Have you decided on the name?" he asked.

"Ruby." Ava looked up with eyes softened by mother's love. "She is a fiery little lady."

"It's a beautiful name," Hudson said, swallowing the sadness that was trying to push through the knot in his throat and ruin this moment of happiness. Liz should be here with him, with them.

"Anything from Liz?" Ava asked.

Hudson had to collect all his strength to answer her question. "Nothing. Still not answering any of my emails, calls, texts. I was thinking of sending a singing telegram or maybe a pigeon but I'm worried of what she might do to the poor bird." His joke didn't really work, everyone was weary of the situation.

"I can't believe she's not going to see Ruby as a newborn," Ava said, and the reality of Liz's absence, now and in the future, landed heavily on them. "Hudson, you need to go to Dublin. She can't avoid you forever, not if you camp in front of her door."

"No." He shook his head. "I did all I could. I told her the truth, apologized for how I handled things, asked her to marry me so she knew I was in for the long haul and begged her to stay, to give me the chance to work things out. But she went anyway. That says it all, I think."

"I'm never wrong when it comes to people. I don't care what she said, she didn't mean it." Ava raised her voice and they all turned to the baby when she made a quick star-shaped jerk in her cot. Tom walked to her and placed a soft hand on her tummy and watched her as she settled again.

"Liz was hurt before by someone she trusted, someone she was engaged to, someone who broke her heart." Ava's tone was soft. Her words made sense. "Even Connor, who was supposed to be her mentor and have her back." Ava shook her head. "The bastard. He let her down, adding more weight to her trust issues.

I can understand why she is struggling to believe your intentions."

There was silence in the room.

"Do you really think I should go to Dublin?" Hudson sat on the chair next to Ava.

"Yes. Show her that you'll stick around, no matter what." Ava patted the back of his hand. "Liz needs to learn to trust. It's a painstaking process and it will take some effort on your part. Tell her that if she needs to be in Dublin it doesn't mean you can't be together. That you are willing to do the long-distance thing and make it work."

"What if she didn't actually love me? And this has nothing to do with trust?"

"I think she does, plus Liz is not the type that says I love you if she doesn't mean it."

Hudson smiled for the first time in weeks. "I hope you are right about that," he said.

"Of course I'm right." Ava clapped her hands softly in front of her and Ruby stirred again.

"Shush," Tom said, and Ava blew him a kiss.

"Sorry," she whispered, then turned to Hudson again. "Okay, first things first, Hudson, buy yourself a plane ticket and get your ass to Ireland," Ava said with a cheeky smile.

"Are you sure?" he asked.

"Yes, you go and deliver that singing telegram in person!" she ordered, and he felt hope floating in his heart but then reality raised its ugly head.

"I can't really leave now. We are on the verge of bankruptcy." It hurt him to say that but it was the truth.

"I've got this, Hudson," Tom said. "I'll find us a new investor, we can give away more equity if needed and the sales team is already working overtime to find new clients. All we need is a few more contracts and we can break even. One big agency and we are laughing." Tom's optimism was contagious. "You go and get your future wife. I'm sure all this drama will still be here when you get back."

"Thank you," Hudson said. "To both of you."

"We are family, we wouldn't have it any other way," Tom said. "We started our company to bring innovation in the industry; not to become millionaires, so as long as we find a way to stay afloat, I'm okay with that."

Hudson smiled, touched by the kindness of his friends. *There's more to life than career and money.* Hudson remembered his grandfather's words and for the first time really understood their meaning.

"Okay, now go," Ava said, returning to her bossy self.

Hudson kissed her on the cheek, then shook Tom's hand and left them to cuddle their newborn who was just waking up.

❧

Liz looked at herself in the mirror while the hairdresser finished pinning her hair up. The makeup was already done. She wore lacey bridal lingerie under the silky robe that she would soon exchange for her wedding dress.

"You look stunning." Simone had shiny eyes and emotions were coloring her tone.

Liz tried to smile back but she was too nervous.

"Maybe you are not the happiest bride I've seen, but you are certainly one of the most beautiful," Simone said, squeezing her shoulder. "Are you sure you want to marry Sean?"

Liz's throat went dry. "Yes."

"But you love Hudson," Simone pointed out.

"Do I?" Liz asked.

"Of course, you do. You're just being stubborn."

A knock at the door interrupted them. While Simone went to answer, Liz looked down at her finger. Sean's engagement ring wasn't there. She lifted her hand closer. Her grandmother's ring was tightly wrapped around her fingers. She remembered how loose it used to be, but now when she tried to twist it around, to remove it, it didn't even budge. She sensed a change in the room and looked up. Hudson's face appeared in the mirror.

It took her a few seconds to realize that it wasn't the fruit of her imagination but that he was actually standing behind her.

"Hello, Elizabeth," he said, placing his palms on her shoulders and leaning down to kiss her cheek.

"Hudson?" She blinked twice as he kneeled to the side of her chair. Her hands were shaking when he took them into his. "What are you doing here?" She clutched his hands, worried that if she let him go he would disappear.

"Marry me." His tone left no doubt that this was what he wanted.

"I can't, I'm marrying Sean," she said, but there was no conviction in her words.

"No, you are not. Because I won't let you walk out of my life." When she looked up everything seemed to be blurry and confused.

"Hudson?" she called for him but he was no longer there.

The insistent ringing of her mobile woke her up. It had been a dream. She looked around, she was in her childhood bedroom, she wasn't about to marry Sean and Hudson wasn't there. Her finger had no ring on it. She looked at the time, it was one o'clock in the morning. She swore under her breath and picked up the phone. Who could it be? She had got herself a new number from an Irish provider and no one other than her family had it. "Hello?"

"Liz, you need to come back, how soon can you be in Boston?" the voice on the other side said with urgency, but her brain was still sluggish.

"Sorry, who's this?"

"It's Connor." The silence between them was heavy.

"How did you get this number?" she asked.

"From your father."

Liz shook her head. "It's the middle of the night, Connor,

can't this wait until the morning?" She blinked her tiredness away.

"It can't, Liz. Your clients are rioting. They are asking for you, they are not staying with COBA unless you are on their accounts," he said, and Liz smiled. *The sweet taste of revenge.*

"I don't work for you anymore, Connor, you fired me." Her voice was ice cold. "Actually, to be precise, I never actually worked for you at all, because you never officially employed me, so I guess I'll just contact *my* clients and let them know I'm still on their accounts." She had not realized that until now, because of Connor's greed, she was holding all the power.

Connor said something unclear and she carried on finally getting off her chest what she had wanted to tell him for more than a decade. "You used me, treated me as if I didn't add value to your firm and denigrated me for years, taking credit for my work knowing that I'd not leave because it would hurt my dad."

"Liz, come on, that's not true." Connor was out of his depth and she knew it.

"It is true, like it's true that I've turned down so many opportunities because of the loyalty I pledged to you and COBA. You gave me nothing in return and the one time I needed a favor, you turned against me to save yourself." She took a deep breath, this felt so good. "I have an interview tomorrow at Kirker Architects. They are offering me a director role and a place on the board, so looks like your loss is my gain. And theirs of course, my clients are coming with me."

Connor drew a sharp in-breath. "I'll employ you, officially. I could also review your salary," he said.

She laughed out loud, then covered her lips with her hand remembering that her parents were asleep in the next room. "I'll pass but thank you for the *generous* offer," she said before disconnecting the call. She leaned back on her pillows feeling her heart booming in her chest. She felt so good. She felt free, finally ready to cut with the past but she also thought of Hudson. She wanted

to tell him about her conversation with
hear his voice, she wanted to be with him
pretend that she didn't miss him.

She thought of what had happened. A
tell her what was going on with Malone, t
him but she understood he was trying to p

the baby away with the bath water, her grandmother used to say.
Maybe this was one time she needed to listen to that advice.

She took her US sim card out of her bedside drawer and put it
back in her phone. When she turned it on her cell went crazy
with notifications. There were texts messages, emails and voicemails. She could see Hudson's name flashing but also Ava and
Simone's numbers. Connor and COBA were also a recurring
feature of this parade. She felt guilt flowing inside the pit of her
stomach and before she listened to the voicemails or read the
messages, she decided to see what had happened to STYLE. She
opened the browser and typed in the search bar.

When several articles appeared with the details of the acquisition withdrawal, Liz felt her stomach churning. She knew
Malone was unscrupulous and she had expected him to twist the
truth to his advantage, it was still hard to see it in print. He was
quoted saying that he was the one who pulled out from the deal
after several experts had expressed doubts over STYLE's real
capabilities. Liz read the articles knowing this was probably the
last nail in the coffin for Hudson and Tom.

She closed her eyes, reminding herself that it wasn't her fault.
It's Malone's lack of integrity that caused this, she told herself, but it
was true that to save her reputation Hudson and Tom had paid
the highest price. The press release had never gone out, she had
not been touched by this and now she was also free from
Connor, free to choose what to do next—but was that what she
really wanted?

She turned the lights on and went to her mirror. She stared at
herself like she had done in her dream. For so long all she had

a successful career, then when she met Hudson she she wanted more, she wanted him and a family. She into her own eyes knowing she ended up with neither. Her interview tomorrow with Kirker Architects told her she could easily have a career if that was what she wanted. But Simone's words were playing in her mind: *There's only one Hudson*, she had said, and that was a painful truth. She didn't want to choose, she wanted both.

She knew that Hudson had made a big sacrifice for her, was she ready to return the favor?

She still had things to figure out but right now STYLE was about to go under, and she couldn't let that happen without trying to find a way to help them. She returned to her bed, picked up her cell again and dialed Simone's number.

"Lizzie! Oh my God, I was so worried about you. It has been two weeks since your last text." Simone's words flooded the silence of the room.

Liz closed her eyes. The guilt swelled in her chest. "I'm so sorry, Simone. I needed to cut all ties for a while. I'm a shitty friend. Sorry."

"Just stop it. I can't find a violin small enough for this." Simone's sarcastic remark made Liz laugh. "You are one of those people who needs to lick their wounds in private. I get it." Simone sighed. "Me, I'd plaster my feelings all over the web for everyone to see but I know that's not you, and it's totally fine. It doesn't make you shitty. As long as it's less than a month."

Liz laughed again. "Thank you."

"So, how's it going?" Simone asked.

Liz swallowed. "Not very well," she said.

"Is it your dad?"

"No, my dad is grand. The usual pain in the ass, or arse like we say over here. He's recovering fine, drives my ma crazy because he never does what he's supposed to and keeps forgetting to take his medicines."

Simone laughed. "Are we stereotyping or do all fathers around the world fit the same mold?"

"Probably a bit of both. Anyhow, the bottom line is that he's doing well."

"So, what's up with you then?" Simone asked.

"I'm miserable here."

"Okay, now tell me something new," Simone said.

Liz closed her eyes. "I know, I know, you told me."

"And?"

"And yes, you were right. There's only one Hudson."

"Yep. I told you that." Simone switched her combative-attitude mode on. "So, what's new?"

"STYLE is going under," Liz said.

"I've heard. Ava is worried, she doesn't say it out loud but I can tell. Also, she gave birth to baby Ruby last week. She is adorable. I'll send you a picture."

"Oh, I'm so sad I missed that but the due date was not for a few weeks."

"Yes, well, Ruby was in hurry, but she's doing great."

"Please send me a million pictures. I'll get some flowers delivered; I wish I were there." Liz's voice was dripping with regret. "And Ava? How's she?"

"She's good, she misses you. We all do."

"Same here." Liz felt emotional. "I can't call her yet, not until I know I can fix things."

"You sound just like Hudson, he wanted to fix things on his own, and look how that turned out. Just come home, we'll find a solution together."

Liz took a deep breath. "I can't, Simone, not yet. My plan starts here. It's important that I see this through." Liz paused for a second. "This is why I'm calling, actually. I need your help," she said.

"Anything."

"Could you send me all my clients' contact details?"

The line went quiet. "Lizzie, I'll get in trouble for that."

"Not really, I have them on my computer at home so you can just forward them to me from there—also remember that I wasn't an employee of COBA. Connor didn't have to pay my pension and medicals but that means that those are *my* clients and not his and I can take them with me to another firm if I want to."

"Oh my God! That's true." Simone's voice was high-pitched. "He had that coming, finally, this is payback."

"This is not revenge," Liz said. "It's leverage."

"Ohhh, that's intriguing. Spill it then, what have you got in mind?"

"It's a gamble, but I think I'm holding a winning hand. Here's what I have in mind," and then Liz told Simone the details of her plan.

CHAPTER 28

Hudson stopped in front of the red door and stared at the metal knocker with the lion head, unsure of what to say and how to say it. He had practiced his speech on the plane, mulling over each word, trying to think of a convincing reply to any of her objections. But now that he was here just outside her parents' house, his brain had gone blank.

He needed some more time, so he jumped down the three stone steps he had just climbed and walked back and forward on the sidewalk—or rather the *pavement*. He stopped to admire one of the old poplars dotted along the street at regular intervals. He looked up at its tacky round leaves, at the basic brown bark, at the weird shape of the branches hanging over the road and wondered if he had made a mistake. After all, Liz left Boston and asked him to stay away. Was it disrespectful of him to be here, to give her no alternative but to talk to him even if she didn't want to?

He heard a noise behind him and turned. "Excuse me?" A woman on the threshold of the house with the lion door knocker was trying to get his attention. From the resemblance Hudson could only assume she was Liz's mom.

"Hello." He walked towards her.

"Is there anything I can help you with? I saw you pacing. Talking to yourself. Are you lost?"

Hudson smiled and marched up to her. "I was looking for Liz. I wasn't sure if it was the right house," he lied.

"Yes, it's the right house." The woman's gaze turned suspicious. "She's not here though."

"Oh." The disappointment on Hudson's face was too obvious to miss.

"She's got a new job. Big important architect firm, they asked her to be a director, on the board even. My Lizzie is finally back home," she said, and he saw her eyes shining with happiness while his own world crumbled.

"It's well deserved, she is great at her job," Hudson said truthfully.

The woman nodded. "Do you want to come in? Liz's due home any minute. She's on her way back: she texted from the train."

Hudson panicked. Liz had clearly moved on and left him behind. It was better for him to do the same. "Thank you but I need to get going," he said.

"Suit yourself," the woman said, he knew she was watching him as he walked away.

"Hey!" she called back. Hudson turned. "Do you want me to pass on a message?"

He stood there for a second, words spinning in his mind. He shook his head to clear away his emotions. "Just good luck with the new job," he said, waving. Hands shoved in his pocket, head low, he walked aimlessly down the road turning left or right at random. He waited for the sense of loss to hit him. Then suddenly, Liz's voice calling his name captured his attention.

"Hudson!" she called again. He looked in all directions but couldn't see her and wondered if he was dreaming.

"Up here!" He looked at the pedestrian bridge. She was at the top, her hands cupped around her mouth to amplify her voice.

When their eyes met, she dropped her hands and smiled. He waved and walked toward her, she did the same. He took the stairs two steps at a time until they reached each other halfway.

"You're in Dublin," she said, her voice trembling.

"Looks like it," he said, and made her laugh.

A group of students ran noisily down the stairs, then disappeared into the off-licence down the road. Hudson and Liz just stood there, looking at each other. When the tension reached an unbearable peak, he stepped closer.

"My mother told me a very handsome man came looking for me." She lifted her chin up to look at him. "I knew immediately she was talking about you."

His smile, those words were the green light he was waiting for. Painfully slowly, he lowered his lips to hers. In an instant that seemed to last forever, bounded together by that kiss, time seemed to be folding back as well as leaping forward. She was kissing him with the same love and passion he felt before, and full of promises. When they finally broke apart, they were breathless.

"Hi," he said.

"Hi," she replied, but then taking a step she returned to her controlled, cool self. "What are you doing here?"

"We need to talk."

She looked away. "I know, I have something to say too, but not here, not yet."

"I can do the talking."

She shook her head. "I need some more time."

"Can I walk you home at least?" He was hurting but he was too happy to see her to spoil the moment.

She seemed unsure. "How about I show you where I grew up?"

He smiled, the tension in his shoulders melting a little. "I'd love that."

"Follow me, then," she said and took his hand.

They walked in silence for a few minutes. "I'm surprised you came," she said, looking ahead.

"Really? I asked you to marry me. That was my way of saying that I'm in this for the long haul. That I really care. Did you think that if you didn't answer my call for a couple of weeks I'd just turn the page and move on?"

"No." She turned to him. "But you've always been very considerate: you stopped texting and calling—"

"—and emailing," he interrupted her.

She smiled. "And emailing, of course, let's not forget that."

He squeezed her hand.

"I knew you were giving me space and I appreciated that."

"And now, are you disappointed?"

She turned to him. Shook her head. "I'm glad."

He stopped and pulled her into his arms. "So why are we doing this? It's stupid and painful. Marry me, Lizzie, we can figure out the rest."

She quivered, closed her eyes. "I can't."

He lowered his lips to hers and kissed her face, her eyes, her nose. Featherlike, his stubble ran across her jaw, when she sighed he covered her mouth with his again. "I can arrange for some romantic settings if you like; flowers, candles, music. I even have the ring with me, all I need is for you to say yes."

"I can't," she repeated and looked at him with unreadable eyes.

"Can't or won't?"

"It's complicated," she said, but then she didn't elaborate and Hudson's frustration made him paranoid. He worried that this was going to be the end for them. Despite the fact that she loved him, he could feel that she wasn't going to choose him. They walked slowly down the road, and when they passed the gate of a park, she walked in. "I used to come here all the time when I was young. See that bench?"

He nodded and she aimed for it.

"I sat here for hours, sketching and daydreaming." When they reached it, she sat down with a sigh. Hudson sat next to her. It was late afternoon but the sun was still high and bright.

"It's a great spot," he said, then leaned back, hooked his elbows against the back of the bench and stretched his legs. He was still tense but was hoping to hide it.

"How've you been?" she asked, studying him carefully.

"Fine," he lied.

"And you?"

"Fine," she answered, looking at the lush lawn ahead.

"I heard about the new job. Congratulations."

"How do you know?"

"Your mother told me."

"Of course she did." She looked away, her jaw tensing as if to make sure no words would escape her mouth. He wondered if she was trying not to hurt him with the truth.

"I've been here hundreds of times before, but it looks so different tonight," she said.

He looked around, the bushes delineating the path were in bloom. The old-fashioned street lamp wasn't on yet, he imagined that later it would cast a soft light against the indigo of the sunset. He turned his gaze back to her. "You are so beautiful," he said, and the glint of pleasure he saw in her eyes was a balm for his hurting heart.

"Thank you."

"I'm in love with you, Liz." He took her hand. "I know that I sound desperate but I don't think I can be without you." It felt so good to touch her again. "You make me want things I didn't know I wanted. Getting married, having a family, making a home. My life was great because I didn't know what I was missing, but then I met you and suddenly I saw the big hole right in the middle of it all."

She shivered at those words and he lowered his lips to hers until they were almost kissing.

"Hudson, why are you doing this?" She sighed. Her voice trembled.

"Because I love you, Liz," he said, gently lifting her chin. "Please don't send me away." He kept his gaze on her. "I know it's terribly selfish to ask you to come back to Boston with me, but I don't care. I'm going to ask you anyway. I have a ticket for you." He plucked a plane ticket out of his pocket.

"A paper ticket? Did you book me a flight back to the nineties?" she said and they both laughed.

"I had to. You've been filtering my texts and emails, I needed to be sure you'd get this," he answered with a raised eyebrow and a playful note in his voice.

"Touché." She laughed, then threw her arms around his neck and kissed him with lips that were still turned up at the corners.

"You are driving me crazy," he said, enveloping her in his arms.

"Yeah, I was just about to say the same thing about you." She spoke the words keeping her lips on him.

"Do you love me?" he asked her suddenly, rushing the words.

She looked into his eyes. "I do," she said.

"Then why? Why aren't you coming back with me? Why don't you want to marry me?"

She entwined her fingers with his. "I can't."

"But this is bullshit, Lizzie!" Hudson's frustration was resurfacing. "If my company wasn't about to go under, I'd be moving here for you. I cannot abandon Tom right now, he needs me."

"I know, Hudson." She lowered her eyes. "I'm so sorry, it's all my fault. You are in this mess because of me."

He lifted a hand to her face, his tone softened. "It's not your fault, it's Malone's fault. If anything, you did us a favor. I'd have hated to deal with that crook for the rest of my days."

"Still, this is going to cost you your business."

"I'm not giving up just yet. All we need is a few big clients, maybe a large architect firm and we will stay afloat."

She rested her cheek on his hand and smiled. Then with a slow move she leaned over and kissed his lips. "The luck of the Irish," she said before leaning against his shoulder. He wrapped his arm over her shoulders and rested his chin softly on the top of her head. Her hair was soft and scented with coconut, as the sun started to set, he closed his eyes, enjoying the moment.

Her phone vibrated in her handbag; she checked her messages. "Mama's checking on me. She's asking if my train was late or if I've been kidnapped by the handsome American who was stalking the house." She turned to him. "She likes you." Liz laughed.

"She has good taste," Hudson replied.

Liz just rolled her eyes. "I need to go."

He wondered if the word goodbye would be next, but she surprised him.

"Are you hungry?" she asked.

"Starving."

"Come on then, you are about to have the best supper in Dublin," she said, standing, then she offered him her hand. When he took it, she pulled him up.

"Meeting the parents, eh? Does this mean that you've changed your mind about my proposal? That I have a fighting chance?"

She looked at him with serious eyes, shook her head. "No, it means the Irish are hospitable people."

He smiled at her. *There is still hope*, he told himself as they walked together out of the park.

"Dinner was delicious, Mrs. Walsh," Hudson said, finishing off the last forkful.

"Thank you, dear, and please call me Shannon."

Liz's father snorted. They all turned to him.

"What?" Liz asked, but he just shook his head.

"This story!" He waved his hand "The fact that he's just a client who was in Dublin for business and popped in to see you."

"And what about it?"

He pointed his finger at her. "I can see that you like him. You've just turned forty. How long are you going to wait around for this one to propose?"

"Dad!" Liz slapped her hand on the table. This was so humiliating. She'd always respected her father's old-fashioned ideas but his words hurt. He wasn't a very nice person.

"You've got this all wrong, sir." Hudson's voice was calm but firm, she realized he wasn't going to sit there without taking her side, she felt her heart soaring. "I'm the one who would like to marry your daughter, I've proposed several times, tried everything really, including begging but nothing has worked so far." Hudson took out the engagement ring he had been carrying in his pocket and put it on the table. She saw her father ogling the ring, he didn't say anything but she could see he was impressed.

"You came here to take her back to Boston, did you?" Shannon sounded emotional.

"I did, but she is not coming home with me." He turned to Liz. "Or have you changed your mind?" he asked.

She looked down at her plate. Her food almost untouched. "I can't go back to Boston right now."

There was a moment of silence, then Shannon spoke. "Anyone want dessert? I made apple cake with custard," she said, but Hudson was looking at Liz, not really paying attention to what she had said.

"I should go," he said, standing up.

"I'll walk you out." Liz followed him out to the door.

They walked down the corridor in silence. She felt her heart breaking but she had made her choice and she had to stick to it now.

When they were outside, she took his hands. "I'm sorry, Hudson."

He nodded. "I understand."

"No, you don't."

"Then explain, because I love you and all I want is to be with you."

"I told you, it's complicated. I cannot come back to Boston just yet, but I do love you, Hudson, that much I can say."

"Is this a game to you? Payback for my misdemeanors?"

"No, of course not!"

"Then what's with all this secrecy?"

"I have my reasons."

He looked at her. "Whatever it is, why can't you tell me?"

"For the same reason you didn't tell me about the press release."

Hudson frowned. "I just wanted to protect you, which I did at a great loss. Why are you punishing me for that?"

"I'm not, I promise."

"What's going on then?"

She wanted to tell him about her plan to save STYLE but she knew it was safer if he didn't know until it was all done. If something went wrong there might be a legal battle and the less he knew, the better it would be for his defense. "I can't explain."

"Okay, I guess you are choosing your career. Fair enough, Kirker Architects are one of the top firms in the world. It's a brilliant opportunity," Hudson said. She saw the anger and the disappointment in his eyes but she knew he was also pleased for her.

"It's just bad timing," she said, and he smiled.

"Yes, the worst," he said, then he went quickly down the steps. "Goodbye, Liz," he said, and walking fast down the road he was soon gone from her sight.

She stood, waiting for her heart to calm and her tears to stop before she helped herself to an extra big slice of apple cake hoping it would help her mood.

CHAPTER 29

It was Labor Day weekend and Boston was in turmoil. The fireworks display at the harbor the night before had been magnificent and reminded him of Liz. Independence Day seemed so far away now, but it had been less than two months. Their first kiss had tasted as sweet as a promise but the summer didn't actually deliver.

Hudson parked at the office and noticed there were no other cars around. Probably everyone else had taken the day off to celebrate with friends and family, he wasn't in the mood. He grabbed his bag from the passenger seat and with a bitter sigh, he slammed the door shut. Tom had insisted they met early to discuss the quarterly plan. He knew their funds were running out but he had nothing else to cut, he had taken a massive salary sacrifice and his own savings were running out. With a sigh, he thought about his grandfather's boat, that was the last asset he had left, he could sell that but it would only finance a couple of months of trading.

He took the stairs and with every step he thought about the many meetings he had scheduled with investors all over the country. They all loved his pitch but then after a quick due diligence they all returned with the same answer: no one was going against Malone who had made it clear was on a mission to bankrupt STYLE. *He's succeeding*, as they were now on their knees and without much hope of getting back onto their feet.

He entered the office and thought of Liz, he was surrounded by her ideas, the colors she had chosen, the flow she had designed. There was so much of her in the place that he could almost smell her scent, coconut and flowers. His stomach churned at the reality that only a few months ago he had been at the top, his life complete. Now he was sliding into the chasm without a way to stop his descent.

Walking down to the mezzanine, he saw the glow: the lights were on downstairs, maybe Tom was already here. As he neared the rail, he stopped to look at the scene. There were sheets of printed paper scattered everywhere on the floor.

"What's going on?" He looked more carefully and noticed they were not placed at random: they seemed to be spelling out one word.

He walked further down to get a better view and read the word out loud.

"YES."

He looked around but there was no one there. "Hello?"

No answer.

He jogged down the stairs and picked up one of the printouts.

It was a page from a contract. He picked up another one —same.

He looked at a few more. Big names signed with STYLE for thousands of dollars' worth of contracts.

"What's all this?" he said almost in shock.

"A wedding present." He heard her voice behind him and turned.

"Liz?"

He was too surprised to speak.

She was wearing a summer dress with a flowing skirt, the snug top left her shoulders naked. Her hair tied back into a ponytail bounced as she walked towards him. She was carrying two flute glasses in one hand and a bottle of fizz in the other.

Hudson wanted to ask her so many questions but he didn't know where to start, he was stunned into silence. His brain couldn't quite fit the information together in a sensible way.

"What's going on? What's all this?" he asked.

"Hi, by the way," she said, coming closer, but he didn't want his heart to reach the wrong conclusion. When he didn't move. She spoke.

"That's twenty-four new clients, the signed contracts are on the floor. Also, an exclusive distribution contract with Kirker Architects in Dublin. They are going to be STYLE's only authorized reseller in Europe, I hope that's okay. Tom blessed it," Liz said, and he felt a smile tugging at his lips.

She took another step towards him.

"How, even?"

"Kirker Architects offered me a fantastic job but I didn't really want to stay in Dublin because the man I love lives in Boston and I want to be with him." She took another step. "They were disappointed, of course. Chatting about things I mentioned STYLE and showed your software. I told them how they could achieve scalability and efficiency by using it. Also, I suggested they could become distributors if they were willing to invest some money."

"Invest? In STYLE?"

She took another step closer. "Yes. Tom drafted the contract. It's all legal."

He looked at the papers scattered on the floor.

"These are internal copies, the legal documents are in a pile on your desk, just waiting for your signature."

"What about your job?"

She was right in front of him now. "You are looking at the new director of the interior design division at COBA."

"Connor gave you an entire department?" He was confused.

"Yes, also a very substantial raise and a three-year contract with STYLE."

Hudson blinked. "How did you manage that?"

"Long story short, all 'his' clients were actually my clients. Turned out they didn't like him much and they were happy to come with me if I were to leave COBA."

"Ah! That's a move," he said with true pride for the clever game she had played.

"It calls for a little celebration even if it's only nine o'clock." She passed him the bottle and lifted the empty glasses waiting for him to pour.

"It's five o'clock somewhere," he said, popping the cork and filled the glasses with bubbly, then he put the bottle on the floor and took the glass she was offering.

"To STYLE's success," she said and the flutes clinked against each other, echoing through the empty room.

"And to us?" he asked with a smile. "Unless I misread the intent of your message."

She took a sip from her glass and then she went to him. Her kiss was so powerful he felt the adrenaline rushing through his body.

"I dreamed of you all the time when I was back home," she whispered. "I dreamt of us together, of our honeymoon, our wedding. I want to spend my life with you, Hudson."

"Why didn't you say that when I came to Dublin?"

"Because I was doing this." She lifted her chin in the direction of the floor covered with papers. "I couldn't explain my plan without making you aware of the details, and I didn't want you to know anything because I wasn't sure I was going to pull it off. I didn't want to get you involved in case my fight against Connor over my clients became a legal battle."

"But it didn't?" he asked.

Liz shook her head. "No, he knew he was going to lose in court, he had no grounds."

"You were brilliant." He kissed her.

"Well, thank you. You were not bad yourself at getting out of Malone's claws."

"You brought it home for us." He was grinning. "I can't believe Tom didn't say anything, he really had me fooled."

"I guess we were enjoying giving you a taste of your own medicine," she said.

"Fair enough, I've learned my lesson." He was too happy to be grumpy.

"So, we are getting married?" His voice shook.

"We are."

He took her glass from her and put it on the floor near the bottle, then went down on his knee and took her hand.

"I don't have a ring handy. I lost the one I bought for you, I'm sorry," he said, but she smiled.

"You didn't lose it, you left it at my parents'." She fished it out of her pocket and held it in her palm.

"On the dining table?" he asked, and she nodded.

He picked it up and held it out to her. "Elizabeth Walsh, will you marry me?"

She grinned. "Absolutely."

"Third time lucky," he said, sliding the ring on her finger.

"It's a perfect fit," she said with a giggle as he pulled her into his arm and spun her around.

Her heart was almost exploding with the intensity of her emotions. *I did it*, she told herself. Against all the odds she had everything she wanted, love and a career, and she also managed to save Hudson's company in the process.

"Now I know, for me happiness is both," she said.

"Both?"

"Yes, love and career. I found the way to have it all."

"I'm glad you did," he said, kissing her. "So very glad."

THE END

ACKNOWLEDGEMENTS

Dear reader, thank you for choosing *Which Way To Happiness?* I hope you enjoyed it.

Women often have to reinvent themselves and overcome the many obstacles on their way to success, especially when trying to juggle family and career, if you are in the thick of it and pulling your hair out, well, sit back, take care of yourself, relax and don't give up – I'm sure that like Liz - you'll figure it out!

Now for the thank yous. First up my amazing husband Pete for his unfaltering support and my children, Olivia and Sebby, then my family (both in England and Italy) – Hello Guys!

A massive thank you to my writer buddy, Mark Jones, for being so generous with his time and genius - It's such a privilege to share the hive-mind with you.

A shout-out to the VWG, some of the funniest, talented and most supportive people in the writing community.

Last but not least, thank you to Clare for her brilliant editing and the entire team at Bloodhound who believed in me and worked so hard to make this project a success.

Lightning Source UK Ltd.
Milton Keynes UK
UKHW010016070121
376479UK00002B/18